DEVIL'S

by

ROXANE BEAUFORT

CHIMERA

Devil's Paradise first published in 2005 by
Chimera Publishing Ltd
PO Box 152
Waterlooville
Hants
PO8 9FS

Printed and bound in Great Britain by
Cox & Wyman, Reading.

The characters and situations in this book are entirely
imaginary and bear no relation to any real person or actual
happening.

DEVIL'S PARADISE

Roxane Beaufort

This novel is fiction – in real life practice safe sex

Riku pushed Romilly back till her knees pressed against the great slab. Mahil was dancing round mouthing incantations. The tribe swayed and chanted as they watched. The warriors lifted Romilly onto the altar and bound her, spread-eagled, ropes about her ankles and wrists. She had never believed in God, not seriously, bucking against attending services in the church on her father's estate or going to those in London, but again she prayed. 'Dear Jesus, save me. I don't want to die.'

She could not move, tears running unchecked down her cheeks and dripping onto the stone beneath her head. Then a large black-haired man with fierce eyes leaned over her, blocking out everything. A cloak of vivid feathers fell from his immense shoulders, and he raised his arms to heaven, evoking his gods.

Chapter One

'I'm bored,' complained Romilly, rustling her skirts and striking her fiancé on the arm with her closed fan.

'How can you be bored, dear heart?' he drawled, a colourful popinjay, leaning an elbow on the edge of the stage box they occupied. He was as much an actor as those who trod the boards, and played to his admirers in the pit who were watching him with almost as much attention as they gave King Charles, theatre-goer par excellence. Romilly would have liked to catch the royal eye, though it was said that his mistresses were hussies.

'This display obviously pleases you, Jamie – all those trollops flaunting their wares, kicking up their legs in lewd dances, but it don't appeal to me!' she pronounced loudly, her lovely mouth pouting, her green eyes sparking with annoyance. She could not confess her true reason – that Nathan Westbury, principle player, was not in this part of the show. She had developed a passion for him, unrequited as yet.

She resented the adulation lavished on the actresses, accustomed as she was to being the centre of attention, Lady Romilly Fielding, the Earl of Stanford's only daughter, beautiful, gifted, with blood as blue as could be, inherited from a long line of aristocrats.

'Dearest,' said Jamie, lifting her hand to his lips and pressing a kiss to the back, the feel of his narrow moustache raising goose bumps on her skin. 'You know I adore you. They are mere entertainers, helping their superiors – that's us – to pass an idle hour. You are my existence, my dove. Why won't you take pity and let me prove to you how much I love you?'

She shot him a straight stare, her face illumined by the candles floating in a trough of water that formed the footlights. 'What you mean is that you want to roger me like any tuppenny whore!' she hissed indignantly.

'No, no – not at all. We're betrothed, aren't we? Soon to be man and wife. There would be no harm in anticipating the ceremony, surely? You drive me mad, Romilly. I want you so desperately. See the state to which you bring me,' and he placed her hand over the bulge lifting his breeches. 'Feel my manhood straining to be united with you. Be merciful and come to Vauxhall Gardens with me before I deliver you home tonight. My coachman will turn a blind eye if I order him to leave us for a while. The seats are wide and will make a capital bridal bed.'

'Sir! You shock me! What a monstrous suggestion,' she whispered, but inside she warmed with excitement, virgin she might be and innocent, but she was filled with an overwhelming curiosity about the congress between a man and a woman. That hard bough inside his breeches intrigued her and she longed to see and touch it, but, 'Even if I agreed, there's my chaperone, Wade,' she reminded, and withdrew her fingers, casting a glance over her shoulder to where the duenna sat.

'A pox on Wade!' he fumed, and one or two members of the audience looked across angrily and hushed him, though disturbances during the performances were commonplace. 'We're never alone.'

'It is customary to guard a young girl's virtue,' she rejoined primly, but wished it wasn't so. Nathan was more than just talented and she daydreamed of having him make love to her, though ignorant as to what this would entail. 'Take me round to meet Mr Westbury later,' she demanded.

'Oh, very well, my angel,' Jamie agreed reluctantly.

She fidgeted and waited for the final curtain to go down. Thoughts of Nathan were a mere diversion. She had never yet met anyone who filled her with uncontrollable ardour, and was heartily tired of Viscount James Milward, the man to whom her father had given her. They had been promised to one another in childhood, an arrangement made between their fathers with money, land and titles the main consideration. She liked him little better than when he was a bullying boy and a spotty youth whereas he, it seemed, had fallen in love with her, delighted with both her person and the prospects of a generous dowry.

He declared that love repeatedly, but she could not be certain of his sincerity. His well-born companions were dandies, living lavishly, constantly in debt, obsessed by the gaming tables, horseracing, cockfighting, prize fighting – anything and everything that involved betting. Consequently marrying a lady with a substantial dot was essential if they were to continue their profligate lifestyle that was based on the laws of inheritance. Romilly's eyes had been opened to this early. She had been taught that it was a wife's place to obey her lord, run his household like clockwork, be modest and diligent and bear him a clutch of heirs.

Of course, like everything else in England since Charles II had been restored to his kingdom, restrictions were relaxed from those dull days when there had been a Puritan dictatorship under Oliver Cromwell. Even so, men still had the upper hand and someone like Romilly, despite her fiery temper and rebelliousness was still compelled to obey her father and, after marriage, her husband.

The orchestra played the finale number. The dancers whirled in a lively jig and then took their bows to thunderous applause. The king rose in the Royal Box and his people cheered. 'I'm going backstage with the viscount,' Romilly informed Jessica.

'Very well, my lady,' Jessica replied, laying a gauzy scarf round Romilly's shoulders, her stance telling her without words that she intended to go along too. Romilly was in her charge, and woe betides her if the Earl discovered that she had been neglectful of her duties towards his daughter. She

7

let her views be known however, adding with a sniff, 'If your ladyship feels it necessary to consort with a collection of mountebanks.'

'Don't be so stuffy,' Romilly retorted, and swept ahead of her, fingertips resting on Jamie's crooked elbow.

The narrow corridors were packed and, 'Well met, Jamie and Lady Romilly,' said a foppishly dressed individual, the long curls of his elaborately curled periwig almost sweeping the floor at her feet as he made a bow.

'Ah, George, my dear fellow, and did you enjoy the play?' Jamie replied, clapping him on the shoulder.

'Capital, capital!' George enthused. 'I'm about to offer my congratulations to the players.'

'So are we. Shall we go together?' Jamie suggested, and Romilly had the impression that he was more relaxed now that one of his bosom companions was there – Lord George Althrope, heir to an estate in Dorset.

Jamie had a close-knit circle of friends. They were always together, as if joined at the hip, all rich and idle and considering themselves masters of witty repartee. Besides gambling, their main interest was women – whores, actresses, society belles, shop girls and maidservants – though there were a few who preferred their own sex.

Romilly had heard about their exploits through her friend, Lady Alvina Segar, who was more informed than her regarding matters sexual. Even so she did not understand the ramifications. Now several others had come along, all talking loudly and smelling very high of orange flower water. They were handsome young men, untouched by the Civil War that had ripped their grandfathers' and fathers' lives apart and executed their King. The aristocracy had gained ground again once his exiled son, Charles, had been returned to his rightful place on the throne. Licentiousness abounded; everyone was out for a good time and none more so than these privileged scions of noble families.

It was fashionable to meet the performers in the dressing

rooms, and no beau worth his salt would leave the building before carrying out this ritual. Many were motivated by lust, for the actresses' morals were notoriously lax. Though a few were genuine in their desire to be serious thespians, the majority were ladies of easy virtue seeking a rich keeper.

Romilly had heard that they had clamoured for auditions once King Charles had issued an edict forbidding men to appear in female roles, as had always been the custom. It had been considered lewd for women to display themselves in public, but he liked the ladies and had seen them on the stage during his years of exile in France. Since men had been forbidden to trail a skirt across the boards, his Majesty had acquired more than one courtesan from theatrical circles, Nell Gwyne being the favourite.

It was not Romilly's first excursion to the dressing rooms and these were shared by males and females alike, divided by curtains that were usually thrust back casually, the players unconcerned about false modesty, existing with a free and easy camaraderie marred only by flashes of professional jealousy.

It was noisy and lively, with both sexes in a state of undress and Romilly quickly spotted Nathan, slim, dark and elegant, seated at a dressing table, his lean face illumined by candles in sconces each side of the mirror. He was in the process of wiping off make-up. He stood as she approached and bowed when she introduced herself.

'I'm Lady Romilly Fielding.'

'Your ladyship does me too much honour,' he replied, and their eyes met in the fly-spotted glass and interest sparked in his, although a big-busted, mature woman was observing him.

Romilly recognised her as Lady Barbara Leyton, subject of much gossip because it was rumoured that she had used her money and influence to help Nathan advance his career. She shot Romilly a venomous glance, which she ignored.

'I so much enjoyed your performance tonight, Mr Westbury,'

9

she continued, aware that Jamie's attention was elsewhere as he and George flirted with a couple of scantily clad dancers. Never in her life had Romilly seen such a blatant display of breasts, rounded buttocks and hairy pudendum.

'You are too kind,' Nathan replied, hand on heart. 'Please be seated so that I may continue removing the greasepaint while we talk.'

'I shall leave you now, Nathan,' Lady Barbara interrupted rudely. 'My husband and I are invited to a masque at the palace. Such a nuisance, but unavoidable. Be good and I'll see you tomorrow.'

She reached down and squeezed the prominent bulge between his legs, and he smiled up into her face. But when she had left in a flurry of silk and expensive French perfume he grimaced and said, 'She's kindness itself, but possessive. It's rather like being married. Are you married, my dear young lady?'

'Oh, no,' she responded quickly, glad that she wasn't, then added, blushing a little, 'but I am betrothed.'

'To that young man you came in with?' he asked.

His striking features were even more fine without the layer of greasepaint. His hair was long, curling to his shoulders, every strand his own, not a peruke like those adopted by the leaders of the bon ton, including the king. Their hair was cropped short, the theory being that it was easier to keep a wig clear of lice than one's own head. Romilly wanted to run her fingers through his lovelocks and draw his face towards her breasts. These were pushed high by a short, tight busk worn beneath an equally tight, low-cut bodice. Her shoulders were bare, the large puffed sleeves of her pastel pink gown slipping down as if dragged by their own weight. A cascade of pearls circled her slender throat and reached her cleavage. There were more pearls on her wrists and adorning her hair, which was piled into a coronet at the crown, with ringlets falling over each ear where the lobes were adorned by pearl drops.

She looked wonderful and she knew it, sure that every man thereabouts would find her irresistible. It was not conceit but habit that made her think thus. She had been pampered and spoiled from infancy, never knowing her mother who had died shortly after her birth, and her grief-stricken father had not married again, devoting himself to his daughter, sole heir and beneficiary. It was small wonder that she was sought after.

Tish! she thought impatiently. I'm tired of fops and want to be in the company of a real man, someone who has known life's discomforts, like Nathan. Being an actor can't be easy. I wonder what it is like to be poor, reliant on one's talent to turn a coin. She wanted to be alone with him, to ask him pertinent questions and, maybe, have him kiss her. He had a beautiful mouth, the upper lip firm and commanding, the lower full and sensual. The thought of him capturing hers in an ever deepening kiss made her wet between the legs. Jamie didn't affect her like this. She had known him so long that he was like a brother.

How was this naughty ambition to be fulfilled? she wondered. Wade was standing in the background, arms folded on her breasts and a sour expression on her face, and then there was Jamie. Even if she managed to give her duenna the slip, he would be lurking around. But something had to be done.

'I'm mighty interested in those clever tricks that make the scenery so convincing,' she said, on a wave of inspiration. 'I'd love to see them, and the costumes, too. Are the swords real or fake?'

They had seen a comedy that night, a bawdy romp that was far removed from the works of Shakespeare or Christopher Marlow, but even so she was providing herself with a splendid excuse for having him conduct her away from the dressing rooms on the pretence of a tour round the theatre's illusionary secrets.

She hit on another scheme, calling across to the chaperone,

'I'm thirsty, Wade. Fetch me a drink. Refreshments are still on sale. Wine for me and ale for yourself.' She knew that she had a penchant for small beer, becoming almost human under the influence of a pint or two.

'I say, bring a couple of bottles of sherry sac for me. You'd like a drink, wouldn't you, ladies? And you, too, gentlemen?' put in Jamie, too occupied in impressing the girls and his friends to notice what Romilly was doing.

Nathan stood up and together they slipped away, down a dimly lit passage and into a further room. It was deserted, but piled high with dress baskets from which costumes spilled, while others hung on crowded rails and bulged from cupboards. There was the glint of mock gold and paste gems from crowns and armour and sword hilts, racks of boots and shoes, and shelves containing hats and stands supporting grey, black and blond wigs for every possible character. Chairs, couches and rugs, thrones and beds gave it the appearance of a second-hand shop.

A conglomeration of stale sweat, dust, must and grease paint filled the air, a heady brew that invaded Romilly's nostrils and fired along her nerves. It symbolised the theatre, that make-believe world where anything was possible – and Nathan was a denizen of this magical place.

He lost no time, placing his fingertips on hers and then drawing her ever closer to his body. He was wearing a white shirt with billowing sleeves. It was unfastened down the front over a hairy chest. Still holding one of her hands, he guided it through the opening so that she touched the warmth of his skin.

She drew breath on a sharp gasp, 'Oh!'

He gave a wry smile, the lines each side of his mouth deepening, as he said, 'Don't tell me that you've not felt a man before, my lady.'

'Er... n-no, I haven't, in very truth,' she stammered, embarrassed that he should know of her innocence. It was as if it gave him an advantage.

'Unusual in one so fair,' he commented in his beautifully modulated actor's voice. It caressed her and penetrated her almost as if he had done so physically. 'Place your arms around my neck,' he added, and she could refuse him nothing.

'Ah... you smell so sweet,' he murmured. 'So young, so fresh, after the much used, aging charms of Lady Barbara.' And he kissed her neck and nibbled her lobes, setting the pendant earrings swinging, and she was in the seventh heaven of delight, nipples crimping, thighs yearning to open to his invasion.

'Don't you love her?' she managed to squeak.

He chuckled, deep in his chest. 'Love her? Indeed I don't, but she wants me and is willing to pay for my favours and in return will make me London's leading actor.'

'And her husband doesn't mind?'

'There's no love lost between them. A marriage of convenience, nothing more. He has his whores and she has her lovers,' he whispered, and his fingers toyed with her breasts, exploring the smooth area above her bodice and dipping into the front.

Such cynicism offended the romantic streak within her, but she had been reared to accept the sense in this. Love marriages only existed among the lower ranks – servants, tradesmen, shopkeepers, not the upper echelon. But now all sensible considerations were far from important. She was where she had wanted to be – in Nathan's arms. He was so gentle, pushing her back against a wicker dress-basket and lifting her so that she was perched on the lid. Then he carefully parted her legs and lifted her voluminous skirt and frothy white petticoats as if unwrapping a precious gift. It was in no way alarming, for Nathan had learned to be a practiced seducer; it was part and parcel of his trade.

By now Romilly was putty in his hands. Her heart was beating wildly and mad thoughts were winging through her brain. If she allowed him to breach her maidenhead and became with child could she yield to Jamie, convince him that it was his and push forward the date of the wedding? More urgent than this, however, was the crying need to experience everything with Nathan, her body urging her to surrender and enjoy and damn the consequences.

He had lifted her breasts from their covering, the nipples like hard cherries, and then his lips found hers, parted and explored them, his tongue tangling with her own in a dance of passion. His hand, meanwhile, cruised up her stockinged legs and found her fork. It was not thought modest to wear drawers, as these were a mannish garment, so her parts were bare beneath a long chemise and frou-frou of skirts.

'Darling girl,' Nathan breathed, combing through her pubic floss. 'You're like a pure young goddess – so beautiful. Let me breathe in your nectar,' and he dived under her clothes and she felt the outrageous shock of his mouth on her cleft.

'Mr Westbury!' she gasped, while her loins convulsed with pleasure. 'What are you doing, sir?'

His face appeared momentarily, dark eyes sparkling, lips wet with her dew. 'I'm supping on ambrosia, the food of the gods,' he declaimed, and then his hand went to his breeches that were gaping open. He withdrew his cock, long and thick and fully erect.

'Oh... oh!' she exclaimed, wide-eyed as she stared at it.

He thrust it into her palm, losing control as he almost snarled, 'Rub it! Don't be shy!'

It felt incredibly warm and smooth and she obeyed instinct more than his instructions as she eased her hand up and down, aware of wetness around the helm and hearing him groan. Her own moist delta ached with a need she did not comprehend, only knowing that she wanted his touch there again – lips, fingers – this monster that was filling her hand. Was this what fucking was all about? Small wonder the world was obsessed by it. So curious a sensation, so compelling that one was blind to all else. Poems were written extolling love – art depicted it, yet it was like the jungle or farmyard, simply Dame Nature's way of insuring the survival of the

14

species.

He held her mons, parting the hair-fringed wings and fondling the seat of her sensation – that sliver of flesh surmounted by a nubbin. She had discovered it long ago and touched it briefly, alarmed by the tingle that ran along her nerves. Frightened and certain that it was wicked to fondle it, she now discovered that Nathan was producing the same feelings, but more acute and demanding. He fell into a rhythm, rubbing the little protuberance steadily and she found herself doing the same to his cock.

The strange feeling in her increased, leading her on and on to – where? Bliss. Paradise. A fulfilment that she could only begin to guess at. And Nathan was plunging his cock into her hand and withdrawing, then pushing back in feverishly.

'Oh, sweeting, don't stop,' he groaned. 'Bring me to the heights, while I do the same for you!'

'I will! I will!' she cried, lifting her hips to meet his slippery touch, unable to stop, chasing that extraordinary feeling.

Then the door was flung open abruptly and Jessica Wade was framed there. 'My lady! Whatever are you doing?' she thundered.

Nathan shot away from Romilly, turning his back on the duenna and rearranged his breeches. Romilly sat up and adjusted her skirts. 'Did I send for you, Wade?' she answered haughtily, maintaining authority, even though her bud was throbbing at the point of explosion.

Wade stood her ground. Gawky and plain, she was obeying her employer's orders, not those of his wayward child. 'You did not, milady,' she said firmly. 'But I was worried when I found you had vanished.'

'She did right to tell me,' thundered Jamie, appearing behind her and pushing to the front. 'What have you to say for yourself?'

Romilly had regained her composure and with it her annoyance. How dare he speak to her like that? 'I am not your slave,' she said regally. 'If I chose to permit Mr Westbury to

15

show me round the property rooms, then that is my business. As I recall, sir, you were engaged in talk with the actresses, were you not?' She permitted the slightest note of reproof to enter her voice.

Jamie reddened, and turned his wrath to Nathan, hand on his sword hilt. 'You, sir, should know the rules. A young lady goes nowhere without her chaperone. Were you a gentleman I should call you out.'

'Then it's lucky for me that I'm lowborn and not allowed to wear a weapon, *my lord*.' Nathan laid mocking emphasis on the title.

'Indeed it is. Had you not been a commoner I'd have challenged you to a duel at dawn with the weapon of my choice – rapier or pistol. Even so, I can have you whipped by my servants.'

'Don't be foolish, Jamie,' Romilly broke in. 'You must trust me. I'd do nothing to tarnish your honour.'

'You have offended me deeply,' he said grumpily, glowering at Nathan who stood there unconcerned. 'Your father shall hear of this.'

'Of what?' she snapped tartly. 'My speaking with an actor whose performance I have just enjoyed? What do you expect him to do? Lock me in my bedchamber?'

'That might be a solution,' he snapped. 'I know he is already concerned about your unladylike behaviour.'

Nathan made for the door, turning with a bow as he said, 'If you will excuse me, I have work to attend. A rehearsal for tomorrow's rendition of *'Tis a Pity She's a Whore*. Come and see it. You might find it amusing.'

With that he raised a brow at Romilly, smiled mockingly at Jamie, and took himself off.

'And what have you been doing, my girl?' thundered the Earl of Stanford.

Romilly outfaced her father, head raised, chin set at a mulish angle, totally unaware of how much she resembled this proud

16

nobleman who had sired her. Not so much physically, of course, she being a slender girl, but in her mien and determination to have her way on every issue.

'Doing? Why, nothing of note, sir. Shopping at the Royal Exchange with my maid,' she responded sharply, drawing her fingers from her gloves and shrugging off her fur-lined cape. But her pulse was racing and she knew by the expression on his harsh features that someone had told him about her dalliance with Nathan.

And dalliance was all it had been, she regretted. *Another few moments and I should have been transformed from an ignorant girl into a woman of experience.*

'I'm not speaking of this morning, chit,' the Earl said heavily, standing spread-legged before the fire blazing on the wide hearth, hands clasped behind his back. 'James came to see me early and Wade has corroborated his story. You were caught in a compromising position with a vagabond actor or some such. Is this true?'

'No, it is not,' she lied. 'And Jamie is a fine one to talk. He's forever ogling the dancers.'

'That's different. He's a man.'

He loomed over her, big and imposing, a peer of the realm and master of vast estates in Devon and Cornwall. She had always held him in awe and had had little to do with him, brought up by nursemaids, housekeepers and governesses. As she grew older he had taught her to ride and hunt and, later, to take her place in London society, but there was never any easy intimacy between them. She was sure there should have been and she missed this – keeping her distance, as he did from her. It was only when he was angry that she felt he was truly noticing her and this made her defiant and equally enraged.

She stood in front of him, arms akimbo, hands on her hips, a golden-haired termagant. 'A man, quotha! So that gives him licence to do as he pleases? I don't think so, father.'

'You know nothing about life, you foolish child. Men are a

17

different breed… they know how to comport themselves and it is their duty to look after the frail sex of their own class.'

'Ha!' she gave a harsh bark of laughter. 'That I can't stomach.'

'We follow the teachings of the Bible,' he shouted, his face turning puce, with a little vein throbbing in the centre of his brow.

'Stuff!' she exploded, her gown swishing as she took a pace towards him in her high heels. 'You hardly ever attend church, only when you have to, at Christmas or Easter if you happen to be residing at Harding Hall. Don't give me this religious clap-trap.'

He raised his hand as if to strike her and, for an instant, she wondered if he would, imagining the shock as his blow descended. 'Wicked, blasphemous and wanton! You deserve to be punished!' he roared. 'Get to your room at once and I'll deal with you later. Meanwhile think on this… I am sending you to Jamaica.'

'Where?'

'To Port Royal in Jamaica, an island in the West Indies,' he retorted briskly. 'Your aunt, Lady Paulina Fenby, lives in the nearby town of Kingston. She's my sister. You've never met her, for she went abroad with her wealthy husband years ago. He owns several plantations, you know. Enormously rich, but that's by the way. I shall write to her at once, saying that you need a woman's guidance and godly company to free you of these silly notions. An actor indeed! You are betrothed to a fine young man. He shall accompany you and, on your return to England, I fully expect you to have given up your wild ways and settled down to be a good, faithful wife.'

'And if I refuse to go?' she challenged, though her stomach gave a lurch and she was shaking.

'You won't,' he declared heavily. 'Not by the time I've finished with you. Prepare yourself, Romilly, for I intend to chastise you. I can't have you smirching our good name. I have always believed in the old adage, "Spare the rod and

18

spoil the child".'

She bowed her head and trembled. This would not be the first time he had punished her for some misdemeanour, but not of late. As a child she had been regularly caned by those in authority over her, from not learning her books to racketing around like a tom-boy, but he was the one to be feared most of all. His palm was heavier, his whip harsher, his rod a whippy, pliant devil of an implement but, most of all, she hurt inside at having offended him, this sole parent whom she longed to please.

Chapter Two

Romilly flounced from the room and up the wide, curving staircase. She wanted to scream at Jessica and give Jamie a piece of her mind. She wanted to find Alvina and talk the matter over. She wanted to run away, putting miles between herself and all these bothersome people! She stamped her foot and slammed her bedroom door.

'You!' she yelled, in the worst rage of her life.

'Now, my lady... be calm...' the duenna expostulated, ducking to avoid a savage swipe across the cheek.

'Calm? I'll give you calm, you traitor! How dare you tell tales on me to my father!'

'He pays me to look after you,' Jessica said calmly, ignoring this temper tantrum. 'And Lord James was angry, too. He visited your father this morning and complained of your behaviour.'

'Father wants to send me to Jamaica!' Romilly raged, pacing up and down like a caged tigress. 'The colonies are savage, uncouth places, with no parties, no theatres, no shops. Dull, dull, dull! I won't go. I won't!'

'I've heard tell that they are none of these. The towns are fine and so are the houses. There are plantations and the wealthy own slaves, making heaps of money from sugar and tobacco,' Jessica said placatingly. 'It might be just what you need, and your betrothed will go with you.'

'No! No! No!' Romilly repeated

'But yes, my girl, yes,' said a strong masculine voice. Her father walked in. He carried a cane in both hands, striking the left one lightly across the palm as he strode towards her. 'Bend over,' he ordered. 'Clasp your ankles. Wade, throw her skirts back over her shoulders.'

'But, sir... my lord...' Jessica protested.

'Do as I say, Wade, unless you, too, want to feel the weight of the rod. I don't know what's got into women these days, always arguing with their betters.'

Romilly hesitated for a second only, then she gripped her ankles, head hanging down, bottom raised, feeling the cold as Jessica hoisted up the silk skirts and the shift. Romilly waited, anticipating the blow but still unprepared when it fell. Her buttocks went numb, then pain flamed through them. She cried out, unable to restrain herself though hating to give him the satisfaction. It was some years since he had beaten her and now she found it all the more humiliating. She was a grown woman and yet he still considered it his right to chastise her as he thought fit. Presumably Jamie would do the same, once the knot was tied. No matter how sophisticated and modern the young bloods thought themselves, they would still treat their wives as possessions over which they ruled.

Her father paused, took off his coat and rolled back his sleeves, his actions proclaiming his intention of making every blow count. Romilly endured, bracing herself, legs spread, well aware that her private parts were on show. Jessica stood to one side, ready to restrain her should she attempt to escape. Her pride refused to allow her to cry, protest or try to flee. He would see that she was made of as stern a metal as him.

It was all very well to make resolutions, but harder to carry out. The cane swished and landed with an agonising crack and she jerked involuntarily, her hinds bathed in fire. Again and again that punishing rod bit into her tender flesh and she could feel consciousness slipping away. She staggered and Jessica upheld her.

'Well, my girl, do you concede to my command?' he asked sternly, and she was dimly aware that he liked this no more than her and was but carrying out what he considered to be his duty.

She prayed this was so, for Alvina had hinted that there

were those who enjoyed inflicting pain and, even stranger, those who actually liked being whipped. The idea horrified Romilly, yet a thrill shivered through her. What would it be like to be mastered by a big, handsome brute of a man? Putty in his hands, to do with what he willed?

Her father straightened and she turned towards him, managing to hold her head high and look him straight in the eye. He was sweating, droplets trickling down his red face from beneath the long grey lappets of his tightly curled peruke. At the moment she both loved and hated him. 'How can you send me away, father? I'm your only child,' she whispered reproachfully.

'It is for your own good,' he insisted, wiping his face with a snow-white handkerchief. 'There is far too much licence abroad these days. London is a hotbed of sin. God knows I'm no prude, but the Court has gone too far and all follow the King's example. I want to see you happily settled and my sister will enjoy helping you. You need an experienced woman to give you advice on how to comport yourself. It won't be for more than a twelvemonth and then you can return and we will celebrate your marriage to James in high style.'

'I have no choice, have I?' she muttered, her bottom bruised and aching, but her stubborn pride undiminished.

'No,' he answered bluntly, and Jessica held his coat while he stuffed his arms into it and then straightened his lace cravat. 'I shall make arrangements at once. One of my merchant ships will be sailing to Port Royal within the month. You will travel aboard her. In the meantime, you'll go nowhere unattended and if there's the slightest hint of impropriety, you'll feel the weight of my stick again.'

'Damn him! To the devil with all men!' Romilly raved when he had gone. Jessica made no reply, busying herself by rearranging the many gowns hanging in the wardrobe. 'How dare he beat me? The bully. As for ordering me abroad... my God, if I only had money and independence. I'd show him!'

A tap on the door, and Jamie was admitted. He looked

sheepish, giving her a timid glance and advancing with caution. 'How fare you, sweetheart?' he asked.

She sprang at him, though the effort cost her dear. He dodged aside as she shrieked, 'How do you think I am, traitor? You tattled about my acquaintance with Mr Westbury, and father has just beaten me.'

'It appeared to be more than mere friendship, my love,' he said, nervously producing a silver box, opening it and placing a tiny dune of snuff at the base of his thumb, then inhaling it.

'Oh, is that so? And what about you and those tarts? How dare you judge me? The upshot is that father is sending me to the West Indies.'

He applied a kerchief to his nostrils and said, 'So I understand, and I am to escort you. It should be entertaining. Your aunt, Lady Fenby, is exceedingly rich and lives in high style, so I'm given to understand.'

'Indeed. But first there is a tedious sea voyage during which I shall undoubtedly be sick, and arrival at Jamaica where my relations are to drill me into becoming a virtuous wife!'

'Don't fret, my darling,' he murmured, bending to whisper in her ear, 'we shall be together and maybe able to find privacy in which to make love. Under clear blue skies and waving palm trees you shall become my pagan goddess, and I'll ram my prick up you and give you heavenly delight.'

If he hoped to impress her with this it had the opposite effect; Nathan's face sprang to mind and not only that – his kisses, his caresses and the sight of his manhood. Desire warmed her loins, spreading from her overheated buttocks, a part of the pain and ache. Hot on this came the realisation that she wouldn't be able to see him again. Jamie seemed a very poor substitute, though this might improve – she had tasted sensual delights and was unlikely to be satisfied with anything less. It was like opening Pandora's box.

Jessica hovered closer, mindful of the Earl's strict instructions and reluctant to feel his wrath. 'Please excuse us, your lordship,' she said to Jamie, bobbing a curtsey. 'But

I must put my lady to rights and make sure that she rests. I believe you are invited to supper. You will see her again then.'

He bowed himself out, one hand on his heart, the other resting on the basket hilt of his sword, and it was then that Romilly cracked, throwing herself across the bed and crying as if her heart would break. Despite her boldness, inside she was like a frightened child. Jamaica was so far away. The other side of the globe!

'Don't upset yourself, my lady,' Jessica soothed, bending over and stroking her hair. 'I shall be with you... and so will your betrothed.'

'If only Alvina could come, too,' Romilly sobbed, tears dripping onto the pillow.

'Maybe she can. Why don't you ask her? Her father and yours are friends, aren't they? This might be arranged.'

At that Romilly sat up, tears drying on her cheeks. 'Perhaps it could.' She flung her arms impulsively round Jessica. 'What a capital notion! She will be here anon, and I shall speak to her and we can ask our fathers.'

It was cool in the cave below the fortress. A stream trickled between the rocks, cascading into a deep dark pool, where several beautiful women and handsome youths frolicked. They splashed each other, gave shrill screams and laughter, fondled naked breasts and thighs, phalli and clefts, totally at ease and ready to give or receive fulfilment. Bejewelled, bizarre and barbaric, they satisfied the eyes and the senses of their lord and master. At a word or gesture they would pleasure him in any way he wanted.

He lay back on a regal couch placed on a dais where he could see them, these spoils of sea battles, inland raids, plunder and pillage. He allowed lust to race through his magnificently honed body that bore scars here and there, relics of many a vicious duel. He was bronzed and fit, rippling with muscle, ready for anything. His hair was wet, rendering it jet-black, falling to well below his broad shoulders for he had just come from the beach, via a secret way. He had been pitting his strength against the waves that thundered in to run up the shore of this tropical island paradise that belonged to him as well as all he surveyed and much that he didn't, the most feared man in the length and breadth of the Spanish Main.

He enjoyed sex and money and conquest, but above all he relished power, and had acquired this in plenty throughout his chequered career. A goblet of vintage wine gripped in one mighty fist, he considered the girls, selecting one or maybe two to bring him to orgasm. He wore a silk robe, open down the front over his muscle-packed belly and thick thatch of black pubic hair from which an enormous penis stood proud. It was fully erect, long and as thick as a bough. He palmed it, rejoicing in the hardness, the smoothness, and the dew seeping from its single eye. He rotated the ring that pierced the glans. This suffused him with a rush of feeling and his cock bobbed, moving of its own volition. He controlled it as he controlled everything and everyone that swam into his ken. But this appendage of his was like a difficult stallion, full of self-will and often refusing to be mastered – mastering *him*.

The urge to climax was almost unbearable, but he took his hand from his cock and concentrated on his surroundings in an effort to subdue the monster. The cavern was huge, a natural formation made by the volcano that had formed this island millions of years ago. It was furnished luxuriously. Many decadent, colourful objects robbed from his prey over the years had been taken there to enhance it.

Massive wax candles, snatched from a church, wept creamy tears that trickled down and solidified on the wrought iron-girandoles that held them. They cast a glow over the scene, though they had not been intended to illumine debauchery. Natural pillars of rock supported the ceiling that reared up into the darkness like the fan vaulting of a cathedral. They reminded him of religious ceremonies, as did the smell of incense, like that wafting from censers swung by altar boys, one of whom had been him long ago. A different time, a different place, before his world had been turned upside down and, in the confusion, honour, family traditions and loyalty to crown and country had been destroyed forever.

With it had gone compassion towards his fellowman. It stripped him of emotions, leaving a void within him that nothing could fill. It was a dark place, and cold, and he had replaced love with lust, encouraged passion fired by cruelty, and indulged in the urge to experiment with each facet of the senses. He had succeeded, exploring every pathway of sexual deviation. He was master of all he surveyed – feared – admired – copied even, by lesser men who wished to share his reputation for wildness and mastery. But try as they might to emulate him, there was only one Armand Tertius, born a French comte but now a pirate king.

He was roused from his musing by the feel of soft fingers trailing down his back. He looked round as the woman snuggled up to him, one thigh thrown across his as he lounged there. She was exotic and lovely, the light glimmering on her dusky skin, her ebony hair coiling into a hundred little beaded ringlets round her shapely head, her proud mien that of an African goddess.

'Is there anything I can do for you, master?' she purred, and reached down and pinched his wine-red nipples, causing a shudder to pass through him to his groin.

His hand clamped on hers, crushing her slim fingers, but she made no protest. 'Perhaps there is, Sabrina,' he growled. 'I need a diversion. I've seen this all before. It is time for fresh blood to be brought here.'

'I understand, master,' she murmured in that intriguing Creole accent, a free woman who chose to be his slave for her own advancement. 'Be patient. I have read the cards for you and foresee that a change is coming.'

'A woman?' he asked, only half believing her ability to foretell the future with Tarot cards that she kept in a sacred bag.

'Oh yes, my lord. Certainly a woman, and a beautiful one.'

'Will she love me?' He was not aware of the wistful note in his voice, but Sabrina was, and her dark eyes were troubled.

'Who could not love you, master?' she asked quietly.

He gave a harsh bark of laughter. 'Many! And if they say they do, then how can I be sure they are sincere, or just protesting love through fear or greed or seeking to fulfil their own ambitions?'

'Does it matter? Do you need love?' Sabrina wound her subtle arms round his neck, sinuous as a snake.

'No! That's romantic shit. All I need is *this*.' He threw her on her back and reared over her. 'And *this*.' His fully erect phallus found its goal and he thrust inside her, using the force of his strong hips as he plunged in and out, finding the rhythm that would take him to the heights.

Sabrina responded quickly, her brilliantly patterned silk skirt falling away, the sequinned scarf that partly hid her breasts opening to his questing hands. She welcomed him between her thighs and raised her legs, scissoring them round his neck, drawing him ever deeper into her scented mysteries. His acolytes, watching this erotic performance, began to ape his movements, lost into a welter of passion, legs and arms entwined, males with females, girls with girls, men with men. It didn't matter, just as long as there were cunts and cocks, breasts and arseholes. The cavern throbbed with excitement and arousal and uninhibited desire.

Armand relished Sabrina's flesh. She was the chief of his concubines and obeyed him explicitly. Sometimes these willing submissives irritated him. He felt the need of a challenge and even as he reached a thunderous climax within Sabrina's body, so he experienced ennui. He had everything, but longed for an extra thrill – that of conquering a personality almost as forceful as his own. A lady perhaps, a royal personage who would put up a fight, marking him with her vicious talons and showing such strength and purpose in defending herself that he would know he had met his soul mate. She might try to kill him, or rouse his followers to rebellion and, when eventually he subdued her, driving her mad with love for him, then he might know the peace that always eluded him.

Restless now that he had released his spunk he pushed Sabrina aside, stood to his impressive height and clapped his hands. The slaves looked up at him in awe as he summoned a giant of a man, with a black beard and scarred face. His head was shaven, his shoulders broad as an ox, his hands like mighty paddles. His chest was naked; the skin tattooed with weird symbols, and a wide leather belt above canvas breeches spanned his waist. These were unfastened, his penis jutting out, swaying from side to side as he walked – a powerful weapon, like that of a bull. Sea boots covered his lower legs, and a cutlass swung from an ornamental scabbard. He was one of Armand's band of cutthroats, his second-in-command, who was feared almost as much as his chief.

'Ah, Johnson, fetch that new girl, the one we took from the *Santa Royale*.'

'She claims to be the governor of Cuba's daughter, captain,' Johnson replied, his deep voice gruff as gravel. Once he had been a mutinous English seaman condemned to death, but had escaped. Like many of Armand's crew he was a fugitive from justice, signing up under the unlawful flag of piracy.

'More likely to be his whore,' Armand stated crisply. 'Bring her here. She shall amuse me for a while.'

'Why bother with her when you have me?' asked Sabrina, standing tall and straight by his side, very conscious of her position in his household hierarchy.

He reached out and pinched one of her prominent nipples. 'It is my wish,' he said sternly. 'Do you dare question this?'

'No, master,' she replied, lowering her head meekly.

'Good. For if I thought for one moment that you were opposing me, then you would take your place on the crosspiece.'

Swinging a long pliable whip, Johnson went to the back of the cave where several prisoners were chained by the wrists to the rocks. He loosened one of the ringbolts and freed a young woman who cried and protested. He dragged her by a loop of manacle, hauling her along till she stood before Armand. She was a dark-haired beauty, though in disarray, her once fine gown torn and dirty. The ship they had taken had been Spanish, though vessels of any origin were fair game for them – pirates, not buccaneers who only attacked the Castilian navy. Armand showed little mercy to merchant shipping of all nationalities. He had no scruples. All that mattered were fat pickings.

My mother would die of shame could she but see me! The thought flashed crossed his mind to be rapidly erased. No time to dwell on the past. The here and now was all that mattered. He deliberately focused on the girl trembling before him.

'Please, sir,' she begged, her huge brown eyes awash with tears. 'Send me to my father. He will pay any ransom you demand.'

Armand was conversant with Spanish and he smiled sardonically as he replied in her native tongue, 'Indeed, and am I to believe you? Are you not a whore transported to the Caribbean in punishment?'

'No, sir, I swear it. My name is Maria Gomez and I've recently left a convent in Madrid. Father wanted me to join him now that mama is dead.'

Armand knew she was telling the truth. She had the air of an innocent girl once surrounded by nuns, but he chose to tease her. 'I don't think so, Maria. You are curious about what takes place during the carnal act, aren't you? Your thoughts dwell on it instead of on prayers to the Virgin Mary. You would like to share my bed, wouldn't you?'

Johnson laughed, deep in his belly, and the slaves tittered too, guessing what was to come. When Armand was being jovial he was usually at his worst. Sabrina settled back to watch, quelling her jealousy and saying, 'Don't keep her to yourself, master. I want a share in such a fresh young body.'

Maria shrank back, trying to conceal her breasts and her hairy mound, though this was part-hidden beneath the rags of her satin gown. She couldn't understand what Sabrina said, but the look in her eyes spoke volumes. Yet, as Armand scrutinised her, so a change took place. She blushed, sighed and reached out as if begging him to hold her, recognising his aristocratic bearing and hoping he would be lenient and do as she asked.

'You would like me to free you, honour you, treat with your father?' he said mockingly.

'Oh, yes. I know you could do it. You are a man of principle, not like the ruffians who ransacked the ship, slaughtered seaman and kidnapped officers.'

'I am their commander,' he corrected. 'They do nothing without orders from me.'

'How could you be so base?'

'I have been taught by experts,' he retorted coldly, stepped forward and dragged her against his firm, bare flesh, letting her feel his burgeoning phallus. One climax was never enough for him. The sap was rising again, sending urgent messages through his whole being, demanding that he take and enjoy this girl. 'On your knees, wench,' he growled.

She hesitated but Johnson placed a hand at the back of her neck, forcing her down till she knelt on the hard floor of the cave. Her legs were bunched under her, buttocks raised high. Johnson grabbed a handful of skirt and ripped it from her waist. Now her rounded bottom was on display, with its intriguing crack, and the plump, split-fig of her pudenda surrounded by crisp black curls.

Armand leaned over and inserted a finger into her virgin delta, smiling mockingly as he discovered it to be wet and slippery. She was gaining enjoyment from this, despite her protestations, confirming his opinion of women. The more they screamed the more they wanted to be ravished. 'Higher, higher,' he instructed the trembling girl. 'I want to see your ripe little cunt.'

It was satisfying to be able to speak several languages, each of which had its own particular terms for the genitals. Maria may have been innocent, but she obviously understood him and lifted her hips even further. Armand enjoyed deflowering maidens. It was hard work, and nothing like as easy on his cock as a well-worn pathway, but had its own special pleasure for the man who liked domination.

His nostrils flared and his grey eyes shone like steel. He could not resist touching her, insinuating a hand beneath her and fondling the ripe breasts with their coral tips that bunched under his caress. She moaned and her bottom cheeks parted even more, as if begging him to penetrate her arsehole and inexperienced cleft.

'And so I shall, my dear,' he muttered. 'But first you'll have a taste of subjection and pain.'

But would it be new to her? he wondered, taking whip from Johnson and snapping it through the air. Convents were notorious for their harsh treatment of malcontents and the sisters, often frustrated spinsters who had never had a man, regularly relieved their desires in congress with other nuns or novices. If they had not actually corrupted Maria then, at the very least, she might well have been flogged for some real or trumped up sin. The idea made his prick throb.

'Don't hurt me,' she sobbed, and this entreaty added further fuel to his fire. He nodded to Johnson who stood, spread-legged, restraining her by the manacles. Then Armand raised his right arm, relishing the movement, the whip an extension of himself and his passion. He brought it down with full force across Maria's backside. She shrieked and writhed. The spectators cried out their enjoyment. Johnson tightened his grip on her chains. Armand narrowed his eyes as lust, sharp as a spear, pierced his groin. His penis thickened and rose past his navel to his waist.

'No... no...' Maria sobbed, the mark of the whip etched on her pale skin, but Armand was beyond listening or stopping. The whip slashed down, landing on a fresh spot and, as she screamed and begged for mercy, so this roused him to an even greater fever pitch and he lashed her ruthlessly.

He paused, arm aching, and Sabrina leaned over the fainting girl. She ran her fleshy pink tongue over her red lips and then opened her mouth and licked the livid marks, wetting them with her saliva. 'Oh, master, how appealing she looks, how young and vulnerable,' and her tongue went lower till it reached the puckered brown rose of her anus, sampling it, and then the pink wings that protected that vital channel of love.

'Stand aside,' Armand ordered. 'She is mine and so are all her treasures. You may use her when I'm done.' He threw aside the whip, pushed Johnson out of the way and lifted Maria, one arm round her shoulders, the other beneath her buttocks.

She cried out in agony, but he didn't stop until he'd reached the divan and laid her down. Then with hardly a pause he was on her and in her, his phallus carving its way through her maidenhead. A moment of resistance and he was inside and Maria was no longer a virgin. The tightness of her clasping his member like a velvet glove, the gush of fluid as her pain was transformed into pleasure, her moans that changed to a keening note of ecstasy, worked like yeast on his overexcited cock. He kissed her neck, her throat, and forced his tongue between her lips, just as he was thrusting his member into her vagina. And Maria stopped struggling. Her limbs went lax as he slid his fingers between their bodies and found the hard nodule of her pleasure button, rubbing it steadily.

'Oh, God, I'm dying,' she gasped and convulsed in orgasm.

'No, you're not dying,' he murmured. 'You're living... have come alive after years of repression. Now feel me reach my apogee, you dirty little bitch.'

He was climbing that stairway to bliss – up and up – only death could stop him now. He reached the peak in a spasm of ecstasy so acute his head reeled. He came back to reality completely drained of spunk and, as always after fucking, experiencing that disillusion and self-disgust that always tormented him.

'What is it, master?' queried Sabrina, as he abandoned the girl and reached for wine. 'Didn't she please you?'

He scowled at her – the blackest scowl she had ever seen on his handsome face, as he barked, 'Another spineless virgin. Is there no female left on God's earth who will fight me?'

'Well, here's a to-do!' exclaimed Lady Alvina Segar, after she had listened to Romilly's tale of woe.

They were in the bedroom, seated on a dainty walnut couch, with a little table drawn close on which stood a silver teapot, milk jug, sugar basin and plate of fancy cakes. Jessica Wade and Alvina's maid, Kitty Rigg, were out of earshot near the window embrasure. Romilly thought it grossly unfair that her friend was allowed to drive out with only the sprightly girl as chaperone. But then Lord and Lady Segar were of liberal views and gave their daughter a great deal of freedom. She had been brought up in the company of her brothers and their friends, the youngest child with married sisters who had families of their own.

'It's too awful, isn't it?' Romilly wailed, springing up and pacing about, driving her fist into her palm.

Alvina helped herself to another iced fancy, then said with a careless shrug, 'I've heard of worse.'

'What?' Romilly stopped dead in front of her, breasts heaving with indignation. 'Are you trying to tell me that anything could be worse than banishment to the Caribbean?'

'Calm down, dear fool,' Alvina advised, laughter lifting her wide crimson mouth and lighting up her face. She looked even more beautiful when she laughed, and this was often.

She was a stunning woman of nineteen, with tumbling red hair and hazel eyes. Fashionable and popular, she was as yet unmarried but had suitors aplenty. There was ample opportunity for a lady in her position to encourage potential lovers as well as prospective husbands, and she had recently surrendered her virginity to a virile groom from her father's stables. Romilly had been shocked.

'Weren't you worried about getting with child?' had been her first question after she'd listened in disbelief to Alvina's graphic description of what had taken place between her and this commoner. It beggared belief and she still wasn't sure if she'd heard her aright. It seemed so crude, so reminiscent of the barnyard, but this was before her dalliance with Nathan.

'How can I be calm?' Romilly raved. 'I am being sent into exile.'

'Very dramatic,' Alvina said, still smiling. 'You say that Jamie will accompany you, so that's all right. And what were you doing with Nathan Westbury anyway? And why did you allow yourself to be found out? Tell me about Nathan. Is he well endowed?'

'Oh, Alvina, he seemed very big, but how can I judge? I've not seen a man's thingy before.'

At this Alvina rocked with mirth. 'Lack-a-day, listen to it. All of eighteen and you've never handled a cock. Shame on you! What about Jamie? Hasn't he tried to seduce you?'

Romilly's face was fiery, but she stuck out her chin and answered sharply, 'Not really. Not like Nathan. I think he wants to, but respects me.'

'Respect, fiddle-sticks!' Alvina retorted. 'Every man wants to find a nest for his prick. I'm sorry, dearest, but these home truths have to be said. You're far too naïve.'

'And you're so confident. I wish I was more like you.'

Romilly looked at her friend, admiring her green watered silk gown, with its tiny waist and low neckline. Her breasts were rounded domes, pushed high by the stiff busk and lacing. Her skirt sprang out over several petticoats, and she wore satin shoes with square toes, long tongues and spindle heels. The emphasis was on bare necklines, throats and shoulders, the gowns designed to look as if they might well slip too low, displaying rosy nipples. There were flowing scarves and capes and feathered hats with big brims, the whole effect one of

34

Arcadian freedom, these styles popularised by the King's bevy of mistresses.

'Darling child, you have everything to be confident about.' Alvina reached out and took her hand, stroking her fingers. 'Think of it as an adventure. Jamaica! Heavens, what sport!'

'Will you come with me?' Romilly sank down in front of her and rested her head against those luscious breasts. 'I can't leave you, dearest friend.'

She breathed in her perfume, a combination of lilies, the scent of her hair and that special, intimate and sweet odour all her own. A strange thought entered her mind of how fortunate was the lover who enjoyed the bounty of Alvina's lush body. She experienced a sharp ache in her womb and a sensation of longing to hold and be held in those alabaster arms.

'It's possible,' Alvina said thoughtfully. 'I've heard reports that the West Indies and the coasts thereabouts are strange and marvellous places, with natives and sea monsters, pirates and I don't know what-all. I should like to see it for myself.'

'Dare I hope that you will come?' Romilly's spirits were already lifting at the prospect.

'I shall speak to my father who will talk it over with yours. Yes, my love, I'd like that. Jamaica! Who knows, I might find my future husband there, or a string of lovers at the very least.'

Chapter Three

'How much longer, Captain Willard?' Romilly asked, seated at the dinner table in the oak-panelled, well-furnished main cabin in the stern of the *May Belle*.

He smiled at her, a ruggedly handsome man, a mariner to his fingertips, controlling his crew, the vessel and his passengers with an ease born of long practice. 'A day or two at the most, my lady, if the wind proves fair. It should do if I'm any judge of the elements, and I've been a sailor since I was fourteen. We'll reach Jamaica ahead of time.'

'La, what a relief that will be,' sighed Alvina, eyeing him encouragingly as she had done since the moment they boarded at London docks. But she'd not made much headway, for he took his duties very seriously. His officers, however, were more susceptible.

Two had joined them that evening, and they were young and personable, swaggering in the presence of the guests, well aware that they held positions of authority, sons of noblemen, following a tradition of seafaring.

'To step on dry land again, I'll second that,' put in Jamie, not a good sailor, subject to *mal de mer*.

Romilly and Alvina had not suffered this condition, but they were lucky. Jessica and Kitty had gone around pale and listless after the *May Belle* put to sea. So had Lord George Althrope, who'd come along for the fun of it. It hadn't been very funny to be confined to one's stateroom for days on end, with a chamber pot to hand.

But after this initial baptism of fire all had begun to enjoy the journey. They rose when they willed, with their servants to wait on them, ate at the captain's table and enjoyed an excursion ashore when they stopped off at Madeira to take on fresh water before beginning the lengthy haul across the Atlantic Ocean. Kitty Rigg, Alvina's high-spirited, curly-headed maid, spent much of her free time exchanging saucy banter with the crew, an occupation scorned by Jessica who behaved like a confirmed spinster. As for Alvina? The officers paid court to her, and of course there was the intriguing Joshua Willard, but he appeared blind to her blandishments.

Romilly was still resentful, blaming the Earl, considering his treatment of her as callous and uncalled for. Despite the fact that he had difficulty in controlling his emotions when she left, declaring that he would miss her sorely, she had not forgiven him. She took it out on Jamie, while he was endlessly patient. She would have respected him more had he shouted at her, instead of idling with George, playing cards and making silly wagers, like how many seagulls would fly across the top-sail within a given space of time, or if a porpoise would surface. Captain Willard was much more to her taste.

'Is Port Royal civilised?' she asked him, while the steward refilled her wineglass.

His blue eyes twinkled as he replied, 'It's fair enough, growing larger all the time. You should enjoy your visit.'

'But you will be leaving us?' She looked at him from under her lashes, alarmed by her own boldness.

'Naturally, my lady. I shall take goods aboard and transport them back to England.'

'To my father's warehouse in Wapping?'

'Indeed,' and he nodded sagely.

They settled down for a game of lanterloo when the table was cleared. Joshua and his officers joined in, whereas he usually excused himself and went about his duties. The players were subject to forfeits and it was a popular pastime at Court where more and more outrageous demands were made on those who lost. Kisses were the price, at the very least. Alvina inveigled herself into giving such tokens to everyone present, including Romilly.

'Get Joshua to kiss you,' whispered Alvina against Romilly's lips, as she held her in warm, scented arms.

'You cheat to get your way,' Romilly accused.

'Of course, sweetheart. What woman worth her salt doesn't? He's hot for it, hard as a broom handle down there when we embraced.'

Romilly shook her off, stood up and said to the others, 'If you will excuse me, I'm tired and seek my bed. Goodnight, gentlemen.'

They all rose and Jamie said, 'Wait, my love. I suggest we take a stroll on deck before retiring.'

Damn, Romilly thought, even as she smilingly agreed. He was forever seeking opportunities to caress her and, while her body responded, she missed the thrill Nathan had given her. The idea of marrying him, tied to him for the rest of her life, did not appeal. She needed someone more exciting, a hardy man like Joshua Willard, or an adventurer similar to the actor. If anything, Jamie was boringly safe. She had known him too long. He was more like a brother than a lover.

It was a warm night, scented with a salty tang and the faint odour of cinnamon from spice islands. The moon hung overhead, surrounded by a retinue of stars, and the ship sailed on, its canvas bellying out, bearing Romilly to – what? Unknown adventures? Or a dull stay with a fussy aunt who would wrap her up in cotton wool and lecture her on what was required of a good, faithful wife?

Jamie gave her his hand as she mounted the companionway, and then led her to the rail, overlooking the dark sea carved by white spume as the *May Belle* drove through it. Such power of motion made the vessel judder. It was exciting and alarming, making Romilly aware of how puny humans were in the face of such an omnipotent force.

She leaned her elbows on the carved balustrade, and then Jamie slipped his arms round her from behind, straining her to him. He swept her hair away and placed his lips on the sensitive nape of her neck. That touch shivered down her spine and connected with her nipples and loins, but she wished it was Nathan or Joshua caressing her. His hands moved over the silk, finding her every curve. She remembered him saying that they might find more freedom to be alone together once on the voyage, and this had proved true, especially at night for Jessica retired early. He had become bolder, insisting that there would be no harm in intimacy as they were to be married, but something deep within her urged restraint.

'I should go below,' she said, but he spun her round and captured her lips with his, tongue penetrating, seeking, demanding. She pressed her hands against his chest, pushing him away. 'No, Jamie,' she said firmly, though her heart was thudding and dew wetting her cleft. 'I've already told you I won't do it till our wedding night.'

He stood back, with frowning brows and sulky mouth. 'Then you don't love me.'

'That's foolish talk. I'm being sensible, and know that you'll lose respect for me if I give in. I'm a lady, not a whore.'

'You're my darling and I adore you,' he protested, throwing himself on his knees in front of her and then pushing up her skirts and grabbing her legs, sliding his hands higher till they reached the buckled garters that upheld her stockings.

Romilly was riveted, knowing she should resist, but unable to control the pleasure that bounded through her as his fingers found the soft, silky skin of her inner thighs and going further, the curly hair that shielded her secrets. Nathan had done this to her but they were interrupted before she climaxed. Now there was nothing to stop her and she wanted this sensation, recreating it herself sometimes, but always daydreaming of Nathan.

Emboldened by her lack of resistance Jamie burrowed beneath her gown. She felt his breath on her pubic hair, then his fingers parting her labial wings and his tongue darting to that sensitive little nodule that crowned her delta. She gasped, clenched her hands on the taffrail and went with the flow. She was unable to help herself, Jamie's tongue and lips a miracle, delving and prying, dipping and sucking. She could almost forget there was anyone there beneath her voluminous petticoats and imagine that his tongue was a disembodied creature, created purely for her pleasure.

She forgot that there might be members of the crew on duty. Someone was on watch all night, so Joshua had said. Thinking of him and wondering if he, too, would enjoy using his mouth on her, brought her ever closer till she reached her extremity, giving a little cry, her hips jerking. Jamie held her still, licking and slurping, taking her down gently from those delirious heights.

His face appeared from beneath the silken covering and he was smiling, his lips glistening with her juice. He stood up and his breeches were undone, his penis jutting forth, not so large as Nathan's but an impressive weapon nonetheless.

'Pleasure me as I've just pleasured you,' he whispered, holding it in his right hand and working the foreskin up and down over the darkly infused helm. 'Touch it. That's right, and stroke my cods.'

She wanted to help him, wanted to hold a man's cock in her palm again. It was weeks since she'd been caught with the actor. It felt smooth and hard and hot, and Jamie groaned as she took it in her fingers, playing with it for her own entertainment as much as his need. It was so fascinating a thing – and he opened the flap in his breeches wider so she could see and feel the heavy balls that hung beneath it.

A transformation was taking place in Jamie. No longer the languid, fashionable dandy, he yielded to his primordial instincts. He thrust into her palm, her thumb and forefinger forming an O, a makeshift orifice into which he could work his needy prick. It was quickly over. He threw back his head and gasped. His cock jerked and his semen shot out in milky jets, once, twice, thrice, wetting her hand and the front of her gown.

Dear God, she thought, for she hadn't known what to expect, will he ever stop? His emission was warm and sticky and she didn't know what to do, till he handed her his kerchief. 'Dearest girl,' he said softly, 'that was heavenly. So you do love me, don't you, poppet?'

'I suppose I must,' she answered, but was uncertain.

'This will get better and better,' he promised as he tucked his cock away and buttoned up. 'Wait until you feel my pork sword within your very being.'

'When we are married,' she reminded primly, having second thoughts now the heat in her blood was cooling.

'If you insist,' he said with a shrug. Having shot his load he was prepared to humour her. 'Come, dear heart, I shall escort you to your cabin.'

He helped her down the narrow stairs and along the passageway. Accommodation was cramped, but they each had a cabin to themselves, though Kitty shared with Jessica and George and Jamie's valets bunked down together. The toilet arrangements were primitive, but not so very far from those to which they were accustomed at home. Water was brought in a jug and poured into a washbasin for daily ablutions, and the call of nature answered in a slop bucket or china pot. In the case of the gentlemen travellers it was convenient to relieve themselves over the ship's rail, providing the wind was in the right direction.

Jamie kissed her at the door, and she could feel his phallus stirring again. How many times a night would he want it once they were wed? she wondered. To say nothing of daytime frolics. The prospect was daunting. Despite what he liked to think, she wasn't in the least in love with him. A romantic at heart, loving poetry and stories of gallant knights rescuing their beloved damsels, she yearned for something more than the mere gratification of the senses.

Jessica was there, waiting to unlace her, brush her hair and tuck her into bed. Romilly endured this, but once Jessica had retired she lay in the narrow bunk and thought about what had just transpired between her and Jamie. She slipped a hand between her legs under her white lawn nightgown, feeling that thrill as her fingers lightly explored the crisp hair, the cleft with its damp wings, and the sliver of flesh between that hardened at her touch. She was wet from Jamie's administrations, and she felt again his tongue and lips and wanted more, but not necessarily from him.

With her emotions at full tilt sleep evaded her. She got up, slipped a lacy negligee over her nightgown and quietly opened the door. The passage was deserted; in fact the whole ship seemed to be sleeping. It rocked gently on the swell, moving ever onward. She wasn't quite sure what she intended, having some vague notion of bumping into Joshua. She visualised him as ever wakeful, guardian of the ship and those who sailed on her, studying maps or the stars as he navigated. She crept towards the companionway that led aloft.

Then she heard a noise and stopped dead as she listened. It came again – a sigh – a moan. Perhaps someone was having a bad dream. The sound was coming from one of the cabins on her right. George's, if she remember correctly. She approached it stealthily and found the door was ajar. Whoever was within had forgotten to lock it. Had it been left open on purpose so that an expected person could enter? Possibly Alvina? Romilly had caught them flirting madly together, witty, cynical members of the young society hell raisers.

She applied her eye to the crack in the door and what she saw exceeded all her wildest speculations. George was there all right, but it wasn't a woman with him. Lieutenant Clive Morrison, one of the youngest and best looking of Joshua's officers, was bent over the bed, his breeches down about his ankles, his naked buttocks raised. George was behind him, stripped to the buff, in the act of applying lubricant to Clive's anus.

'Oh yes, sir… yes!' squealed the young man. 'Do it, please do it. Let me feel your todger inside… that's right… stick it right up me. Oh… ah…!'

'Keep still, you tart!' George commanded, heaving against his bare rump and sliding his cock between those taut cheeks, finding the slippery orifice and penetrating in one hard jab.

He slid his hands under Clive, finding his erection and rubbing it fiercely as he pistoned his hips in and out. It was a most extraordinary sight, and though Alvina had hinted about bum-boys and some men practicing sodomy with their own sex, she had scarcely thought it possible. But here was proof and she couldn't deny it. Her nipples tingled and she pinched them into peaks of pleasure, and her nubbin ached and demanded attention. She slipped a hand down between her legs, frigging herself as she watched George's antics with his lover.

It seemed that he wanted to prolong the experience and, just when she thought he was about to finish, he withdrew his fiery domed cock, reached for a whippy cane and started to whack Clive. The young man stifled a yelp, but spread-eagled himself on the quilt, groaning with pleasure more than pain as the rattan stippled his buttocks. George's eyes were shining and he laid on the punishment with enthusiasm, his stiff prick swaying from side to side and dribbling pre-come. Romilly couldn't stop working her clitoris. It ached, it burned, it grew larger and harder and she slowed down, waiting for George to resume arse-fucking Clive.

She didn't have long to wait. He threw the cane aside and leapt upon him, driving in his engorged member. Clive was handling his own penis, matching George's rhythm. Romilly fell into it too, reproducing their sensations, using her fingers to share their ecstasy when, finally, George emptied his spunk into Clive at the moment when the youth spurted onto the counterpane.

George sank down at Clive's side, cuddling him and stroking his hair. This made Romilly aware of her solitary state. There was no one to caress her in the afterglow. Silent as a shadow she sped up to the deck.

Joshua hadn't been able to settle after dinner. Perhaps it was that game of lanterloo with his exceptionally pretty female passengers. He could see what Lady Alvina was – a light-minded aristocratic baggage playing with men as her fancy dictated. But the other one, the delicately beautiful Romilly, was a different kettle of fish entirely. He'd stake a year's pay on her being a virgin. And as for that dandy who was her betrothed? Joshua foresaw trouble ahead and he hardly knew them.

The foppish George was as transparent as glass, obviously ready to thrust his cock into any opening offered, be it male or female. Joshua did not condemn this. He had spent too many years at sea to criticise men for seeking relief among their own kind. Necessity was the mother of invention and he turned a blind eye to any device his crew might use for satisfaction. For his own part, his hand became his mistress when the pressure in his testes was too great.

On shore he took his pleasure where he willed, but without commitment. He was an abstemious man. The sea was the love of his life and he needed no other, yet Lady Romilly had captured his imagination and he had gone on deck because the first mate had come to him predicting a change in the weather, but mostly in the hope of maybe seeing her.

The mate was right; Joshua was aware of the increased swell lifting the stout oaken hull. He sniffed the stiffening wind as he went on deck. The dark clouds gathering on the horizon were obscuring the moon. He issued brisk orders and men scampered aloft like monkeys, furling the main sails. Then to his surprise he came across Romilly, and approached, more concerned about her safety than anything else.

'My lady,' Joshua said, appearing out of nowhere and bowing as he addressed her. 'May I ask what brings you here at this hour of the night?'

'I needed to feel the breeze on my face,' Romilly lied, not quite sure how to handle the situation now it had arisen. She was very aware of her damp pussy and the naughty scene she had just witnessed that roused her so much.

'It is unwise to be alone,' he said, with a sternness that made her tingle. 'My men have been long at sea and this makes them restless. They are looking forward to landing so that they may enjoy the bounties of women once again.'

'You think one of them might rape me?' she said, pretending to be frightened, but was all too aware of the flimsiness of her attire. The wind was stronger now. It flattened her negligee against her limbs, ruffled the lace on her bosom and tangled with her unbound hair. Such a state of undress before a comparative stranger gave her a delicious sense of wantonness.

'I wouldn't go as far as to say that,' he demurred, casting an eye around, seeing that the seamen were carrying out his commands. 'The punishment would deter them, I think, but you are putting yourself at risk up here on your own. Where is your chaperone?'

'Asleep. Besides, there are times when I like my own company and don't appreciate her prattling.'

'Or that of your fiancé, Lord James?' he asked seriously.

'He's well enough,' she replied with a toss of her head, annoyed at having him brought into the conversation. Then, on impulse, she came out with a blunt question. 'Are you married, Captain Willard? Or is it true what they say about sailors – that they have a wife in every port?'

He was standing close beside her at the rail, just as Jamie had done earlier. She was very conscious of his strong body in its plain dark blue coat and breeches. There was nothing flashy about his attire; it was serviceable and functional. He wore his own hair, chestnut brown and curling to his shoulders and he was clean-shaven. She wondered as to his age, and placed him in his late twenties. He was confident and trustworthy and she liked him enormously, feeling his arm at her back as the strong motion of the water threw them closer together.

'Married, my lady?' he said with a smile, looking down at her with those keen blue eyes. 'No, mine is a roving life and

'I'd not expect a woman to wait at home for me to return, maybe after months away at sea. It would not be fair on her.'

'But if she loved you she'd not mind waiting, surely?' Romilly said quickly, wanting him to make some move, hold her hand or kiss her, perhaps, but he seemed preoccupied, staring at the sky.

'I'd not ask it of her,' he said at last. 'Besides, it would distract me from my duty. I'd always be longing to sail home and this wouldn't be good for my career. One day, maybe, when I've had enough of the sea and retired.'

'But captain, don't you long for love, a woman's touch?' His arm tightened about her as the vessel dipped and rose, timbers creaking. This stalwart person was a challenge. She wanted him to be weakened by desire for her, setting aside his principles and letting passion sweep him away.

He continued to look down at her, making her feel small against his tallness. Just for an instance she was sure he was about to pounce, sweep her into his arms and take her, then and there, on the scrubbed boards of the deck.

It lasted a heartbeat, no more, then he said steadily, 'I am not without feelings, my lady, but now is not the time or the place. Let me take you back to your cabin. The wind is rising and I think we are in for a storm.'

'But…'

'No buts. I shall feel happier if I know you are safe below. Come,' and he took her firmly under the elbow and did not stop until she reached her cabin door. He bowed again and gave a little quirky smile that told her he was aware of their attraction towards one another, then he left.

Romilly flew into her cabin, shut the door firmly and threw herself across the bed. A tiny spark had been ignited between Joshua and her, and she determined to encourage it even though it might never blaze into passion. She was betrothed and he a dedicated mariner, but hope springs eternal in the human breast and Romilly felt decidedly hopeful. She curled up under the quilt and went to sleep with a smile on her face, ignoring the ever strengthening rise and fall of the ship, the sound of the wind and crash of the sea hurling itself against the fragile timbers.

Romilly was riding round the estate at Harding Hall, the family seat of the earls of Standford. She was chasing a fox, the pack of hounds forging ahead, the leading huntsmen shouting, 'Tally-ho!' and their horns blaring.

It was a blustery day, the rain lashing the trees, but the riders were indomitable, her father urging her on. 'That's it, girl! Go! Go!'

She saw a hedge ahead, saw his stallion take it in a mighty bound, dug her heels into her mare's sides, encouraging her to go full stride. The mass of greenery came closer. The mare leapt. Romilly lost her seat, tumbled to one side and off, hitting hard, hard ground, jolting every bone in her body.

'My lady! My lady! Wake up!' shouted Jessica, as Romilly opened her eyes and found herself on the cabin floor.

'What's happening?' she said, the dream fading as reality struck.

'The storm! The terrible storm!' Jessica cried, hurrying around as well as she could in the dangerous tilt of the cabin. She was scrabbling to pack a few necessities in a leather valise. 'It's a hurricane, so the captain says, and we've to abandon ship.'

'What?' Romilly repeated, stupefied, getting up and managing to stay up by clinging to the bedhead.

'He's ordered his men to launch the longboat and we're to take our chance in it. The vessel is going down, my lady! Oh, merciful heavens! Make haste!'

The lamps swung crazily on their gimbals overhead and every object not clamped down was sliding and crashing everywhere. The sea lashed against the portholes, the *May Belle* bobbing like a cork, then dipping with dizzying speed into the troughs of the huge waves. There was no time to dress and Romilly grabbed her over-robe and Jessica flung a blanket around her. Then they struggled to open the door, tumbling out into the passage. Alvina was there, clasping her jewel box to her breasts, equally dishevelled. Kitty was sobbing hysterically, till her mistress slapped her across the face.

'There you, Romilly! Come on! We've got to get on deck and into the boat. It's the only way,' shouted Jamie, white as a sheet, while George was attempting to buckle on his sword. Their valets were lumbered with bags containing the gentlemen's clothes. Water was pouring down the companionway, but somehow Romilly managed to climb it.

Dawn was breaking over the chaos on deck, everything at an alarming angle, ropes dangling, winches squealing, one mast snapped and lying across the stern like a felled tree, the others gaunt and bare, the sails tightly furled. She saw the grim faces of the sailors as they tried to lower the two boats that would not hold all of them, never in this world. Some would have to rely on casks, planks, anything that would float and support a man and keep him from drowning.

Joshua was there, a formidable figure, magnificent and courageous and she wanted him at that moment, blindly seeking to be caught up in an emotion as vast as the fury of the elements. He seized her, lifted her and thrust her into the longboat that was hanging precariously over the side, the men fighting to lower it. Alvina climbed in, followed by George, Jamie, and their frightened servants. Romilly clung on, closing her eyes against the pounding sea, expecting the boat to be smashed to smithereens at any second. It jerked, the winches squealing as gradually it swung out from the steep sides and reached the ominously treacherous sea. Several sailors had volunteered to man the oars, and in a matter of moments the longboat bounced and jostled but succeeded in keeping afloat, the *May Belle* retreating into the distance. The last person she saw was Joshua, standing at the prow looking in their direction, before the vessel vanished, overwhelmed by a massive wave.

'My God!' Jamie exclaimed, holding her tightly, the oarsmen battling to make progress.

Alvina was ashen-faced but brave, comforting Kitty and Jessica. The valets, Tom Harraway and Gaston Pruet, showed a fresh side to their natures, helping those manning the oars to the best of their limited abilities.

But the storm had not abated and, although the men pointed to a distant hump on the horizon beyond the turbulent waters, shouting, 'There's land ahead!' it seemed that their chances of making the shore were slim.

Romilly clung to Jamie. The mountainous waves lifted the boat like a cockleshell, as if using it as a plaything. They were drenched. Some of the oars snapped and the last thing she knew was being flung into the water, sinking down and down, lost in the savage depths of that unrelenting sea.

Chapter Four

Built by Spanish conquistadors two centuries before, Armand's fortress was practically impregnable. Not completely so, of course, as the Dons had lost it to the French and the French to the English. Constructed by slaves, it was comprised of stone quarried from the caves and trees felled in the surrounding jungle. Enclosed by a high palisade with a platform for marksmen, it had a huge gate that would have withstood a battering ram. It should never have fallen to an enemy, but on each occasion had been betrayed from within. But no one dared do that to Armand Tertius, the most feared swordsman in the Caribbean.

He had taken the island from his predecessor five years before, making it his stronghold. It was on the map as San Juliano, but had been dubbed the *Devil's Paradise* by those who lived under Armand's regime, as well as by his enemies. From there he despatched ships to carry out his illegal trade – the *Scorpion*, the *Sirocco*, the *Golden Queen*, all fast, well-armed frigates manned by a fierce band of freebooters, who called themselves *The Brethren of the Coast*.

He lounged in a throne-like chair that had been intended for a cardinal. His long legs were stretched out and his booted feet, crossed at the ankle, were resting on the refectory table centred in the Great Hall. This is where he met with his lieutenants and planned enterprises as thoroughly as any admiral. There was nothing slapdash about this organisation. Other pirate leaders might mock, though never in his hearing, but such precision paid off, as that morning's share out was about to prove.

Yesterday the *Sirocco* returned loaded with booty to the

snug little inlet below the fort. Fortunately they had weighed anchor before the freak storm struck. Now those who had manned her gathered to receive their dues. Armand cast a cynical eye over them, knowing them for what they were; a polyglot gang of desperadoes. They came from every country in the world, criminals fleeing from justice, outlaws and mercenaries, lured by the dream of wealth and freedom. He never lacked recruits. They admired his success and reputation for fair play. He didn't cheat his men and whenever he raised his colours mariners rallied round. His nearest port of call was Cayona, capital of Tortuga, a pirate hangout.

Did any of his men have a shred of loyalty? He doubted it, and never showed a moment's weakness. He didn't hesitate to order flogging, marooning, and even hanging miscreants. He was a natural born leader and they avoided any dispute with him or the hard-hitting Johnson, his second-in-command. His other officers were respected, too. Peter Quidley the doctor, Hector Arkwright who doubled as carpenter and ship's surgeon, Giles Medway the quartermaster, Sancho and Browne, boatswain and first mate, and the keeper of the books, Henry Moorcross. He combined the duties of accountant and secretary, a vital member of staff, and now Armand studied him from under curving black brows.

Henry sat at the far end of the table with an open ledger in front of him, a squat brass inkwell and a quill pen to hand; ready to strike off each man's name and payment as they filed past him. Armand trusted him to the letter and was glad to have him around, for he was educated and learned, and provided good conversation. Armand found he was jaded sometimes, wearied of Sabrina and his other concubines. They never talked, only fucked. Even that morning Sabrina had angled to be present, wanting to sit beside him and distract him by playing with his cock, but he denied her. This was man's business, and she was greedy and would have been assessing the loot as astutely as any pawnbroker.

His lips twitched as he glanced at Henry, who was a serious,

51

tight-featured person with an almost puritanical mien. Wearing black broadcloth he looked more like a bank clerk than a freebooter. Armand knew he was a pederast. That was the reason why he had been forced to run from England to escape a gaol sentence, his life in tatters after one of his lovers had squealed. Fortunately for him no one here gave a fig about his taste for sodomising youths. Each to his own was their motto.

As Johnson said, when in his cups, 'Get it any which way you fancy, Henry, my old cully, for you might be dead tomorrow... nay, even later today! Life is bloody short in the Indies.'

Articles had been drawn up and were strictly adhered to. The captain and officers got a larger share than the others, whether or no they actually took part in a raid or sea battle. Special provision was made for those who were wounded or lost a limb during an engagement. Penalties were imposed for any breach of regulations, the project organised like a naval campaign.

The prize was not a large one, but there was a heap of captured weapons and ammunition, some bales of silk, a chest full of doubloons, various articles of clothing, a quantity of food and several casks of wine. Those who had avoided being killed while resisting the pirates had been set adrift in an open boat, taking their chance of reaching a friendly shore, and the ship was stripped of anything useful and then scuppered. But they had taken one prisoner, a violinist.

'We'll get him to join us, captain,' muttered Johnson from behind Armand's chair. 'He'll have no bloody choice. Either that or...' and he sliced a gnarled finger across his throat from ear to ear.

'But we already have one fiddler,' Armand pointed out, disgruntled because there hadn't been any women aboard. There were females aplenty on the island, slaves and native girls, but he always hoped that someone more stimulating might turn up.

'We can do with another, sir,' Johnson pointed out. 'The lads like a bit of music, a jig or two or a few songs. It helps break the monotony, if you know what I mean.'

'Indeed I do,' Armand said dourly. His life was too calm at the moment. He missed a challenge to lift his spirits. One could have it too easy. 'No females aboard?'

'No, sir. The lads will just have to make do with the brown wenches for the time being. Are you planning a trip to Cayona soon? Jolly doxies there. Lasses who were transported because they were whores, and they make a fine living when the boats put in. Hell, I can't wait to see 'em. Big tits, big arses and juicy quims. They're English and French and all sorts, but they know how to treat a man.'

'Curb your enthusiasm; you're positively dribbling,' said Armand coldly. These rogues spent wildly, drinking, gambling, whoring till they had emptied their pockets and had to go to sea again. It suited his purpose, but sometimes made them hard to control. Lust ruled their existence – lust for riches and the women they could buy for gold.

The men saluted him as they passed, after pausing to chat with Henry and pocketing their money. The weapons went into the armoury; the other goods set aside to be sold in Cayona, while the food and wine enriched the fortress's larder and cellar. The business was almost concluded when the lookout knocked for admittance. He had been on watch at the top of a tower, scanning the ocean for miles around.

'A ship has run aground, cap'n,' he reported, a lean fellow wearing canvas trousers and a tattered shirt, his tanned arms tattooed against mosquito bites, his hair confined by a crimson bandana.

Armand glanced up, his eyes razor keen. 'Where?'

'On the rocks near Seal Bay,' the man answered promptly.

'Any survivors?'

'Don't know, cap'n.'

'Have a party go down and take a look,' Armand said, stretching and rising to his full, impressive height. 'In fact, I'll go myself.' He buckled on his sword and took up the brace of pistols hanging from the back of his chair.

Were there really mermaids? Romilly pondered, gradually regaining consciousness. She could have sworn she heard them singing.

She wanted to see them, those legendary creatures who sat on rocks, combing their long golden hair, full-breasted and beautiful with glittering fishy tails. It was said that they lured sailors to a watery grave.

Water! She was in water, little wavelets washing over her as she lay on damp sand. Daring to open her eyes, imagining she might be dead and on some celestial shore, she found she was in a cove, backed by forest and high cliffs. The sun was hot and the sky blue, dotted with woolly clouds. She hadn't drowned, but as memory returned she sat up, and then struggled to her feet, searching round frantically. Where were the others?

To her intense relief Alvina tottered from beyond an escarpment, followed by Jamie and George. Romilly flew towards them, swept into soggy embraces. 'Thank God you're safe!' exclaimed Jamie.

'Where are we?' Romilly cried.

'Lord knows,' responded George, every trace of affectation gone. Whatever the outcome of their dire experience it had brought them all down to earth with a bang.

'Where are the crew and Captain Willard, and what has happened to Jessica?' Romilly asked, wringing her hands in anguish.

'And Kitty?' Alvina added woefully.

'And Tom and Gaston?' said Jamie. 'They were in charge of our belongings. I had a whole new wardrobe for the trip.'

'Never mind that! The ship, did it sink?' Romilly was impatient, beginning to realise their perilous situation.

She also became aware that her nightgown and over-robe were soaked and torn, clinging to her curves, outlining her limbs and breasts in a most immodest fashion. Alvina was similarly half naked, and the men had lost their shoes, hats and periwigs, attired only in breeches and shirts. They were unarmed and without food or fresh water. Their chances of survival were limited unless rescue arrived soon. Shading her eyes and looking out to sea she spotted bits of wreckage being washed ashore and the horrifying sight of bodies drifting aimlessly like rag-dolls. Were she and her friends the only survivors?

'Oh, my God!' exclaimed Alvina, standing beside her and viewing the floating dead. 'What are we to do? I've lost everything, except this,' and somehow she had clung to her jewel box.

'What use is that now?' Romilly cried despairingly. 'We can't eat it.'

'Hush,' warned Jamie, clutching her arm. 'We're not alone.' He jerked his head in the direction of the dense vegetation to the right of the rocks. Romilly looked towards it and her blood froze in her veins. What had appeared to be bush and scrubby trees began to stir and form into shapes of men, with gaudy patterns daubed over their bare brown skin, wearing feathers in their hair and carrying spears. Sunlight glistened on the primitive ornaments banding their wrists and necks, and their appearance was so fearsome that terror gripped her.

They emerged boldly and their leader, a thickset man whose cock was covered by a bark sheath, advanced and shouted in a strange, guttural tongue, gesticulating as he spoke.

'Now look here, fellow,' Jamie began, standing his ground, accustomed to pulling rank. 'These ladies and myself have been cast ashore. We need food, clothing and shelter. I demand that you supply it.'

'Don't be so silly, James, you noodle,' Alvina said crossly. 'He can't understand a word you're saying. I'll try a different approach.'

She turned on her most winning smile, made sure that her wet robe was slipping off her shoulders displaying prominent nipples, then addressed the leader. 'Good morrow, friend. Can you help us? We are hopelessly lost, and would be eternally grateful.'

And all the time she was glancing at him playfully from under her long lashes, and letting her gaze drop to the large object hidden by its pliant wooden covering at the fork of his thighs. His hair was blue-black, cut in a severe bob, and his lower lip was distended by a disc, his nostrils pierced by porcupine quills. Reassured by her smile he turned to the other warriors, gabbling excitedly. They lowered their spears. They circled their captives, particularly interested in the women, though they had George lower his breeches and examined his penis and balls, and then made him bend over so they might look up his bottom.

Romilly was too frightened to resist, yet resented the familiar way in which the natives handled her, though they seemed driven by curiosity more than desire. Their brightly painted bodies were almost hairless, their hair black as ink, their eyes dark and glistening. They were short of stature, with lean flanks and bare cocks that bounced as they walked. Only their leader had his protected. Romilly had never in her life seen so many male appendages all at once. She didn't know where to look.

'Nature's afterthought,' remarked Alvina, scathingly. 'The prick and balls are not a pretty sight at the best of times, whereas a woman's pussy is neat and tucked away.'

'How can you jest about it?' Romilly objected, trembling as one brave with sharply filed teeth took her right nipple between his fingers and rolled it experimentally, making a comment to his companions who laughed uproariously.

They were not brutal in their handling, filled with interest and enjoyment as they pinched breasts and drove impudent fingers between legs. 'Let them do it,' Alvina advised. 'We don't want to antagonise them, do we? Follow George's example. He's not objecting as they finger his arsehole.'

'Perhaps he's enjoying it,' Romilly snapped back,

remembering seeing him with Clive Morrison. Was it only last night? It seemed a lifetime ago.

'I wouldn't be surprised,' replied Alvina with a giggle and a sudden 'ouch' as one of the men became a little too forceful, sinking his forefinger up to the second knuckle in her love channel.

The leader became tired of this game and ordered his band to gather up what they could salvage from the wreckage and then tie their prisoners' hands behind them with vines as tough as rope, and march them into the jungle.

It was like walking through a dim, cool cathedral, the trees forming a canopy over their heads, hung with exotic orchids and purple blossoms. Parrots flew up on rainbow-hued wings, and giant butterflies perched on the flowers, extracting the nectar. It was a colourful, wild, overwhelming place.

'Eden must have resembled this, before the fall,' Romilly whispered to Alvina. 'How beautiful it is, and how alien.'

'Thieving bastards, they've taken my jewels. Do you think they'll make us their queens?' Alvina muttered, limping along beside her. The forest floor was rough and prickly, though their captors didn't seem to notice, but George and Jamie were winching and complaining.

'Who knows?' Romilly answered.

'Perhaps they'll eat us,' Alvina suggested wryly.

'Cannibals?'

'There's a distinct possibility.'

Jamie and George weren't much help, grim-faced and pale, the situation beyond their comprehension. They were dandies who had done nothing more violent than follow the hunt, pursuing deer or foxes. Though wearing swords and attending classes run by French fencing masters, they had never been called out to fight a duel in order to defend their honour. And as younger sons of the gentry their fathers hadn't insisted they spend time as army officers. Life had been easy and luxurious – up till now.

The tribesmen prodded the prisoners in the back with their

spears, not hard and with considerable good humour and wide smiles. Romilly couldn't believe they were looking upon them as dinner! But if not what was their purpose? She dreaded to think.

After what seemed an eternity they came out in a clearing, dotted with palm-thatched dwellings. At once they were greeted with excited shrieks and women and children came running, leaving their cooking fires and huts, eager to see what the men had caught. The females were bare to the waist, and had brief woven aprons that barely covered their clefts. Their little ones were entirely naked, dusky-skinned, black-eyed and high cheek-boned, with the same slightly oriental features as the adults. In all, they were a handsome people.

They chattered and circled the newcomers, while the warriors preened themselves and strutted, proud of bringing home such a fine catch. Impudent fingers touched Romilly. She seemed to attract the most attention, with her wheat-gold hair, green eyes and peaches and cream complexion. Alvina came second. It was apparent that her fiery locks were a novelty. The native women made big eyes at Jamie and George, but it was clear that white people were nothing new. They had visited this tropical land before.

Then a weird figure emerged from one of the huts, and the crowd parted to let him through. He was older than the rest; a person of authority wearing a woven shirt dyed purple, berry juice decorating his face with triangular designs. A plumed headdress added to his height, and his chest was covered in necklaces of polished stones and animal teeth. His intelligent eyes flashed over the captives as he paced round them, sniffing their scent, stamping his feet and shaking a seed-filled gourd. The leader of the warriors handed him Alvina's jewel case, which he opened and examined the contents.

'Are you their chief?' Jamie fronted him up, and Romilly admired his courage.

The man shook his head. 'No, I Riku... shaman. I see spirits... talk with ancestors.'

It was astonishing to hear him speaking English. 'You know our tongue, how so?' questioned Jamie.

'Ah, I have dealings with white man long time…'

'Can you help us? Our ship went down in a storm.'

Riku nodded sagely. 'I know, the gods foretold her coming,' and he stuck out his arm and pointed at Romilly.

Jamie reacted angrily. 'How can this be? What are you, some gypsy fortune teller?'

Riku drew himself up straight, pride in every line of him. 'I tell true. This woman… she is for our ruler, Chief Awan.'

'What?' Romilly gasped. This was all getting just too much.

'But the lady is to be my wife!' Jamie exclaimed.

The shaman's sacred adornments jingled as he shook his head. 'Awan will wed her.'

He barked an order to some of the women, and at once Romilly and Alvina were hustled across the clearing to the biggest of the huts and pushed inside. Two of the women were older and in authority over the rest. The interior was dim, but as Romilly became used to the light, the source of which was a gap in the roof, she saw several couches balanced on stumpy feet. These supported frames made of thick branches crisscrossed with lianas to form a base, covered by palm-leaf pallets and woven blankets. There were also pitchers, ewers, and other domestic articles similar to those used in England.

'It could be a lot worse, but I want my jewels returned,' commented Alvina as her wrists were freed. She stretched her arms thankfully, and Romilly was soon able to do the same.

Her damp clothes were uncomfortable, but she attempted to adjust them to conceal her body. A kindly, smiling young woman shook her head and prevented her, indicating that Romilly should strip. She clapped her hands and others came in bearing calabashes of steaming water. Ignoring Romilly's bashful protests, she was quickly divested of what was left of her garments, and Alvina was treated the same. She, however, made no objection, proud to display her perfect

59

figure. She was happy to receive so much attention when the admiring attendants stroked her alabaster skin and combed their fingers through her russet pubes.

Romilly stood bashfully, an arm across her breasts, the other hand cupping her pubis. Then the leading girl said, in broken English, pointing to herself, 'Jacy... serve you.'

'How do these savages have a knowledge of our language?' Alvina pondered. 'It seems we're not the first castaways,' and she gave herself up to their ministrations.

'Do you still think we may be the main course?' Romilly said timidly, though relaxing as Jacy lowered her dark head and nibbled one of Romilly's nipples. Desire darted down to her loins and she could feel wetness forming in her secret folds.

Alvina chuckled as one of the other girls knelt at her feet, opened her foxy fork and applied a darting pink tongue to her love bud. 'I think they want to eat us for sure... but it's pussy they're after.'

'The shaman said I was intended for the chief,' Romilly gasped, though it was becoming increasingly difficult to concentrate on anything but the extreme pleasure given her by those skilful lips. As when Nathan and Jamie had tongue-fucked her, the sensation was exquisite. She forgot to be ashamed or embarrassed, wanting Jacy to go on and on... and on. She did, and Romilly experienced a rush of voluptuous pleasure that flooded her and made her cry out with the force of it.

Somewhere, in the background, she heard Alvina's moans rising higher and higher as she, too, climaxed.

Their reaction seemed to inspire the girls. While Jacy gently laid Romilly down, and Alvina's paramours continued to caress her, the rest were enjoying one another, the air charged with the odour of female essences. Romilly had never dreamed such actions existed, women lying with women, legs entwined, breasts rubbing against breasts and thighs pressing against eager deltas. She was aroused again and wanted another orgasm.

Jacy smiled knowingly and reached up to kiss Romilly's lips. She could taste and smell herself on the woman's mouth, and welcomed the soft probing organ as their tongues met fervently in a dance of desire. She had never felt so horny, not even with Nathan. Her nubbin throbbed like an enormous swollen bud ready to burst into bloom. Jacy nodded to a couple of the others who came across to fondle Romilly's nipples. Jacy unwound the strip of cloth that covered her own female parts and reached down to part her labia major, and stretch it open. Her inner lips were wet and swollen, and her clitoris was large and upstanding.

Romilly yielded to the urge to show off her own pink parts, for Jacy's were of a pewter-grey colour. She held her wings apart and opened her crack wide so that the girls might take a good look. They murmured in admiration, and each wanted to rub Romilly's stiff bud. She closed her eyes and gave herself to pleasure. Fingers played with her puckered nipples, others toyed with her anus and Jacy went down on her.

Romilly's head sagged back and her throat arched as she sobbed, 'Oh yes, yes!' and she held the girl firmly to her, using her hair as a bridle.

Jacy sucked the hard clit into her mouth and rolled her tongue-tip over its aching head. She used her fingers to gently pull the labia back so that the nub stood out like a tiny cock robbed of its foreskin. Romilly's sensitive nipples sent tingles of joy down to that seat of all sensation, stimulated by the busy fingers of Jacy's companions.

Through half-closed eyes Romilly saw Alvina writhing under the hands of other girls, and the sight of her friend enjoying spasms of lust roused her even more. She was approaching that plateau where nothing could stop that delirious plunge into bliss. Jacy's tongue worked its magic. Romilly's nipples were flicked, rolled and mouthed. With a scream she reached the peak and tumbled over into ecstasy, coming in a welter of pleasure that left her shaking from head to toe.

It seemed as if a wave of awesome female sexuality had taken over the hut. They satisfied one another; they were loving friends and understanding companions, banding into a flourishing sisterhood. It was a state that could never have been entered into with a man, no matter how much of a soul mate he was. They were earth goddesses, giving their womb blood to nourish the soil, giving life to their young, caring for those around them and forming a deep, abiding bond. Romilly's eyes were opened in that moment of revelation and she now understood her feelings towards Alvina. Should anyone have threatened this lovely person she would have fought to the death in her defence.

Riku's entrance rudely interrupted this epiphany. The girls unwound themselves from each other and bowed to him respectfully. A man was once more in control, a holy man, moreover, who claimed he could communicate with the gods and the dead.

An old crone was with him, her bright eyes peering out from under a mane of grizzled hair. Jacy whispered to Romilly, 'She is Mahil, a great sorceress. She will find out if you have been with a man. Chief demands it. '

'I won't let her,' Romilly insisted indignantly.

'What's going on?' Alvina demanded, sitting up and fixing the weird pair with a haughty stare.

'The hag wants to examine us to see if we're virgins.'

'Damned impertinence!' Alvina exploded 'How dare she? Doesn't she know that we're ladies and not to be tampered with?'

'I don't think any of that is significant here,' Romilly said sadly, and huddled on the bed, arms folded protectively about her bunched knees.

Mahil snapped her fingers at the watching women and four flung themselves on Romilly, bearing her down on her back. Two held her arms above her head, while the others forced her to raise her legs, knees widespread. Then the sorceress and shaman leaned over, peering into Romilly's wide open cleft. They muttered together in a strange language, and Mahil inserted a finger into her victim's vulva.

Romilly stiffened at the sudden pain as the women pressed against her hymen. She withdrew with a satisfied nod, and turned to where Alvina was standing like a cornered tigress. 'Don't bother to try me,' she said briskly. 'I lost my maidenhead ages ago. Look,' and she crouched and thrust her fingers into her vagina, withdrawing them wet and sticky with her love juices.

Mahil and Riku shrugged their assent, and gave them over to the women to be prepared for the feast and Romilly's introduction to her bridegroom. She was bathed and perfumed and her hair was washed free of salt water, and Alvina was treated in the same way. Then two beautiful white robes were produced, diaphanous and flowing, of so sophisticated a design that they could only have been manufactured in a civilised country.

'Where on earth did they get these?' Alvina wanted to know. 'I wish there was a mirror; I want to see myself. The chief may demand a virgin bride but I'm willing to be his concubine, if he's handsome and vigorous and well hung. I could use a big cock right now.'

'Are you never satisfied?' Romilly asked.

'Hardly ever, sweeting.'

Drums throbbed in the background, and they became louder. Mahil and Riku led the procession from the hut to where torches flared and a great fire blazed. The route was lined by warriors, standing to attention, spears uplifted. Flutes played, high and reed-like, and human voices wailed a litany. It was spine chilling and ritualistic, and Romilly's fears returned threefold. So foreign a people, and totally beyond her understanding.

Behind the flames stood totem poles surmounted by hideous demon faces – a jaguar, a snake, a skull. Before them lay a large flat altar stone, and beside this, guarded on either side, stood Jamie and George. They had not been washed and cleaned up, and Romilly had the horrified notion that they might be intended for human sacrifice, the stone to be smeared with their blood in honour of the deities. She prayed this would not be so, hoping against all hope that when the chief penetrated her it would be suffice, her virginity all that would be required.

The drumbeat increased, thundering out, the beat whipping the onlookers into a trancelike frenzy as if, indeed, the gods were manifest. 'Oh,' Alvina muttered in Romilly's ear, 'rather you than me, dearest. These are barbarians!'

Riku pushed Romilly back till her knees pressed against the great slab. Mahil was dancing round mouthing incantations. The tribe swayed and chanted as they watched. The warriors lifted Romilly onto the altar and bound her, spread-eagled, ropes about her ankles and wrists. She had never believed in God, not seriously, bucking against attending services in the church on her father's estate or going to those in London, but again she prayed. 'Dear Jesus, save me. I don't want to die.'

She could not move, tears running unchecked down her cheeks and dripping onto the stone beneath her head. Then a large black-haired man with fierce eyes leaned over her, blocking out everything. A cloak of vivid feathers fell from his immense shoulders, and he raised his arms to heaven, evoking his gods.

'Awan! Awan!' chanted the tribe, while the shaman presented Alvina's jewels to the chief and then fell flat on his face at his feet. Mahil, in a religious fervour, took up a knife and slashed her arms and body, bleeding copiously.

Awan was naked beneath his cloak, his body gleaming and muscular, his skin mahogany. His erection was large and stiff and his intention plain. He intended to thrust it into Romilly. He reached out and ripped her robe aside. She lay helpless, her treasures on view to him – to all of them. A handmaiden stepped forward carrying an earthenware jug. She tipped it slowly and a stream of oil trickled down across Romilly's breasts, past her navel and disappeared into her crack. She was being prepared for the chief and, almost, she wanted it to be over. The suspense was terrible – dread and fear of the unknown and yet a curious kind of submission – the female turning her body into a vessel for the dominant male's seed so that the human race could continue. It was a primitive, frightening feeling.

Awan was ugly, with coarse features, running his spade-like hands over her slippery body, lingering on her hard nipples and reaching down to hold open her sex-lips, ready to plunge that enormous phallus into her tender opening. The drums quickened their beat. The tribe swayed in unison and Romilly shut her eyes tight, waiting for the agony that would surely shoot through her as he inserted the monstrous, shiny dome.

Then a single shot rang out across the clearing, followed by deathly silence. Awan's penis shrank visibly as he swung round. Romilly opened her eyes. A tall man with a commanding bearing strode across to the altar. He was white, though swarthy, and wore a belled-sleeved shirt and close-fitting velvet breeches that left little to the imagination, and supple leather boots that reached his thighs. His long black hair coiled way beyond his shoulders and his face was a mask of fury.

'Awan!' he thundered, and even the warriors cringed, for a gang of villainous looking men, all armed to the teeth, backed the newcomer. 'Haven't I given orders that any prisoners are to be brought to me? You're disobeying and I could have you hanged!'

'But, sire… I'm sorry…' Awan stammered, robbed of his dignity, shamed before his people.

'You know full well that this island and all who live here belong to me. So does anything that fortune drives this way… ships, goods, prisoners.'

Awan fell to his knees and clasped the stranger's boots. 'Mercy, mercy…' he begged. 'You our king… our emperor,' and the tribe followed suit, kneeling and wailing and begging forgiveness.

The men who stood solidly at the stranger's back, brandishing cutlasses or cocking pistols, waited but a single word from their leader to fall upon and butcher the hapless natives.

He stood, hands on hips, looking around with blistering scorn. 'You all know me.' His deep, heavily accented voice rang out and even the shaman and sorceress cringed and pressed their faces into the dust. 'I am Captain Armand Tertius, your lord and master. I protect you and, in turn, you belong to me. I allow you to have your chief, but he must yield everything up to me. He owns nothing.'

'The woman... my bride,' Awan muttered, and Armand spun round and glared at him.

'You have half a dozen wives already. News reached me that you'd captured these people and had the audacity to think you could take one of the women to wife. How dare you? They should have been brought to me.'

'Mercy, mercy,' the wretched chief repeated, shaking like a leaf.

The captain approached Romilly and a shiver went through her as he stood over her and subjected her to close scrutiny. He was the most handsome and striking man she had ever come across, with all the hauteur of someone highborn, maybe truly a king. What was he doing in this godforsaken place?

'Well, well,' he said slowly, and bent and lifted one of her tresses to his lips, inhaling deeply. 'Are you Lady Romilly?'

This shocked her. 'How do you know my name?'

'We found Captain Willis and some of his men wandering on the shore, also your servants and those of your male companions,' he answered, and she was puzzled by the enigmatic expression in his steel-grey eyes.

'Where are they?' she demanded, concern overruling fear.

'Safe,' he replied, then took out a dagger and sliced through her bonds. He made Awan hand over his robe and placed it round her as he assisted her to rise.

Alvina, meanwhile, had been acknowledged, also Jamie and George, and Romilly began to hope their troubles were over, until Armand announced, 'You will be taken to the fortress and there I shall decide what is to be done with you.'

'What do you mean?' demanded Jamie. 'We are English citizens and should be cared for and then delivered to the nearest port belonging to our country.'

The men with Armand gave great bellows of sardonic laughter at this, and he towered over Jamie and said, 'You forget, sir, you are not in Europe now. I am master here and I abide by no such rules. I may enslave you, sell you, demand a large ransom.'

'And the women? Lady Romilly is my betrothed.'

'Ah, the women... yes,' Armand replied thoughtfully, fixing Romilly with those piercing eyes. 'I may include them in my harem. Who knows? It will be as the fancy takes me.'

Chapter Five

Screaming, kicking and protesting, Romilly was lifted as if no lighter than a feather, wrapped in the chief's cloak and slung over Armand's broad shoulder. She hung head down, her hair cascading to well below his waist. It was an ignominious position, but there was absolutely nothing she could do.

He set off across the clearing in long, loping strides, and she bounced and cursed him at every step. The tribe parted as if before a tidal wave, letting him through. They were subdued, the festivities over. Romilly tried to see what was happening to her friends, and heard Alvina shouting as she, too, was flung like a sack of potatoes across the shoulder of a big, bearded man. Jamie and George were manacled and forced to walk. They had no alternative, with muskets boring into their backs.

Their new captors were in fine fettle, laughing and cracking coarse jokes, in English mainly, their sallies bringing a blush to Romilly's cheeks. She was very conscious of Armand's powerful body pressed close to her breasts. She could feel his heat; smell him, a pungent combination of sweat, verbena oil and a personal odour that breathed out from his pores and hair. She remembered his hawk-like features and arrogant manner. This added to the fire blazing inside her, and out, for he had wrapped the feather cloak tightly round her, as if insuring that no eyes should look upon her nakedness but his own. Such possessiveness was humiliating yet gratifying. She was nothing but a weak female in the grip of the alpha male. Part of her rebelled, but the other, guided by instinct, relished such a mighty protector.

He strode on effortlessly and she couldn't tell how far they had gone, but was aware that the terrain was different, the path rising steadily and broad paving slabs had replaced the forest floor. The ground fell away on either side and the air was fresher, the tops of the trees lying below. Armand did not change his pace, but finally stopped when he reached a large wooden gate. He threw back his head and hailed the guards within. The gate rolled open to let them through. Now they were crossing a courtyard and into the shade of a building whose walls rose sheer above them. Romilly gave up trying to ascertain their surroundings, hearing his footsteps ringing on stone, aware that they were entering a room.

He set her down with such forced that her teeth rattled, and she staggered and clung to him to balance herself. He held her lightly and, glancing up into his swarthy face, she saw his lips curving in a sardonic smile and little flames, like amber jets, flaring in the black pupils of his eyes.

'Welcome to my castle, *mademoiselle*,' he said.

'A fine welcome indeed!' she raged. 'Is this how you treat your guests, you villain?'

Alvina had been unceremoniously dumped close by, and she was furious too. 'You're a rogue, sir, a black-hearted thief who should be strung up. Where are my jewels, you scoundrel? I saw you take them from Awan. Are they also part of your spoils?'

'Shall I stop her row, captain?' enquired the one called Johnson, part amused, part exasperated, ruefully dabbing at the bloody scratches her talons had left across his craggy countenance.

Armand shrugged. 'Sabrina will deal with them. Take them to her quarters.'

'And the men?'

'Lock them up till I decide their fate.'

'Don't despair, sweetheart,' Jamie called across to Romilly, 'I'm certain I can find a way out of this. I'll settle on a price.'

'You're very sure of yourself, *monsieur*,' Armand mocked.

'I'm sure of one thing… money talks, especially to someone

like you.'

Armand laughed and Romilly both hated and feared him, and yet there was something about him; he was impressive, even desirable, though she loathed herself for entertaining such a thought.

They were in a lofty hall with a massive fireplace at one end. Rooms led off from it, like the yawning mouths of caves. There was a refectory table in the middle, with benches and stools on either side and an oaken carver at the head. The thick grey pillars that rose to the ceiling were decorated with banners and flags, crossed pikes and other relics of skirmishes fought and presumably won by the ruffian who now appeared to own the place. It was hard to categorise Armand as such, for he carried himself like royalty, and the tribesmen had feared him and his own bullies accorded him respect.

She searched the room, hoping to find Joshua or Jessica and Kitty, but there was no sign of them. What had been their fate in the hands of these freebooters?

'This way, my lady,' said Johnson, and he was truly alarming, every inch the desperado, a swaggering bully, though there was a twinkle in his eye as he viewed the women.

Romilly and Alvina followed him up an immense staircase, hand in hand and very wary. They passed servants going about their duties, and many tightly shut doors, finally coming to one at the end of a passage. Johnson knocked and a dusky maiden in a single chiffon scarf wound around her lissom frame opened it. It was transparent and formed little barrier between his lewd gaze and her breasts, and the dark triangle that marked the division of her thighs.

The room was airy, though like all others in the fortress the windows were narrow and facing into the courtyard below. Only musket slits gave access on the outer walls. A woman rose from a luxuriously draped divan as they entered, and her beauty struck Romilly. She was raven-haired, her head covered in a multitude of beaded plaits. Her body was magnificently proportioned, a sari draped across one shoulder and falling to her feet, tight and revealing. She was a person who gloried in her body and liked to display it. She sashayed across to them and then stood, hand on one hip, looking them up and down.

'Who are these, Johnson?' she asked in a rich, husky drawl.

'More captives, Sabrina,' he replied, one big hand fondling the slave girl's breasts. 'We took them from the Indians. That fool Awan was about to marry this one,' and he pushed Romilly forward. Sabrina gave her a searching stare, frowning a little, and narrowing her cat-like eyes.

'They are from the wrecked ship, like the others,' she mused, walking round to view them from every side. 'But a cut above, eh?'

'They say they are ladies,' he replied. 'And there were a pair of gentlemen with them who claim to be lords.'

'That fits in with what the cards foretold,' Sabrina murmured mysteriously, then gave a sharp order to the slave. 'Fetch their servants, Aponi.'

The girl scurried off while Sabrina conducted Romilly and Alvina to the couch, and had a lithe male slave pour wine into cut glass goblets for them. 'That's right, Marcus, treat the ladies politely and I may let you satisfy them later.' She turned to Romilly, adding, 'Would you like that, my lady? He's a fine, virile stud. I can vouch for that. Tireless, my dear, always willing to oblige, especially if you give him a tiny flick of the whip.'

He was Caucasian, though with a deep tan, and his hair was flaxen, his eyes pale blue, but he acted in a subservient manner, doing precisely as Sabrina ordered, keeping his lids lowered. He wore a thong that cradled his genitals and Romilly avoided looking at him as she said, 'I have scant knowledge of men, madame.'

'Call me Sabrina,' insisted their hostess, and she sat between Romilly and Alvina, her pungent perfume seducing their senses.

'I'm Lady Romilly.'

71

'And I'm Lady Alvina.'

'Are you virgins?' Sabrina enquired. 'How fortunate if you are, for this will stimulate Armand's appetite.'

Aponi returned before they could reply, and Romilly gasped as she saw Kitty and Jessica with her, but they were much changed in their dress. 'Oh, my lady, thank God you're safe!' cried Jessica, rushing across to her.

'Madam, ah, my dear madam!' Kitty exclaimed and Alvina stood up and embraced her, then she held her at arm's length.

'Gracious heaven, what *are* you wearing?'

'Mistress Sabrina had us rigged out like this. Our own clothes were in rags. These are comfortable, so much cooler than stays and lacing and skirts.' Kitty did a twirl, showing off her single garment that consisted of a length of flowered material that just about covered her ample charms.

'Well I shan't feel right until I'm wearing sober, civilised clothing again,' said Jessica, shame-facedly. 'You can hardly call these dignified or modest.'

Romilly thought this new mode of dress suited her starchy duenna. She looked years younger and her hair, once confined in a tight bun, was hanging loose, softening her face and curling down her back.

'I like it, and can't wait to try it myself,' said Alvina.

'So you shall,' Sabrina promised.

'The captain says you are to prepare them and join him for supper,' Johnson pronounced with a monstrous leer, happy as a king amidst this bevy of women, finding even Jessica bed-worthy. 'Her ladyship here was about to be shafted by Awan. That means she's bound to be a virgin, for that crafty old devil Riku the shaman wouldn't have dared fob his chief off with used goods, now would he?'

'Have you been with a man, Lady Romilly?' Sabrina asked bluntly. 'Answer truthfully, for this will make a difference to your fate.'

'It is the second time I have been put through this embarrassing ordeal,' Romilly snapped, head held high, spine stiff. 'That impertinent shaman and the vile old crone with him asked me the same thing and dared to examine me. Yes, Sabrina, for what it's worth, I am a virgin.'

'Good,' Sabina said slowly, while Marcus positioned himself behind her and stirred the warm air with a peacock fan mounted on a bamboo pole. 'And you, Lady Alvina?'

'I'm a woman of experience,' she retorted proudly. 'So your leader can put that in his pipe and smoke it. No one tells me what to do.'

Sabrina's pleasant expression changed dramatically. She sprang up, seizing a short-handled whip and launching herself on Alvina. The thong flicked her flesh lightly, but enough to make her bare arm sting. She out-faced Sabrina and for a long moment there was a tense battle of wills, then, 'You'll find everything is different here,' Sabrina hissed. 'We abide by Armand's laws and those of the *Brethren of the Coast*. No snotty-nosed cow who thinks she's above him can get away with insolence.'

'Out of my way, bitch,' Alvina growled.

The whip twitched again and this time it struck her across her barely covered buttocks. Alvina couldn't stifle a yell.

'Don't defy her, my lady,' urged Kitty. 'They are a ruthless bunch and it's best to give in to what they want. Trust me, I know.'

'They haven't hurt you?' Alvina asked anxiously, rubbing her own stinging flanks.

'No, no, but I'm not sure of our fate. There is talk of a slave auction in somewhere called Cayona. I don't want to be sold, my lady. I want to stay with you,' and she started to cry, the usually feisty lass who could give any man the rough edge of her tongue.

'Don't worry, I shall put a stop to this nonsense,' promised Alvina, but she and Romilly exchanged a worried glance.

'I want to see your master,' Romilly demanded. She felt responsible for the safety of her friends. If it hadn't been for her they would never have found themselves in this situation.

Johnson slapped his thigh and roared with laughter and Sabrina raised an eyebrow. 'Do you indeed? You're brave; I'll give you that. Do you know what you're saying? It's not wise to toy with a tiger.'

'I shan't toy with him. I intend to negotiate.'

'On your own head be it. I'm warning you that he is renowned for his black moods and evil temper.'

'I want to see him *now*.' Romilly refused to be put off.

Sabrina shook her head, hoop earrings gleaming. 'Can't be done. He's given orders not to be disturbed till supper. You'll see him then and not before.'

'But…'

'Relax, young lady. I expect you are hungry. Eat with me and then we'll find you something gorgeous to wear tonight. Armand is a man of taste who appreciates style and breeding. He misses France and his own kind.'

'He's from Europe?' Romilly was annoyed with herself for betraying interest. Interest meant caring, and she had no intention of getting any closer to the man than was strictly necessary.

'I thought as much; a nobleman, I shouldn't wonder,' Alvina cut in, but Romilly refused to discuss him.

Sabrina's slaves brought in dishes of delicious food. There were pyramids of fruit, cold chicken served in rich sauce and crusty bread still warm from the oven, and sweet potatoes and unusual vegetables. Romilly realised how hungry she was and tucked in with relish. Kitty and Jessica were ordered to eat with the other servants but given no freedom, under house arrest.

The food settled comfortingly inside her, the wine was heady, the atmosphere one of sensual delight, and Romilly lay back on the couch unable to keep her eyes open. When she awoke later it was already dark – the darkness that comes so abruptly in the tropics. Marcus went round taking a wick to the candles.

'Time to start preparations,' said Sabrina, bending over her.

Bemused with sleep Romilly gathered her wits, looked for Alvina, and found her already yielding to Aponi's ministrations. Kitty was there too, working on her mistress's flame-red hair, which refused to be tamed. A mane of curls it suited her nature to perfection – unruly, rebellious, a law unto itself. Romilly was becoming more like her by the minute. Though they were in an untenable position, she was learning to fight and stick up for herself, her independent nature coming to the fore.

She consented to rise and visit Sabrina's privy, a civilised affair consisting of a wooden seat over a shaft that led down into darkness. There was a pitcher of water for flushing it. The offices at Harding Hall were little better, and the bathing facilities impressed her even more. They were led down a spiral staircase into the foundations, coming out in a cavern, lit by braziers reflected in water that trickled into a pool from an underground stream.

Romilly could hear the hiss of waves on the beach somewhere outside. Jessica was ordered to officiate over her toilette, and Kitty to assist Alvina, while Aponi ran about with fresh towels, jugs of hot water, and creams to make their skin silky smooth. Marcus assisted her, not in the least embarrassed to be attending naked bathers. Sabrina organised everything, a stern taskmaster never hesitating to use her whip.

Romilly found her fascinating. African people were a rarity in London, though some of the great ladies kept little black pageboys in silk suits and turbans to run errands, treating them like exotic pets. Sabrina was half-caste, her skin honey-gold, her body statuesque with full breasts and a supple waist. She was so beautiful that Romilly wondered if she was Armand's lover.

Sabrina slipped a hand under Romilly's towel, her nails skimming across her buttocks as she said, 'We must hurry; he doesn't like to be kept waiting. Into the pool and let me wash you.'

Alvina was already immersed, giving little shrieks as the water wormed its way into her nooks and crannies. 'Oh... that's cold!' But her protests changed to moans of pleasure as Marcus went down the stone steps that surrounded the watering hole, lathering his hands with scented soap and commencing to anoint her all over. No area was sacred, neither her breasts nor between her thighs.

He was hardening, his cock straining against the codpiece. He released it from its imprisonment and Sabrina didn't stop him as Alvina slid her arms around his neck and drew him closer. Their lower halves were concealed by the watery cascade flowing over the rocks, but Romilly watched as her friend's legs appeared, milky white and shining with droplets, and hooked around the young slave's waist as he raised and then penetrated her.

'Don't try that trick with him,' Sabrina cautioned Romilly, though she was breathing hard, excited by the spectacle. 'You are for the master.'

'We'll see about that,' Romilly answered heavily, averting her eyes from the antics of her promiscuous friend.

'Such disgraceful behaviour,' huffed Jessica. 'She's no better than she should be! As for yon black-a-moor; no gentleman worth his salt would have put her in charge!'

Unfortunately Sabrina heard her and the whip landed unerringly across Jessica's backside. 'Are you talking about me?' she snapped, and lashed her again.

'"If the cap fits wear it",' Jessica responded sharply.

'Hush,' Romilly warned, but it was too late. Sabrina fell upon the hapless duenna, lashing out mercilessly, the whip singing as it cut through the air, landing with brutal force. Jessica hopped about nimbly but could not avoid the blows. Sabrina was too skilled and eventually her victim dropped to her knees, head bowed as she tried to protect herself. Then tiring of this game her tormenter threw the whip down and lowered herself into the pool, her draperies floating around her as she moved across to join Alvina and Marcus in their amatory play.

Romilly ventured in and Sabrina paid her special attention, hands skimming over her body and limbs, bringing her to a tingling state of arousal. To lie back with her head resting on the pool's rim was a blissful sensation. She allowed her legs to float, becoming used to the unusual sight of her own nakedness. Sabina's caresses were gentle, making the excuse of soaping her, and Romilly relaxed, limp as a puppet whose strings are slack, remembering the native girl, Jacy, and the way in which she had pleasured her. Would Sabrina do the same? She forgot the disapproving Jessica, forgot even to be sorry for her because she'd been lashed. Nothing mattered but that this sensual bath went on.

Sabrina smiled and idled her fingers around Romilly's labia, skimming across the hard pea of her nodule, making it throb. She was rousing but not satisfying her and after a while she gave her a final rinse and then said, 'Come, let us get on, you are to be dressed for the master.'

Romilly opened her eyes reluctantly, coming to herself and shocked by her wanton delight in Sabrina's caresses. It was as if she was under a spell, and she did as the Creole ordered, dripping water as she got out of the pool, and allowing the slaves to dry her then rub oil into her skin until she felt completely boneless. She was then conducted back to Sabrina's apartment.

Seated on a stool before a mirror in a gilded stand, she watched as they brushed her hair so that it swept down like a golden curtain. Jessica carried over a pink silk robe threaded with silver and it was carefully dropped over Romilly's head and fastened, Greek fashion, with a girdle that crossed over her breasts and underneath them, lifting the rounded globes. The neckline was revealing, the material transparent, showing the curves of her buttocks, the tiny waist and flat belly, the light gold floss that covered her pubis.

Sabrina had changed too, into an embroidered scarlet skirt slit to the thigh and a tiny bolero that gave glimpses of her breasts at almost every movement. Alvina, similarly dressed to Romilly, though in purple, posed in front of the mirror, exclaiming, 'It's like a masquerade costume! I love it. When I get back to London I'll introduce it to balls at Court. The King will adore it!'

'You know the King of England?' Sabrina asked, momentarily jerked out of her complacency.

'Well, not exactly... not personally... but I have seen him close up and been to parties at the palace.'

Sabrina recovered her poise, saying with a dark note in her voice, 'I'll wager they are nothing like the gathering you are to attend tonight. Armand excels himself when it comes to entertaining.'

'I can't possibly appear like this!' Romilly exclaimed. 'It's indecent.'

'And lovely, look.' Sabrina made her stand at the looking glass while she fastened a circlet of flowers around her unbound hair. The silk of Romilly's robe was so fine that the candlelight shone through it, haloing her limbs, and its lines flowed to her bare feet, hiding nothing. It was embarrassing and her cheeks flamed at the thought of Armand seeing her like that, and would there be others?

'He'll be alone?' she asked, her voice shaking.

Sabrina shrugged. 'Feasting with his men, I expect, and maybe your companions. Don't fret; I'll be there and Lady Alvina. Who knows that may happen? That's what makes it exciting, isn't it?'

It was with fear, trepidation and a sickening sense of excitement that Romilly followed Sabrina from the bedchamber, down the central staircase and through double doors into the Great Hall. She was aware that Alvina was on one side of her and Sabrina on the other. Johnson and Marcus brought up the rear.

It was the same large room to which she'd been brought earlier, but now crowded with men lounging around the long central table, servants on the trot, lovely slave girls ready to perform their every desire. The air was hazy with tobacco smoke, and their loud voices drowned out the two violinists and a man seated at a spinet who were supplying the music from a small platform near a window. Romilly's heart was racing and she saw one man only. Armand lounged elegantly in the magnificent carver that dominated the table, clad in crimson brocade trimmed with the finest Mechlin lace, smooth-shaven with his hair curling around his shoulders and across his chest, a nobleman not a pirate, who could have graced the French king's court.

He stood as the ladies entered and so did his companions, for it seemed he had surrounded himself with his officers that night, and they had retained a semblance of good manners. Romilly was surprised and delighted to see Jamie and George, both wearing smart clothing. Joshua Willard was there too, and Lieutenant Clive Morrison, whom she had last seen being sodomised by George. They bowed, hand on heart, and Joshua said, 'Well met, your ladyships.'

'Indeed, sir,' they both replied, and dropped into curtsies.

'Be seated,' said Armand, every inch the host. 'It is some time since I have entertained such distinguished company.'

'There was Maria Gomez, the Governor of Cuba's daughter,' Sabrina reminded with a sultry smile.

'Ah yes, but we returned her to her father,' Armand pointed out.

'For a ransom?' Jamie said, and Romilly felt safer now that he and Joshua were present. Even sitting beside Armand at the head of the board no longer seemed quite so intimidating.

He shot Jamie a smouldering glance, his fingers playing with the stem of his wineglass. 'We came to an agreement,' he replied.

Jamie leaned forward eagerly, his elbows resting on the table. 'And we can do the same?'

'It is possible,' Armand said noncommittally. 'But tonight is not the time for serious discussion. Eat, drink and enjoy the moment, *mon ami*. Meet my officers; the doctor, the surgeon, the accountant.'

'You keep a tight rein, sir,' Joshua commented while he looked across at Romilly, his eyes speaking volumes in which she read admiration and concern.

'One has to, don't you agree, captain?' and Armand ignored Romilly after that first greeting, going into seamanship in great depths.

Alvina was on his other side, happy to be surrounded by so many men. The pirate leaders were personable and appeared to be educated. Even Johnson became less belligerent, as if the company of genteel ladies was rubbing off on him. But Romilly was still all too conscious of her immodest attire. Although Armand didn't appear to be impressed by it she could feel the tension stretching between them, like a wet hempen rope that grows tighter and tighter. Although the food was temping she could eat nothing, but Armand handed her a glass.

'Drink,' he said, and she was too frightened to refuse.

It was burgundy with a slightly bitter under-taste, and she wondered briefly if he was drugging her. She had heard of cases where a girl lost her virtue under the influence of wine mixed with laudanum. She wanted to place it on the table, but Armand was watching her steadily and she drained it to the last drop. There was something in his eyes that made her wonder if she might have fared better with Awan. This man was strange, whereas the native's needs had been simple. She began to realise that Armand was complicated, maybe a little insane. It wasn't a comfortable thought.

Good food and alcohol were making the other captives relax. So far they had been treated well, provided with necessities and unharmed, but Romilly found it hard to believe that there wasn't a hidden agenda. Course followed course, and had this been a normal supper party the ladies would have retired to the solar, leaving the men to their brandy, pipes and risqué talk, but here there were no such rules. The trio played on and

Romilly recognised some of the pieces that she had often heard at concerts or the opera house. It was very odd indeed, to hear this music in a pirate's lair.

'You like it?' Armand asked, and though he hadn't moved she felt as if he'd come closer.

'I do,' she replied. 'This is a piece from Monteverdi's *L'Orfeo*.'

'You have seen the work on stage?'

'Oh yes,' she replied. 'And you?'

'Before I left Paris,' he said, and there was an intriguing tinge of regret in his voice. She wanted him to say more, but his mood changed mercurially and he issued a command to Johnson. At once the musicians were hustled from the stage and their places taken by two strapping white women, one blonde, one brunette.

They were big built, their skin contrasting with the leather straps that drew attention to their large breasts and organ-stop nipples. The tiny thongs they wore were open-crotched, blatantly showing their denuded pudendum, large clits and anal holes. They strutted and flaunted in high-heeled boots, goddesses and proud of it, demanding adulation.

Johnson officiated, slapping each of them on the naked backside and announcing, 'Ladies and gentlemen, I give you Mad Meg and Milly the Bruiser. These are both champion wrestlers chosen to visit our island from Tortuga. Those who wish can place their wagers now.'

'If only I had cash!' groaned Jamie.

'Me too,' agreed George, another compulsive gambler addicted to the sport.

'A loan could be arranged,' said Armand coolly. 'At a high percentage, of course.'

'Naturally,' both men agreed, forgetting their hazardous position as gambling fever took over.

Armand nodded towards the dark-clad, sober-looking person across the table. 'Arrange it, Henry. Anyone else?' and he looked directly at Joshua, but he shook his head.

Romilly feared for her betrothed and his friend, but they were blind to everything but the thrill of placing a bet.

Mad Meg and Milly the Bruiser were professionals to their fingertips. They prowled the stage like lionesses, despising those who were willing to risk all. Romilly had the gut feeling that they distained the male species anyway, much more amenable towards Sabrina who went up and spoke to them, exchanging caresses. This action inspired the men even more and they roared their excitement. All save Armand, who sat motionless, a cynical smile playing around his lips. Mad Meg looked at him deliberately, then laughed and fingered her vulva, wetting it with her dew and sniffing and licking it, while Milly held a wooden staff between her legs, gripped it with her muscular thighs, and rubbed her slit against it. His expression did not change.

At a signal the wrestlers launched themselves and fell to the floor, folding their long legs round each other, straining and heaving, grabbing at breasts and cunts, giving a display of lesbian arousal that brought cheers from the audience. This spurred the contestants to greater heights and they squirmed in ecstasy, mouths at each other's pink clefts, fingers teasing nipples, mouths feeding on mouths. Then Mad Meg took up the pole and drove it between Milly's bottom cheeks, who snarled and spun round, fetching her a vicious blow to the side of the head.

Punching, clawing, kicking, they fell to the boards again, and every movement of those sturdy legs exposed their female parts, the thongs torn off in the fight. Johnson leapt forward and captured one of these trophies, wearing it on his bald pate, then burying his nose in the place where Mad Meg's pubis had been.

Romilly was astounded by their performance. She had never seen anyone wrestling before, not even men, and to witness females using such violent tactics proved that the description of them as 'the weaker sex' was a downright lie. There was nothing weak about these Amazons.

'What do you think of them?' murmured Armand, close to her ear, his breath a gentle breeze that sent ripples down her spine to her loins.

'Remarkable,' she responded, though finding it difficult to talk, his presence and the drink making everything hazy. Her limbs felt weighted and her mind confused.

'You've not witnessed such a thing in London?' he continued, and little shocks ran through her as she felt his hand resting on her knee under the table. It was warm and firm and her covering flimsy.

She dared not look at him, staring ahead, yet her heart was racing and she knew he was aware. His fingers were gathering up the silk, baring her flesh. He caressed the area and travelled higher, very slowly, as if letting his digits register the softness and smoothness of her skin. Romilly sat as if turned to stone, but inside frissons of excitement travelled through her, from spine to breasts to nipples, and then shooting down to her clitoris.

She pulled herself together sharply. No amount of alcohol and aphrodisiacs were going to make her lose control. He was a murderer! A sea-wolf! No doubt those same fingers that stroked her mound had dabbled in men's blood. Without even glancing at him she moved away and her robe slithered back into place. She felt more than heard his chuckle.

No help was forthcoming from Alvina. She was absorbed in the antics of the wrestlers; half rising and shouting as Milly the Bruiser sank her teeth into Mad Meg's breast. She responded by a punch that landed unerringly on Milly's jaw. She gave a grunt and slumped down, stunned. The men cheered and applauded, those who'd risked their money on Meg, that is. The others sat glumly and these included Jamie. George was jubilant, however. Henry was kept busy, doling out winnings or marking down losses. Jamie was now in debt.

'Your fiancé in trouble,' remarked Armand, making no further attempt to touch her. 'How is it that you are betrothed to such a man?'

'It was arranged by our fathers,' she answered, and the Earl would have been proud of the way she was comporting herself, a lady to the core.

'You don't love him?'

'I do, and I respect him, which is more than can be said of my feelings towards you and your gang of cutthroats, sir.'

His face darkened and his mouth set in a grim line. Then he said, 'You have too much to say for yourself, *mademoiselle*,' and before she could stop him he gripped her round the throat and drew her to him. His face hung above her for an instant, and then he captured her mouth with his, forcing her lips apart and thrusting his tongue within. She beat on his chest with her fists but he was persistent, and suddenly her wanton flesh took command. Her lips became soft and yielding and every fibre in her being melted under the onslaught. It lasted a second, no more, then she tore herself free. Her arm swung back and she slapped him across the cheek. It was a resounding slap that could be heard above the general uproar, followed by a deathly hush. Even the wrestlers stared, Meg supporting the dazed Milly.

Armand recovered and moved like lightning, standing up and dragging her with him. 'You need a lesson in manners, Lady Romilly,' he announced, his voice darkly menacing. 'And I have the very means by which to teach you.'

Chapter Six

Merciful heaven, how did I come to be in this sorry state? Romilly whispered to herself. Sometimes ill fortune finds us. We don't ask for it. We don't invite it, but it comes anyway.

Rough stone pressed into her breasts. Cold attacked her up-stretched, manacled arms. Everywhere her body connected it was uncomfortable, unnatural, designed to cause pain. She had been denied sight too, a blindfold tied over her eyes, the knot tangling with her hair. Robbed of dignity, stripped naked and fastened face forward to the wall ready for chastisement, her back, buttocks and thighs were exposed to whatever treatment Armand decided to give her.

She waited, the apprehension growing. Time had no meaning any more. She could have been there five minutes or hours. Where was he, that devil who had marched her from the Great Hall, down steep stairs to this dark, forbidding dungeon? And for what? Simply because she defied him. Jamie had tried to stop him but it was useless. Joshua protested too, so had Alvina, but there was nothing anyone could do. Armand was master of all he surveyed.

The silence stretched out endlessly, then she heard a movement behind her and smelt his aroma, feral, perfumed, vital. It cut across the odour of damp, but exacerbated her fear. She shivered as he prodded her with something. It felt like leather – a whip handle perhaps? He was so close, covering her from shoulders to heels. His lips were at the nape of her neck, his erection a firm staff prodding between her bottom cheeks. His tongue licked her ears, and then went lower to where her spine and shoulders met. She moaned, the pleasure intensifying as he caressed her gently, one hand going round to penetrate her cleft, his finger playing with her nubbin. He rubbed the head, rotated it, tormented it, then concentrated on where the labial wings joined that sliver of flesh. He was a highly skilled seducer, and kept her hovering on the brink while she writhed, begging for the ultimate pleasure.

He stopped, withdrew the bounty of that deliriously wonderful frottage, leaving her quivering with disappointment. Silence enfolded her again, and she missed the beat of his heart and the pressure of his cock, like a bar beneath his velvet breeches. Her nerves were stretched to screaming point. Had he left her? Was she to spend the night alone in the fearsome place, maybe prey to his hellions who were still carousing in the Great Hall? It was as if she had already been there forever – on the rack – waiting for him to release her from the torment of her lust.

Her arms ached, pulled taut and chained above her head. She was completely in his power. Vague pictures of Nathan floated in her mind, and Joshua and every man she had ever imagined taking her virginity, including England's monarch. Now it seemed she had no choice. If Armand wanted to wrest it from her, then she was helpless to prevent him.

'Do you intend to rape me?' she shouted. He might not be there but at least she could issue the challenge even if it did meet empty air.

'Rape you?' he replied, closer than she had imagined. 'I've never had to resort to rape.'

'You will if you breech my maidenhead,' she retorted

He chuckled and the sound penetrated her ears and tingled along her nerves. 'I don't think so. You are gravid with need. You want me to initiate you… to make you into a woman, not a selfish, pampered girl.'

'Unmannerly oaf! You know nothing about me!' Her anger was overriding other sensations.

'Be silent, silly chit, or I shall gag you. You know nothing about life, but have now found your mentor and master.'

'No man is my master!' she cried.

'I am.' He was quietly persistent.

'Never!'

'You will say it. Call me master.'

'No!'

The following silence drowned out everything except her breathing. Then, without warning, the whip whistled as it fell across her, so swift and so agonising that she was struck dumb. But for a second only, then a scream rushed from her throat to her mouth and echoed round the vault. It was leather that had bitten into her tender skin, a riding crop or whip – not a long instrument of pain but something short and easy to control, able to be used precisely.

Romilly hung absorbing the fire, just as she had taken it into herself when her father caned her. Now there was an entirely new element, or was it that she dared acknowledge the truth at last? Pain and heat communicated with her sex, adding to the arousal Armand had already produced in her clitoris, and it forced her to recognise something concealed in the darkest recess of her being. A strong male was dominating her, just as the Earl had done, and she was grateful!

She recovered a little and braced herself for another blow. Not the whip this time. His open palm slapped her hard across the bottom. It stung, burned, augmented the pain of the fiery weal left by the lash. Armand did it again, raining harsh smacks over her backside until the whole area throbbed. She needed to relieve her bladder, clenching her sphincter desperately, but his next spank was the final straw. She let go, warm urine gushing down her inner thighs and forming a puddle at her feet. It was the worst moment of all, reducing her to a sobbing child who has just wet herself.

'Where's the oh-so haughty milady now?' he whispered. 'You've just pissed like a mare in a field.'

'Bastard,' she retorted.

Armand didn't stop, using the crop again till she was almost delirious, her fevered imagination dreaming of him thrusting his cock into her, carrying her to his bed, using her as he now abused her. She wanted to be released, wanted the torture to end, wanted Armand to take her and satisfy her.

'Don't hurt me any more,' she begged. 'I feel like a slave you're punishing... a servant... a menial. I'm not like that. I'm the daughter of an earl. I've never been treated thus.'

He thrust the whip handle between her buttocks, moving it up and down till it became saturated with her sweat, urine and sex juice. 'A slave is all you are... my slave... and you will address me as master.' He thrust the handle against her and she feared it would enter her anus. 'Say it,' he growled.

'Muh... master,' she faltered, hating him, but worn down by pain and desire. Words sprang to her lips that she stopped herself from uttering, foolish things like, 'Take me. Do what you will with me. Destroy my wretched virginity... fill me with your spunk... I need you. I want you!'

She baulked when the words 'love you' followed. She didn't love him. Never could. She remained silent as Armand unfastened the chains and took her into his arms. She hurt everywhere, yet the powerful hunger in her vagina was all consuming. Surely he wouldn't leave her thus, unfulfilled and virginal still?

When she spoke it was as if someone else was pleading, 'Take me.'

'I intend to,' he answered, 'but first I'm going to wash you.' So saying, he took up a large wooden bucket and sloshed it all over her, making her start and scream and shiver.

His chamber was draped in black and purple and the furnishings were ornate, weirdly fantastic pieces from every corner of the globe. The bed was an ornamentally carved four-poster, with heavy velvet curtains, coverlet and pillows, and a graceful Venetian scene painted on the tester.

Wax dripped down the ivory candles in silver sconces six feet tall. They illumined all except the far corners, and these remained dark and sinister. Tapestries hung on the walls depicting hunting scenes, with men on horseback and deer with anguished eyes, blood spurting from their throats as they were pulled down by packs of snarling dogs. The fireplace was huge but empty. In that temperate climate it was more of a showpiece than a useful adjunct to comfort. A small table was drawn close to it, with wine and goblets, cheese and rye bread and fruit. Armand ignored all this and drew Romilly to the bed. She was still naked, and thankful that they had not encountered anyone on their way from the dungeon.

Armand loosened his jacket and embroidered waistcoat and took them off. His shirt came next and beneath it his torso was copper-hued, rippling with muscle and scarred, too. Romilly wanted to trace over those old wounds with her fingers and listen to him relating stories of how he got them. But she did neither, sitting as still as stone while he kicked off his shoes with their square toes and fancy buckles. His finery suggested that either he had a good tailor somewhere near or he wore stolen plumage. He would have passed muster at one of King Charles's assembles. He unbuckled his belt and his breeches slithered low about his hips. Romilly averted her eyes.

'Look at me,' he ordered, and pushed them down further.

His exposed phallus stood out from the nest of wiry black hair that coated his lower belly. It thrust towards her, swarthy skinned and curved. The foreskin was retracted over the swollen helm and pierced by a thick gold ring. She had expected it to be huge and resemble Nathan's, but was unprepared for this revelation. It was shocking, even alarming, but very arousing. She was excited and apprehensive enough about this act that was made so much of by humans, but it was unexpected that his cock should be adorned in such a way. Would it cause her discomfort or joy? She had no yardstick whereby to measure fornication. The aphrodisiac was still confusing her, adding to the shock sustained by her beating.

Armand stood there, hands braced on his hips, giving her

the full benefit of his manhood. There was no hesitation, no modesty; he simply took pride in it. The cock quivered and became even larger and he came towards her, taking her head between his hands and looking down into her face. His hairy chest brushed across her sensitive nipples. His cock seeped dew around the ring. Romilly waited with baited breath. Armand laid her back, holding her arms out at her sides and lowering his head to kiss her. His hair fell forward, tickling her face. She closed her eyes, resistance melting like snow in sunlight, She felt almost boneless and of little consequence compared to his ruthless passion.

But the quilt chaffed her sore back and she hissed, 'You hurt me, you brute,' twisting her face to one side to avoid his mouth.

His relaxed expression changed to one of anger. 'You deserved it. I shall hurt you again if I choose.'

He handled her harshly, running his hands down her body, cupping her breasts and rolling his thumbs over her nipples. He spread her legs and examined her delta. Going down on her, she felt the outrageous surprise of his lips on her crack, slurping at the pink wings, nibbling the hard pleasure button till she gasped and shuddered and came, not in gentle waves, but in one violent explosion.

Armand knelt between her thighs, lifted her pelvis and thrust his member against her vulva. The pain was excruciating and she screamed. He continued to press into her inch by inch, and raised her legs to clasp his waist, bringing them ever closer as he ruptured her hymen.

She could feel that mighty prick deep within her, and pain faded, replaced by pleasure as the ring rolled against the lining of her vagina. She pumped with her hips, wanting more, and he increased his movements, faster now, losing grip on anything that resembled tenderness and care. He lay full-length on her, crushing her, and she felt another orgasm building but couldn't attain it, her love-bud needing his mouth or fingers. He was beyond caring what she wanted, concerned only with his own satisfaction, driving into her until he arched his back, neck strained and she felt his prick throb inside her, not once but thrice, filling her with his seed.

Disgust and self-loathing swept over her and she struggled from under him, wanting nothing more than to be cleansed of this man's emission. How could she have submitted to him? It would have been better had she seized his sword and driven it through her heart. Now she was a wretched creature no better than the poor slaves who served him and his crew. To make it worse he showed no sign of remorse, lying there looking at her, arms folded under his head.

Romilly left the bed, snatched up his shirt and threw it round her, its folds reaching to mid-thigh. Armand laughed, 'And why, pray, are you borrowing my clothes?'

'I need to cover myself; I feel contaminated,' she answered pithily.

The laughter left his eyes, leaving them angry. 'You didn't ask me if you could.'

'I don't have to ask you for anything.'

'Don't you understand? I'm king here. I can have everything I want.'

'Except me.'

'I've already *had* you.'

'Not really.'

'Close enough. My sheets are smeared with your virgin blood.'

'I hope you're proud of yourself, monster. Now I want to rejoin my friends.'

'You are sleeping here, with me.'

'And if I refuse?'

'You'll be chained to my bed.'

She tossed back her hair, saying mockingly, 'Are you so afraid that I'll run away? Armand Tertius despised by a woman. Not too good for your reputation, eh, captain?'

He was out of bed in a flash, gripping her fiercely by the upper arms and shaking her. 'You've still not learnt, have you, bitch? You are at my mercy. I can take my fill of you, fuck you legless, bugger you, beat you till I tire of your insipid charms, and send you to the slave block to be auctioned to the highest bidder.'

Romilly had had enough. She was bruised and bloody, hurting inside from his thrusts, sore from his invasion of her maiden delta, dazed with wine and drugs. She capitulated, though she knew it to be but temporary; they had much to sort between them, he and she. So she crawled back into the bed and he shackled her by one wrist, the iron cuff fastened to a ringbolt attached to the bed-head.

After this he dressed and slung on his sword, then headed for the door. 'You're leaving me?' she shouted at his uncaring back.

He looked over his shoulder at her and the arrogance of him caught at her heart, yet infuriated her. 'I shall be back, you can count on that,' he answered, his fascinating, accented voice belying the heavy promise contained in his words.

'Lack-a-day, I wonder what's happening to Romilly,' Alvina murmured, stirring in George's arms. Ordered to entertain the pirates during Armand's absence, the pair had been copulating with her lying across the table and him performing above her.

She had been drinking steadily, and such an exhibition did not embarrass her. In fact, she found that doing it before so many men, all cheering and egging her on, had added to her arousal. Sabrina was jealous, full lips pouting, and this made Alvina all the more determined to put on a good show. The coffee-coloured woman thought she was queen bee around there, and Alvina was delighted to put her nose out of joint. As for George, he was only too willing to oblige. Man, woman or dog, it was all the same to him, just as long as he could get satisfaction.

Alvina disengaged herself from him, meeting Jamie's worried eyes. He wasn't joining in the revelry, neither was Joshua.

They surveyed the scene glumly and Jamie had difficulty in controlling his temper. Alvina dragged a shawl about her nakedness and filled a glass from a wine bottle.

'I don't think he'll hurt her,' she said consolingly, knowing he was fretting about Romilly.

'That's not the point,' he raged. 'I'm in an awkward position. She's my betrothed and he has probably deflowered her by now. She may even fall pregnant, and if we get out of this mess alive I shall have to honour our agreement and play father to her bastard brat.'

'Is that all you care about; your title and reputation?' Alvina questioned, sipping the wine and watching the antics of a girl who lay on the floor.

Her slim body was coated in sauces, fruit and vegetables from the supper table. Cooling gravy trickled down her honey-coloured skin and formed puddles in her navel. Several seamen where bending over her and licking her clean, paying special attention to her crack. One leaned above her and stuck his cock in her mouth, and two stood on either side while she masturbated them.

Alvina imagined relating the scene when she got back to Court. The dandies would express mock horror, rolling their eyes and making elaborate gestures while their pricks hardened under their breeches. She would be the toast of London. It did not occur to her for one moment that they might never return. She had always been cushioned by wealth and couldn't see it stopping. A letter to the Governor of Jamaica explaining their plight and he would pay Armand what he demanded, looking after her until a ship arrived to take her home. Retelling her adventures would provide hours of amusement at parties. And if Romilly lost her cherry on route, good luck to her. All would end well; Alvina was sure, ever the optimist.

She wandered round the room, avoiding the arms outstretched to trap her, but dismissing those who were so bold as to try, with a warm smile and a shrug. These men were tough and rough, accustomed to desperate women who traded themselves for gold in order to survive. Alvina had seen their type in the slums of London and hanging around the places of entertainment. Whores were whores the world over, and she thanked God that she hadn't been born in straightened circumstances. Sex for her was fun, not work.

The fiddlers were playing, but no longer serious pieces. Instead they scrapped away at lively jigs and the men capered and danced and the girls tripped lightly, skirts flying out, displaying long legs, bare bottoms and pudendum.

She reached Joshua and said, 'Well, captain, and what do you make of all this?'

He was leaning with his wide shoulders against a pillar, arms folded over his chest and feet crossed at the ankles. She had never seen him unkempt before, but now he was in need of a shave and the clothing supplied him was of poor fit and quality. Clive was with him, looking truly miserable, usually a pin-neat officer, but now scruffy. He was trying to put a brave face on it, but she could tell he was apprehensive.

'I wish to God I had a few stalwart lads from the British navy with me,' Joshua said in clipped, angry tones. 'That would soon teach these blackguards a sharp lesson. I'd hang them all from the yardarm, that confounded French leader of theirs, too.'

'Really?' she murmured, teasing him though he was unaware. 'But I thought he was something of a gentleman.'

'Gentlemen don't seize and carry off ladies,' Joshua snapped, and Alvina thought, well stab me, he's sweet on our Romilly!

Aloud, she said, 'That's true,' and made big innocent eyes, adding, 'Do you think he wants to marry her?'

'No, my lady, I don't,' he stormed, and her heart leapt at the sight of his rage and she wanted to bed him without delay. Here was a real man, not a fop.

The scene around them was degenerating into debauchery, only the officers showing any sign of restraint. But suddenly the door crashed open, framing Armand, and he was furious.

'Get out, the lot of you!' he thundered and turned on Johnson. 'Are you so foxed that you can't keep order? I left you in charge.' Then Sabrina came into his line of fire and he grabbed and shook her, rousing her from her alcoholic frenzy. 'Have you no control? I thought I could trust you.'

'I'm sorry,' she said, slurring her words. 'But you know what they're like when the drink is in them.'

'Oh, I do indeed,' he said menacingly, and turned towards his prisoners. 'Tomorrow we will hold a meeting and decide your fate. Meanwhile, you will be conducted back to your rooms. Never fear, I shall respect your safety. Ask for anything you want and it shall be yours... except freedom, that is. Sabrina, you will take care of Lady Alvina.'

'And Lady Romilly?' Alvina piped up, unafraid. He was only a man, after all, and she had many tried and trusted ways of dealing with men.

He looked down at her and she quivered at the intensity of his eyes and the sheer, undiluted sexuality of the man. 'She is in my chamber, chained to the bed,' he said crisply.

'You can't!' protested Jamie, making as if to strike him.

Armand smiled darkly, answering, 'I can and have. She doesn't seem to be upset.'

'You villain,' growled Joshua. 'If I had my way you'd be tried and hanged.'

'I expect so, *monsieur*, but this is my island and my regime and my whim whether you live or die. Now, goodnight to you all. I have pressing business that needs attention.'

He bowed and took himself off, leaving Alvina wondering if he was about to return to Romilly and what he was like between the sheets. The images conjured by her imagination made her mouth dry and her lower lips wet.

It is always difficult to sleep in a strange bed and Romilly was chained too, which meant that her movements were limited. Her bruised body needed someone to cherish and heal it and, strong though she imagined herself to be, she couldn't stop the tears from flowing.

There were strange noises all around; the whine of insects, the clamour of the party, doors slamming, women's shrieks of laughter, men shouting, the clash of steel on steel as the more quarrelsome among them crossed swords. Where was Armand? She didn't know which was worse – wanting him to come or fearing his arrival.

As for the loss of her virginity? She had half expected a dramatic transformation to take place once it happened but, apart from tenderness between her legs, nothing had changed, or so she at first thought. But now, lying on his bed in the candlelit room, she realised that she *was* different. Armand had marked her as his own as surely as if he'd branded her with his crest. She would never forget him, no matter what – the first man to enter her body and rob her of her innocence.

At last she fell into a deep sleep induced by Armand's potion and sheer exhaustion. No one disturbed her for the remainder of the night.

She was awakened with daylight streaming in at the narrow windows and Jessica bending over her, shaking her gently by the shoulder and saying, 'Wake up, my lady.'

'What? Where am I?' Romilly said groggily, then her movements restricted by the manacles, suddenly recalled everything. 'Oh, sweet Jesus, that man! That brute. Get these things off me, Wade. At once, d'you hear?' Her voice rose imperiously, momentarily forgetting her ignominious position.

'I'll call someone. No wait, I've a better idea.' Jessica produced a hairpin, inserted it in the lock, twiddled it for a second and it sprang open.

'Where did you learn such a trick?' Romilly asked, amazed that her duenna should have the skills usually associated with a thief.

Jessica smiled and tapped the side of her nose mysteriously. 'Ah, my lady, there are many things you don't know about me, have never bothered to ask, but I had a life before entering your service.'

Romilly wanted to hear more but sat up gingerly, groaning as her injuries sprang into life. At once Jessica was all concern, patting and soothing, fetching over the water jug and basin and bathing her mistress's hurts even as she grumbled and complained. 'That beast. I'm ruined. I'll never forgive him. Never!'

'Did you meet a fate worse than death?' Jessica enquired, colouring even as she spoke those dire words, while Romilly found the chamber-pot and used it, her blushes almost as red as her duenna's when she remembered passing water in front of Armand.

'Indeed I did. He had his way with me,' Romilly confessed, unable to meet the chaperone's eyes.

Jessica clapped a hand to her mouth. 'Oh, you poor thing. I feared as much but hoped against all hope that he might have retained a vestige of manners. What will Lord James say?'

This made Romilly really angry. 'Why are you thinking about him? What about *me*? I may be diseased because of his vile touch or, worse than that, with child by him.'

'There is a doctor among his officers,' Jessica said, patting her consolingly, then helping her into a silk dressing gown that lay across the foot of the bed. She added almost shyly, 'He's a fine man who hasn't adopted piratical rudeness, a member of their band by misfortune not choice. I was speaking with him last night and he was most respectful, a perfect gentleman. His name is Peter Quidley. I'm sure he will attend you, if I ask him.'

'No one is attending her,' Armand insisted, startling them as he entered the room forcefully. 'She's not harmed. Only her pride has been dented and it's high time. Far too full of her own importance. She should think herself lucky it was me who deflowered her, not one of my rapscallions.'

'Yes sir, I'm sorry, sir. I meant no harm but am concerned for my lady.'

97

'Very commendable,' he said ironically. 'A worthwhile trait in a servant. But I haven't quite decided whether I shall allow you to stay with your mistress, or maybe take you to the slave market.'

'To be sold? Oh no, sir... please,' Jessica begged, prostrating herself at his feet. 'She needs me and cannot manage alone.'

'So you still put her needs first? I wish I could command such devotion.' His face was set in severe lines and his voice flat.

'You must have known it once,' Jessica continued from her submissive position.

'Oh yes, I wasn't born a pirate,' he answered heavily, his eyes brooding as if he dwelt on events long ago. 'I was tricked out of my inheritance by unscrupulous, greedy relatives.'

'Isn't that what all criminals say in their defence?' Romilly put in, springing from the bed and glowering at him.

'This happens to be true,' he said coldly.

'Pigs might fly!' she retorted, denying the strong pull she felt, drawn to him as magnet is to steel. Had matters only been different she would have sent Jessica away and welcomed him, reliving all those strange and exciting sensations of the previous night.

'Dr Quidley tells me you are a sensible woman,' he said to Jessica, indicating that she should rise. 'This being the case, I suggest that you advise your mistress to comport herself with dignity and control her waspish tongue.'

'Dare I ask if you have come to a decision regarding her future, and those of her companions?' Jessica ventured, more confident now that she had been found a sober brown dress, white apron and coif. Outlandish attire made her uneasy.

'I am assured by Viscount James and Lord George that Lady Romilly's relatives in Port Royal will pay their ransom, sending word to the Earl of Stanford.'

'You'll set them free?' Jessica cried.

Romilly couldn't believe her ears. 'Generosity, from *you*?'

98

she scoffed. 'There must be a trick in it somewhere.'

'Shut your spiteful mouth,' he snarled, and she rejoiced in finding his Achilles heel.

'That is no way to speak to a lady,' chided Jessica, and it was as if she had grown in stature, a controlling mature woman. Even the roughest of Armand's crew had not attacked her or offered her injury and she had found a protector in Peter Quidley.

'My good woman, your charge is no lady,' Armand snarled. 'Neither is that blue-blooded strumpet, Alvina.'

Romilly lost her temper. Without thinking of the consequences she slapped him across the face with such force that his head jerked back. His hand shot out and grabbed her wrist, bending it back. They glared into each other's eyes and she was astonished by what she read there. His pupils where black pools in which she saw herself reflected and she wanted to get closer and closer, drowning in them. He was so near, his chest brushing her breasts, the contact making her nipples crimp.

'That's the second time you've hit me,' he said angrily. 'Haven't you suffered enough?'

He pushed his thigh between hers and she could feel the hardness of his erection, remembering the cock-ring, the feeling of being filled to capacity, the discomfort followed by ecstasy. She shocked herself by the hot, wanton desire to experience it again. Reacting violently she tore herself free and took several paces back. This was better. She was all right just as long as he didn't touch her. Armand, however, would have none of this.

'Get you gone, woman,' he ordered Jessica.

'But—'

'Get out!'

With a worried glance at Romilly, Jessica scurried through the door. When it closed behind her Armand advanced on Romilly, tore open the robe and dumped her facedown on the bed. She kicked and yelled but he ignored these fruitless protests. Holding her down with one hand he opened his breeches and released that mighty, ring-pierced cock. It was wet with pre-come and he spread some of it over struggling Romilly's arse.

'What are you doing?' she spluttered. 'Oh God, you can't mean to…? Can you? That's unclean, dreadful, against the law.'

He chuckled and pushed a finger into her virgin nether hole. 'The law? You think this means anything to me? I'm about to introduce you to another way of taking.'

As he spoke he dallied with the head of his prick, caressing her crack for what seemed ages, rousing her despite herself, the glans contacting her nubbin from behind, exciting her so much that she was almost mad for relief. She wriggled her hips, attempting to lure him into her vagina, but he had other ideas in mind.

Suddenly his shaft pushed against her anus with unstoppable force. She could feel herself stretching and feared she might split asunder. His jism made it less painful than it would have been if she was dry, but even so she shrieked and near pissed herself. He ground against her relentlessly, till the gold ring and his fleshy helm pushed past her restricting muscles and sank into her depths.

'Christ, you're tight,' he gasped, moving within her.

'I am, and I hope it hurts you,' she hissed. 'I'd like to mangle your cock and damage it so that you'd never more be able to violate me. I'd like to clamp round your tool, squeeze it to death and never set it free, tear it off and keep it within me, forever useless.'

He was panting hard, but managed to growl, 'You're enjoying it so much, are you? Such violent talk suggests one thing only… raging desire.'

'You flatter yourself,' she muttered, praying that the torture would end, or that she might feel pleasure from the encounter, but there was nothing but discomfort.

He bayed like an animal and she felt hot jets of semen

gushing into her fundament. Weakened and depleted as he was she struggled from under him, and immediately his cock escaped from her rectum and he lay flat on his face, head to one side, eyes closed as he breathed in raged gasps.

If I only had a knife, she thought passionately, I could stab him in the back, plunging it into his black heart!

'Don't even think about it,' he said, opening his eyes and staring straight at her.

'How did you know?' she asked, angry and puzzled and afraid of his power.

'I know everything about you. We are as alike as two peas in a pod. Soul mates.'

'I'm not. I hate you, hate you, hate you!'

He turned to lie on his back, relaxed as men are after shagging women, but on the alert, too. 'So you want to leave me and go to your aunt in Jamaica, do you?'

'Yes.'

'And marry Lord James and lead the insipid life of a society wife?'

'That's right.'

'And I'm supposed to believe this fairytale?' He had risen by now and was standing behind her, his fingers playing with that sensitive spot at the back of her neck. She shivered involuntarily, even though his spunk trickled down her inside thighs, cool and cloying.

'Believe it. I've never hated anyone as much as I hate you.'

He laughed quietly, released her and said, 'We'll see about that. If I was a gambling man I'd wager that you'll soon be begging me to keep you.'

'Never.'

He was ready to leave now, saying, 'Tomorrow we are sailing to Tortuga and there, if I decide this is for the best, a packet-boat will carry a letter to your aunt, telling her of your plight and how much it will cost to free you. Meanwhile, Sabrina will stretch you with the butt-plug.'

Chapter Seven

I've never known such discomfort in all my life, Romilly complained inwardly, lying on a couch in Sabrina's apartment with a dildo inserted in her arse. Aponi and Marcus were in attendance.

'Such a to-do,' the Creole had exclaimed when Romilly yelled at this intrusion. 'This is the smallest size and they will gradually get bigger, till you'll be able to take the master with ease. Lie there and be good. Then we'll see what you can wear to dazzle Cayona in the morning.'

Alvina had been permitted to join her, and she was now sitting on a chair close to the couch comparing notes. 'I like it here,' she said. 'I've never been fucked so much. No chaperones or parents or older brothers keeping an eye on one.'

'Have you had Joshua Willard?' Romilly was still interested in the upright and honourable seaman.

'No,' Alvina said, encouraging Marcus to wave the feather fan just that little bit faster. It was a very hot day. 'Don't be so mean. You have the highly desirable Armand.'

'Who I don't want. D'you see what they're doing to me, just so he can take his perverted pleasure in my bottom? He's hateful.'

'Oh, dear, aren't you protesting a little too much? You don't sound sincere. Anyway, Joshua is mad in love with you.'

Romilly's heart leapt, and even the pain in her rectum was slightly mollified, but, 'Don't be foolish,' she chided.

'It's true, dearest. Both he and Jamie are most dreadfully put out because Armand took your maidenhead.'

'Doesn't anyone here have more to do than gossip?' Romilly

102

asked, exasperated.

'Apparently not. Men are bigger scandalmongers than women, I vow, and just because this lot are pirates it doesn't make a hap'orth of difference. They chew the fat and comment on the love affairs of others like a gaggle of old washerwomen.'

She dived a hand under Marcus's sarong and played with his genitals. His response was immediate. Sabrina, watching idly from her place near the couch, said to him, 'Go on, do it. I want to see you at it. Then you can diddle my pussy. Hurry, slave,' and she flicked his backside with her whip, hard enough to sting and make his cock lift.

'Can't you remove this tiresome thing from me?' Romilly grumbled. 'How much longer do I have to endure it?'

Sabrina smiled, showing a flash of perfect white teeth. 'You're right. It is time for something bigger. Aponi, fetch the next size. Don't pay no mind to what I'm doing to you, Lady Romilly. Keep your eyes on your friend and Marcus.'

This was easier said than done. When Sabrina withdrew the plug Romilly felt she was being disembowelled. Her torment wasn't over, however. Aponi carried in an even larger one and though Sabrina greased it well, Romilly insisted that she introduced it to her anal opening slowly and carefully. Eventually it slid inside her and, 'Make believe it's Armand's magnificent prick,' the Creole whispered lecherously.

Meanwhile Alvina was with Marcus, stretched out on Sabrina's bed while he slurped at her cleft. When she mewed like a kitten, then threshed wildly in climax, he followed this up by thrusting his cock into her. Despite what Romilly had said she found such an exhibition arousing, willing to let Sabrina fondle her clit till she came, the muscles of her back passage clenching round the carved ivory lingam.

'There, that's not so bad, is it?' Sabrina crooned. 'Now I want it, too. Marcus, come over here and bring me off. Aponi, you shall attend to my breasts and later, if you please me, I may let you enjoy a good frigging.'

103

After a while Romilly became bored with voyeurism. She wished her ordeal was over, cursed Armand for his selfishness and inwardly bewailed her lot. But there was a gleam of light at the end of the tunnel. It seemed that Armand was prepared to negotiate and send a letter to her aunt, Lady Fenby, demanding a substantial sum of money for their safe passage to Port Royal and freedom. She knew that her aunt and uncle were exceedingly rich planters and would be happy to extend a loan to be paid back by the victims' fathers. Soon the ordeal would be nothing but an unpleasant memory, and the fact that she wasn't overjoyed was cause for concern. Surely she wanted to be free, didn't she?

My life has been turned topsy-turvy, and it's all the fault of that villain, Armand Tertius. I wish I had never, ever met him, she vowed, and wriggled uncomfortably on the object buried in her fundament, put there for the sole purpose of increasing his pleasure. Typical, she raged. God damn all men!

'Where's Jamie?' she shouted suddenly, needing to vent her wrath on someone. 'He's not bothered to seek me out.'

'His movements are restricted,' Sabrina answered lazily. She had just come and was resting on the bed with Marcus on one side of her and Aponi on the other. 'We can't have prisoners roaming at will. They might get some silly notion of trying to escape. Impossible, I assure you.'

Later Sabrina had her slaves bring clothes from a walk-in wardrobe, and Romilly was astounded by the richness and variety of those on offer. There were gowns and cloaks, petticoats and furs, hats, gloves, shoes and every refinement of female attire, all of excellent quality.

'Where did all this come from?' Alvina asked, letting gold chains and pendant earrings and any amount of jewellery run through her fingers and back into their casket.

'Loot, no doubt,' put in Romilly acidly. Though relieved of the plugs she was sore and uncomfortable.

'You're right. All these treasures are spoils of war, as it were, selected by Armand for sale or to clothe any visitors he might have,' replied Sabrina.

'Enforced ones.'

'Whatever.' The Creole gave a shrug of her shapely bare shoulders.

'I don't want to wear anything he has stolen from some other unfortunate.' Romilly was offended. Surely he could have provided her with something other than cast-offs, not that she wanted to be obligated to him in any way whatsoever.

Sabrina smiled, a woman of the world. 'Everything here is of the very finest quality. Some of it will go to Cayona to be auctioned tomorrow, along with surplus slaves.'

'That's horrible. A traffic in human flesh!'

'And doesn't your aunt own plantations in Jamaica? I dare swear that the workers are slaves, transported from Africa. I come from such stock, so you have no call to be uppity, my fine lady.'

This silenced Romilly. She had never before questioned her father's wealth and its source, assuming it was inherited. No doubt most of it was, but he traded abroad, importing tobacco and sugar and now she realised slaves produced this. It gave her food for thought, but the idea that Armand might dare put her on the block, or even her servants, was abhorrent. The man was a monster! She resolved to refuse him if he came near her again with his demands, his masterful possession of her that reduced her to a similar kind of slavery. I'll die first, she vowed.

'And what do you think we should do, my lord?' Joshua glanced across to where Jamie and George were seated in the shade, playing cards. Peter Quidley had joined them; another stranded Englishman who, through force of circumstance, had ended up on Devil's Paradise.

'I don't much care, just as long as we get away from this godforsaken spot.' Jamie had been cast down ever since Armand had taken Romilly.

'And you, Lord George?' Joshua was disappointed in their

lack of action. If any man had touched his betrothed! By God, he would have been hell-bent on revenge. Even though Romilly could never wed someone of his station, the idea of her being fucked by a pirate made him see red.

'Me, old boy? I just want to get back to London in one piece. The life here ain't bad, I suppose. Warm and sunny with plenty of wine and women… youths too, for that matter, but I miss the theatre and coffeehouses, the chat with witty fellows, keep up with Court gossip and some such. Yes, I want to go home. What say you, Clive?'

'I'm in total agreement. Can't wait to see London again.' Clive shuffled the cards and spread them out. No one, except the doctor, had any money, so they were playing for pebbles.

Joshua was well aware that Clive could act the 'sea-wife'. Not that he had ever taken advantage of the young man's predilections. He was non-judgemental about such matters. Being so long at sea had taught him many lessons, not the least of which was to mind his own business. He had enough to do commanding his ship without bothering about who was sharing whose hammock.

Now he was restless, needing to launch into action. The island was idyllic, and from where he sat he could see the ocean, watch the white horses running up the golden beach, smell the fragrance of exotic trees and enjoy the juice of pineapples and other strange fruits. It could have been heaven on earth, instead of a playground for that scoundrel Armand and his gang. Joshua was a member of the merchant navy and bitterly resented his ignominious position. If he could only lay hands on a lively ship, a few gunners and stalwart lads, then he'd give these rogues a run for their money and see them hanging from the gallows at Tyburn Tree.

'Can I get you anything, master?' lisped a golden-brown slave girl, all big eyes and black hair, a tiny person, doll-like and enticing.

'Go away,' said the doctor firmly. 'You'll get no trade here. These gentlemen are prisoners.'

This reminder made Jamie fling himself back in his rattan chair, exclaiming, 'Dammit, Quidley, d'you have to say that? I was doing my best to forget, and going to ask her to bring us another bottle of rum.'

'For which I would pay? I don't think so, my lord. My advice to you is to do as Tertius suggests. If you go along with the plan, then we shall shortly be in Cayona where he can send a messenger to Port Royal, negotiate with Lady Fenby, and arrange an exchange.'

'Will he honour such an agreement?'

'Of course. You don't know him, but I can assure you that he comes from French aristocracy, an old respected family but, on the death of his father, the old Comte de Tertius, he was robbed of his inheritance on some trumped-up charge. He went to prison and was then deported to the West Indies. That is how he became what he now is, but old habits die hard and he has codes of behaviour to which he always adheres.'

'Not with regards to my fiancée,' Jamie reminded dourly, and his hand went to his left side where, normally, he would have worn his sword.

The doctor lifted his lean shoulders and said, 'He is susceptible to a lovely woman, naturally. And she is exceptionally beautiful. If he found the right lady, then I think he would settle down.'

'A vagabond like him? You jest, sir!'

Peter shook his head with its long brown locks streaked with grey at the temples. 'No sir, I don't. We are all of us not getting any younger, and I myself would like to marry, leave this island and practice medicine and my doctoring skills among respectable folk. I have an eye on Lady Romilly's companion, Mrs Jessica Wade. A charming woman who would suit me admirably, but alas I am committed to this way of life.'

'Can you never leave?'

'Not unless I obtain a pardon.'

'How did you come to be here?'

107

'I sailed from England several years ago, part of a venture organised by London merchants who financed a ship to explore the Indies, bringing home samples of flora and fauna. We were captured by Tertius and given the option of joining them or being marooned. I wanted to live and continue my work, so I consented and, strangely enough, have learned a great deal while attending the pirates' wounds, working among the inhabitants and adding to my collection of drawings and examples of flowers, seeds and native remedies.'

The more Joshua heard the more he liked the neatly built, pleasantly looking medical man. If I get out of this alive I'll put in a word for him with the authorities, he resolved, but meanwhile the future looked uncertain.

Just for a moment he allowed his thoughts to dwell on Romilly. What Quidley said was true: she was indeed a rare and beautiful example of womanhood. He wanted her with a desire that was like fire in his belly, and would have gladly taken her on, had he been given the opportunity, even though she had now been soiled by a pirate's spunk. But even this notion excited him, and he could not control the thickening of his cock as he imagined her, naked and suppliant, in Armand's experienced hands. This shocked him, for his parents had been God-fearing people, regular churchgoers who raised him and his four siblings to be pillars of society. He'd had women, of course, during the course of his career, but had always been ashamed afterwards. Now he was twenty-eight and ready to fall in love, marry and establish a family.

The presence of Sabrina and her shameless sisters had stirred emotions in him best forgotten. The pirates were licentious and bawdy. There was constant reference to sexual matters during their conversations. Joshua could see the last remnants of civilisation slipping away from him if he didn't escape from there soon. Maybe if he travelled to Jamaica as Armand's messenger, he could arrange matters so he could sail back to Devil's Paradise and attack the pirate stronghold.

As if reading his thoughts the doctor glanced up from his

cards and reminded, 'Lady Romilly and her companions will be held hostage, you understand. Any rash move on your part will result in their deaths.'

At the slack of the tide the helmsman expertly steered the *Scorpion* into the crescent-shaped harbour of Cayona. Armand trusted him to pilot her through the narrow, dark-blue streak of water that marked the passage to the land-locked port of the fortified island of Tortuga. It was the refuge of privateers, pirates and buccaneers and the governor, who received generous handouts for his trouble, had granted them semi-official French protection.

Armand gave a signal and his gunners fired a convivial salute. It echoed round the wharves and reverberated among the wooded hills. Gulls rose, circling and screaming over the forest of masts as several ships, riding easily at their moorings, gave answer in a noisy volley. Roused from the siesta that was the only way to pass the scorching heat of the afternoon, some of the inhabitants ambled out to welcome the newcomers.

One who heard but did not go was Catherine MacGowan, known as the Cat. She was landlady of the *Kicking Donkey*, one of the most notorious taverns in the whole of that lawless island. She went to her window, took up a telescope, pointed it towards the quay and squinted through it. A smile lit her sun-browned face, blue eyes sparkling as she recognised the ship. Armand was back! Tough though she was, donning breeches and fighting alongside the men sometimes, she had a weakness for him and was fiercely jealous. She hoped that one day, *one happy day*, he would make her his bride and take her away from the dangerous hurly-burly of everyday life in the port. She didn't go to meet him, however. She had her pride, and although her breasts tingled to feel his hands and her sex ached to have him inside her once again, she spruced herself up and sauntered down to the bar to wait his arrival.

Cat was bold, beautiful and took her pleasures with either sex. Once she had been a footpad, a pickpocket and thief and had narrowly escaped the hangman, convicted at London's Old Bailey. She had pleaded her belly and was locked up in the notorious Newgate Jail where her child was born. Destitute, she was indentured as a servant to a family who were seeking their fortunes in the West Indies. They were pious Puritans and never let her forget that she was a sinner. She endured it because of her son, Paul, but eventually ran off with a dashing rascal who took her to Tortuga. He bought the *Kicking Donkey*, was surrogate father to her bastard, but was eventually slain in a brawl.

Impatience ran like liquid fire through her blood, but she gave no indication. Love was for weaklings, and she had no intention of walking that road again. She poured a tot of brandy and stalked into the taproom, greeted by her regulars. They were full of the news, chorusing in several different languages, 'The *Scorpion* has just dropped anchor. Tertius will be here at any moment. Watch your backs, boys.'

'He'd never stab anyone in the back,' Cat shouted, glaring threateningly, arms akimbo, a tall woman who could stand her ground. They quietened and she sat at one of the tables, greeted by a youngster who she was considering taking as her latest lover. Going by the name of Phil, he was all of nineteen to her twenty-eight years.

'You're soft on Tertius,' jeered a man, speaking English with a foreign intonation. He was handsome, with a hawk-nose and black oily ringlets falling across the shoulders of a dandyish sky-blue silk coat.

He wore no shirt, but a lavishly embroidered waistcoat, tight breeches and boots made of supple deerskin. The sword with a Toledo blade and basket hilt that swung from a baldric over his right shoulder proclaimed him to be no fop, but a hardened fighter.

'Shut up, Lafette,' Cat said, her mane of curly flaxen hair giving her the aspect of a fallen angel. 'No man gets to me. I don't need the aggravation.'

'You need a stiff cock though, I'll warrant.'

'And can get one anytime, anywhere.' She held Lafette's dark eyes – wolf's eyes, gypsy eyes. He was angry because she had never yet taken him to her bed and made no secret of her dislike. He was a powerful leader, almost as powerful as Armand, and hated being thwarted.

Half a dozen of his men were with him, for he rarely travelled alone. He had too many enemies and was quite likely to end up with his throat cut in one of the sordid alleys that led from the waterfront. He was recklessly brave, owned two ships and scoured the seas relentlessly, seeking rich pickings. Were it not for the fact that he greased the Governor's palm, he would have been handed over to the authorities long ago.

'You'll never find a man who will fuck you like I can,' he boasted, and she could tell that he believed it. She glanced down to where his cock lay, and could see it was engorged beneath the breeches, stretching up almost to his waist. No empty boast, then? But there was something about him that repelled her. He was too smooth and snakelike.

To rile him she turned her smile on the lad at her table. He was staring at her, obviously besotted. She ran her fingers through his brown hair, causing mayhem in his groin area. He gasped and seized her hand. She chuckled and pressed her breasts against his shoulder. Her bodice was low-cut, her cleavage pronounced and he blushed fiery red. She guessed he was on the point of spilling in his underwear and felt motherly, as she did towards her son. One day perhaps an experienced woman would take pity on him too, and relieve him of his spunk.

Lafette was watching her through lowered lids and she didn't relish having an audience. She stood up, held out her hand to the boy, and said, 'Come, Phil, let's go out back to my private rooms.' Her scornful stare defied Lafette to comment, or anyone else for that matter, and leaving the pot-man in charge she took the youth into her parlour.

Fired by Dutch courage he tried to kiss her, but was too clumsy. She enjoyed being in charge and drew him down on

111

the couch of her well-furnished room. She had filled it with gifts from her customers and spoils of piratical adventures in which she had taken part. Cat was rich enough to retire, but would have been bored to death.

To stop her heart from beating madly in anticipation of seeing Armand, she lifted her skirt, giving Phil a full view of her sparse pubic hair. He goggled, moaned and clasped himself between the legs, almost beyond control.

She reached down and stopped him, withdrawing his grasp on his cock and saying, 'No, not yet. Don't lose it till I say you can.' She unbuttoned him and drew out that long, pink, fresh young prick, but was careful not to caress it, thus precipitating a premature explosion.

'You're wonderful... wonderful...' Phil spluttered, hardly daring to move lest the pressure prove too much.

'And I'm going to show you how to pleasure me,' she promised, then lay back and lifted one leg, resting it against the couch. Her skirt fell back, revealing her shapely thighs and tempting cleft. She wore no stockings, only high-heeled mules with metal buckles. 'Come closer and take a good look. Have you seen a woman's cunt before?'

He went even redder. 'No, I've not.'

'Don't be shy. You're a virgin, aren't you?' This was even more exciting.

'Yes, but don't tell my mates. They're always talking about the women they've had.'

'Pay them no heed. They're probably lying anyway. This is my pleasure spot, and I'm going to show you how to stroke it.' She lifted a finger to her mouth and licked it, then applied the moisture to her labia, parting the swollen folds and anointing her love-bud. A moan escaped her as she gently massaged it, lifting her hips so that the little organ poked from its hood, rosy-pink and hard. Phil stared, riveted to the spot.

'What are you doing?' he breathed jerkily.

'This is my treasure, my little nubbin of delight.' Cat was

112

roused even further by his innocence.

'But I thought women needed a man's prick inside them.'

She gurgled with laughter that ended in a gasp as the pleasure began to course through her, every nerve responding to the steady friction of her fingertip flying over her clit. 'This is a story put about by men. A lusty cock feels good, but not unless my bud is rubbed. I can get my pleasure with women, too. They know where and how to caress it. I am about to teach you a valuable lesson that will stand you in good stead for the rest of your life. Women will adore you for it, if you treat their nubbins as I'm doing now. Watch.'

Her hand moved faster and she arched her back, chasing the pleasure. Now she was beyond the point of no return, vaguely aware that Phil was holding his cock and rubbing it in unison with her rapid movements. Who would come first? She had a notion it would be her. She was rising to that plateau where all she needed was concentration to lift her even higher and tip her over the edge. Her nipples tingled, her clit was fiery hot, the need within her growing to immense proportions till she was overwhelmed with a rush of intense pleasure. As she came she saw one face before her. Not Phil's, but the swarthy, arrogant features of Armand.

Romilly was excited, yet annoyed. She couldn't wait to leave the ship and step on to the wharf, but her attire infuriated her. She wore a big, shady hat, elbow-length gloves, high heels, silk stockings and lace-edged lawn petticoats, but the gown allotted her did not meet with her approval. She was still grumbling about it to Alvina as they waited to be escorted ashore.

'It's so outmoded. Scarlet hasn't been worn for ages. Everyone who is anyone wears pastel shades now. Look at the waist, so high it's almost under my armpits, and the collar! Ye gods, the neckline is square. It must be all of ten years old. And as for this necklace and earrings, they're nothing but paste.'

'Would you expect him to provide you with real gems? No doubt those are in his strongbox. Stop complaining,' Alvina said, cross at being interrupted when she was making eyes at a crewmember engaged in lowering the gangplank. She was attired in emerald green. 'I think these strong colours are flattering. I may introduce them when we get home. And I like the cut of the sleeves.'

'Come along, ladies,' Armand said, finely dressed and wearing a broad-brimmed hat with an ostrich plume.

Goods for sale had already been taken ashore, including half a dozen slaves that were surplus to requirement. Romilly shuddered as she realised she could have been among their number. Jamie and George had been kitted out with fashionable suits, and their valets were neatly attired. Kitty wore a low-cut dress with a full shirt that finished at her ankles, and Jessica was more soberly clad, though she looked years younger now, flattered by the doctor's attentions.

'Love moves in mysterious ways,' Alvina said, nodding towards her. 'Who would have thought that your duenna would fall prey to Cupid's arrows?'

'Who indeed?' Romilly rested the tips of her fingers on Armand's outstretched arm and permitted him to help her cross the swaying gangplank, with its dizzying drop to the water.

The goods were already being loaded on a cart, ready to be transported to the auction house, while the slaves, tethered by their wrists, walked along behind. They were well fed and in prime condition. A sick slave wasn't worth much and it was up to those selling them to ensure they were healthy.

'Where are we going?' Romilly demanded, missing her mentor, Sabrina. She had been left in charge back at the island.

'Firstly, I want to introduce you to an old friend of mine. Then we'll stay in my house while Captain Willard makes the trip to Jamaica, to talk with your aunt and uncle.'

'I could try to escape,' she challenged, lifting her hem from the dusty, unpaved walkway.

'You could, but I don't advise it. You're my hostage, remember, so it will be unwise to try any tricks.'

Despair swept over her. It was so hot there, although the sun was down. Her hat and the parasol she held aloft offered little protection. She shrank against Armand, afraid of the dregs of humanity that teemed on the quayside. Beggars, like those that haunted the London streets, held out crippled limbs or displayed empty eye sockets or unhealed sores. Mariners without ships tugged at Armand's arm, seeking employment. There were women of every race and colour, some turning out to meet their men with babes in their arms and children clinging to their skirts. The rest comprised gaudily dressed whores bawling obscenities and touting for business. The buildings were mostly ramshackle, though there were some set back from the quay, white stone structures that housed the wealthy and a range of others that were brothels, gambling dens and taverns, mostly made of wood with straw roofs. An open-air market was in progress where everything could be bought, from a parrot to a sack of yams or a fresh chicken.

The place stank of rotting vegetables, dirt, corruption and human waste. Romilly and Alvina were not greatly inconvenienced by this; London was little better, though greater cleanliness had been introduced since the Great Plague struck in 1665. It was common practice to urinate in the streets, and chamber pots were emptied out of the top windows, with the warning cry of, 'Gardeloo!'

It was the heat that was unbearable and Romilly could feel the sweat soaking into her tight bodice. Her skirts were hot and heavy, her gown made of substantial satin, and the parasol did little to shield her from the glare.

'How can genteel white women survive in this dreadful climate?' she said, removing her hand from Armand's arm as they walked beside Alvina and George, Jamie and Joshua, with their servants bringing up the rear.

'One can get accustomed to anything. "Needs must when the devil drives",' he answered philosophically.

'Well I never shall. I'd rather freeze on the Arctic wastes than spend a moment longer here.'

In that fraught second he seemed no longer even remotely attractive. Neither did Jamie or Joshua or any man there. It was her father's fault that she was in this sorry situation – another bothersome man! What use were they? And God had made them in His image! This didn't commend the Almighty to her in the slightest.

'I've never known a wench to grumble as much as you.' He was part amused, part irritated.

'Believe me, I haven't even started yet.' She was determined to make him suffer, though doubted that anything would penetrate his thick hide.

Having seen the cart and slaves on their way under Johnson's eagle eye, he now guided the rest of them down a side street where the crowd was thinner and the quality of the houses better. He stopped at a tavern where flares cast a lurid glow on the sign swinging overhead depicting a donkey with its hind-legs raised in a savage kick. Light streamed through the leaded glass windows for it was almost dark. Inside someone was scrapping a tune on a fiddle. Men were singing, laughing, talking, but this ceased momentarily when he walked in through the open door.

Then uproar followed. 'It's Captain Tertius! Well met, cap'n! How fare you, sir?'

It was noisy and boisterous, voices clamouring on all sides in a mixture of French, English, Dutch, Portuguese and Spanish, all of which Armand appeared to understand. Romilly was glad she was wedged firmly between Alvina and Jessica, with a couple of Armand's stalwarts bringing up the rear. Dozens of eyes were going over her, appraising, curious or downright lustful.

Armand returned this noisy greeting and ordered drinks all round. 'Where's Cat?' he asked the pot-man, an ugly hunchback who gave a toothless grin, bobbing and ducking as he filled glasses and tankards.

116

'She's in the parlour. Hi, you, go and tell her the captain's here,' he answered, administering a swift kick at the ragged black boy assisting him.

A table was cleared, chairs too, and Armand and his party were soon ensconced at its knife-scarred surface. Wine was served to the ladies, but Romilly sat like a frightened kitten, glancing round at the faces, some ferocious, others friendly, all villainous. Smoky lanterns dimly lit the room, the furniture consisting of battered trestles and benches, the floor strewn with sawdust. A few women hung around, casting predatory glances at the finely dressed ladies who had just invaded their territory.

'Who is Cat?' Romilly asked Armand, wondering what further shocks were in store for her.

'The landlady,' he replied, and then looked up as a tall, wiry man came across to their table.

'Good evening, Tertius,' he said, his upper lip curled into a sneer. His eyes were like those of a bird of prey. His face, too, resembled that of a predator; untamed, cruel and very handsome.

'Ah, Lafette.' Armand did not invite him to join them. 'And how are you?'

'I'm well and prospering.' Without waiting to be asked Lafette straddled a stool, never taking his wild eyes from Romilly. It was disconcerting and she felt as if he was stripping her. He raised his glass, toasting her over the rim. 'Aren't you going to introduce me to your companions, Tertius?'

'If you insist. This is Lady Romilly and Lady Alvina, with Viscount James and Lord George, and Captain Willard, master of the ship on which they were travelling before being cast ashore during a storm.'

'On Devil's Paradise?'

'The same.'

'How fortunate... for you if not for them. What d'you intend to do with them?' As he spoke, Lafette continued scrutinising Romilly and the expression on his face made the lustful glances of the other men seem innocent by comparison.

'You ask too many questions, *monsieur*.'

It would have been possible to cut the air with a knife, and the rest of the taproom became quiet, transformed into one large listening ear. Both men were armed, both powerful and dangerous, guarding their turf jealously.

'Braggarts,' Romilly whispered scornfully to Alvina. 'Awan was a better man than either of them, and he was a savage. Armand thinks himself an aristocrat, and Lafette's clothing is splendid but soiled and he flaunts a ruby as big as an egg on the dirty hand resting on his sword.'

'But my dear, look at the gold rings in his ears and his raven curls,' Alvina murmured. 'Oh, my goodness, you must admit that he *is* a handsome brute.'

Sometimes Romilly despaired of her friend, who seemed obsessed by men and that which lay in their breeches. Now she seemed to be relishing this new adventure, drinking in the admiration of every man there, showing off her beauty, the green gown a perfect foil for her titian hair. It appeared that she relished her role as captured lady and would be happy to stay there as queen of the islands.

'Lady Romilly belongs to you now, Tertius, but I want her. Why don't be play cards with her as the stake?' Lafette suggested recklessly, raising an interested murmur from those watching the interplay between these leaders.

'Not so fast. I hold her hostage. There's no way I'd involve my business with you.'

'Are you suggesting that your doxy is too good for me?' Lafette half rose, his face that of a snarling panther, hand flying to sword hilt.

Armand was on his feet in one lithe movement, kicking the table over with a crash, bottles and glasses splintering on the dirty floor. Lafette pulled out his sword with a singing scrape of steel, but Armand was even quicker. With a movement too swift for the eye to see he whipped out his blade, the deadly point pressing against Lafette's chest. Silence reigned in the tavern now, all eyes on the protagonists. Duels were two a penny, life cheap, but these men had reputations as the finest swordsmen in the Indies. To see them fight to the death would be something to talk about for years to come.

Trestles were dragged back and space made. Armand and Lafette circled each other in a fencing stance with swords outstretched. Then Lafette lunged, his blade glittering. Armand stood erect and met the attack. Their swords kissed, light like liquid fire running down the steel from blade to blade, from tip to hilt. Lunge. Parry. Riposte. Lafette slipped but recovered himself. The men roared and women shrieked.

'What fools men be.' Alvina wasn't impressed. Several of her acquaintances had died at dawn in Hyde Park over some real or imagined insult, despite the fact that there was an edict against duelling.

'But what will become of us if Armand is slain?' Romilly had gone cold all over. She told herself that she didn't care what happened to him but feared the worst if she should fall into Lafette's hands. And yet the thought of Armand lying dead on the ground filled her with dismay. The strong body that had possessed her, those shoulders rippling with muscle, the sinews and tightly packed armour of his stomach and the mighty phallus that had robbed her of her virginity – all lifeless! She couldn't bear to think of it.

'Stay close to me, Lady Romilly,' Joshua said, his arm round her offering protection, and she leaned against him gratefully.

'No need for your help, I can take care of my betrothed,' Jamie interrupted, bristling like a turkey cock.

'And I can look to myself,' stated Alvina, leaping to her feet, ready to hit anyone with her furled parasol. 'George, a broken bottle is a handy weapon. See to it.'

The blades flashed and Armand was the better duellist, his feet in constant motion like a dancer, standing back then charging forward, sidestepping Lafette's wild swipes, bending gracefully in a sudden feint. Lafette's swordsmanship was crude by comparison.

A riot was taking place in the room, knives out and cutlasses too, men hacking and snarling, old enmities coming to the fore. The women's screams were hysterical, but the hardened harpies threw themselves into the fray, clawing with their nails, attacking with the jagged edges of broken glass. Then like a thunderclap a shot reverberated beneath the roof.

'What the hell's going on?' A woman stood in the doorway like an avenging angel, a smoking pistol in her hand.

Chapter Eight

She was the most ferocious female Romilly had ever clapped eyes on. Tall, almost alarming of aspect, she gave her a feeling of awe, coupled with envy that someone so beautiful could also be so commanding.

The effect on the crowd was astounding. The duellists lowered their rapiers. Men slunk against the walls, nursing injuries, while the women, eyeing her warily, kept their mouths shut for once. She cast a fierce eye around her property, noting damage and rounding on the hunchback.

'I told you to keep order and look after the bar, Starling. What the hell's been going on?' She lashed out at him with her open palm while he ducked and cringed.

'Captain Tertius is here,' he whimpered, as if this explained everything.

'I can see that, you dolt.' She swung round on Lafette. 'As for you, I warned you about making trouble. Any more of it and you're banned!'

He looked as if he longed to run Armand through the back but was prevented by the rough code of honour to which they all adhered, no matter how reluctantly. He sheathed his weapon and went to sit with his confederates, grabbing a tankard and downing the contents.

'How is it with you, Cat?' Armand said, and after slipping his sword back in its scabbard walked towards her, took her in his arms and hugged her.

Romilly was startled by the pang in her heart. Surely she didn't give a fig if he embraced another woman? But this one was unusual, a bossy madam who acted with the freedom and independence of a man.

Cat smiled delightedly, her arms linked round Armand's neck as she looked into his face. 'All the better for seeing you, darling.' Her voice rang with sincerity. 'It's been too long.'

'And how is Paul?' Armand accepted the warm salute from her crimson mouth.

'He's living at the mission outside town, being educated by the priests. I see him every few weeks. He's growing so tall now, you'd never believe it.' Her expression softened, then sharpened again as she looked over his shoulder to where Romilly and Alvina stood, their gowns splashed with liquor from the overthrown table.

'And who are these flash bunters?' Cat asked from the haven of his arms, their intimacy plain for all to see.

'Prisoners. Lords and ladies washed up on my shore when their ship sank. The captain is with them and their servants.'

'You want these women? Fancy something more refined than me?'

He shook his head. 'It's a matter of money. I'm holding them hostage and expect a large sum for their return. Captain Willard, master of their wrecked ship, will carry my demand to Lady Romilly's relatives who are planters in Jamaica.'

'You've fucked the golden-haired one.' Cat brought this out as a statement of fact, not a question. 'I can see it in her eyes when she looks at you. Not the redhead, she's a hard-faced bitch who knows her way around.'

Armand gave a lopsided smile. 'Sometimes you are just too perceptive.'

'But you'll stay with me tonight? She's only a simpering chit. You need a real woman.'

Romilly listened to this conversation and became more and more disgusted, with herself as much as him. How could he have treated her so, knowing he had other women eager for his body?

He did not agree to Cat's blatant request. Instead he said, 'Come and meet them.'

Cat ordered slaves to clear up the mess, sweep aside broken

122

glass and mop spilled liquid. The tables and benches were put back in place and Cat invited Armand's enforced guests to sit with her. She ordered whatever they wanted to drink and was friendly on the surface, but Romilly knew she was assessing her every movement and watching Armand's reaction.

Alvina was angry. 'I know it was only borrowed plumage but this dress is stained with rum, wine and ale, when the table was turned over by that pair of imbeciles.'

'Don't fret, dear, I'm sure some man will fix you up with another,' rejoined Cat, sitting with her arm linked through Armand's.

'You come from London, don't you? I can tell by your Cockney twang. Whitechapel, was it?' Alvina asked.

Cat registered surprise. 'How come a fine trollop like you knows the slums?'

'I was engaged on 'good works', taking food and clothing round to the poor and needy,' Alvina said with a grin. 'That was the excuse, anyway. In reality I was rogering an exceedingly handsome highwayman with a twelve inch prick.'

'Alvina! You never told me about that!' Romilly sat up, shocked.

'I don't tell you everything, dearest. A girl has to have some secrets. Don't you agree, Cat?'

'Absolutely,' and Cat slipped a hand into the opened front of Armand's shirt and toyed with his nipples, then felt the bulge in his breeches.

Romilly couldn't help watching and was certain it grew larger under Cat's experienced fingers. She felt quite sick. Involuntarily she moved closer to Joshua. He offered more solace and strength than Jamie or George who were subdued, as was Kitty and the valets. Jessica was flushed and seemed as if she was enjoying every moment, but then, Dr Quidley was looking after her. That grave, considerate man was on friendly terms with Cat. It seemed by their conversation that she was his sometime patient, as was her son, Paul.

123

These almost domestic details put the pirates into perspective. They were human beings after all, not ravaging demons. Too human by far, when it came to sex, and she tried not to look as Cat fondled Armand's private parts. Memories were hard to control, flooding in, making her hot inside. She leaned closer to Joshua, needing another man to come between her and lustful thoughts about Armand. She should be cuddling up to Jamie, but Joshua was much more to her liking.

'Lady Romilly, can we meet later, if at all possible?' He gripped one of her hands under the table, keeping his voice low as he said earnestly. 'I've been told that we are to be conveyed to Armand's house on the outskirts. I don't know what can be done, but I'm willing to risk all if I can help you escape his clutches.'

She glanced across and met the full blaze of Armand's eyes. He looked angry enough to strike her dead. Without more ado he stood up. 'Time we were going, ladies and gentlemen. There are coaches waiting outside.'

Cat bowed her head but recovered swiftly, accompanying him to the door. Bright moonlight shone on two carriages with coal-black drivers in uniform and cocked hats. Men with muskets sat beside them, and postilions occupied the saddles of the leading horses. They, too, were fully armed, a sharp reminder of the dangers that abounded.

'Inside ladies, and you too, gentlemen,' Armand instructed, then gripped Romilly's arm, whispering harshly, 'Not you. You're travelling with me.'

She was given no chance to argue, the iron step of the front coach lowered so that she might climb in. Lighting was supplied by little lanterns hung in the four corners of the boxlike structure. Armand followed her, shouted a command and the vehicle moved off, jolting and swaying.

He flung himself back on the deeply padded seat and ordered, 'Come here.'

Romilly wanted to refuse, but couldn't bring herself to do so. 'Why do you want me to sit beside you? And why didn't you stay with your paramour?' she asked waspishly as she obeyed him.

'Cat? No paramour. She's an old and trusted friend.'

'So it seems.'

'Do you care?'

'Certainly not. You mean nothing to me.'

'Is that so? And what about this?' His cock was exposed and he grabbed her hand and folded her fingers round it.

'Vile beast!' she hissed, but couldn't help moving them, feeling that rock-hard appendage.

He bent and ran his lips over her half exposed breasts and throat. She closed her eyes, fighting the intense pleasure his touch evoked. His cock leapt in her hand and she traced the path of the golden ring. It pierced his helm, in one side and out the other. 'Didn't this hurt when you had it done?' she enquired, as breathless as if she had just run a mail.

He laughed. 'Of course, but it was worth it. One day perhaps, if you stay with me, I'll have your labia ringed and you will see how much it adds to the pleasure.'

'If I stay with you?' She could hardly think coherently as his lips found her mouth and fed on it. She turned her face away, clinging to sanity and adding, 'I thought you were going to send me to my aunt.'

'Oh yes... that. I may or again I may not. You won't know and it depends on my mood and your behaviour.'

'But I thought... you said... are you going back on your word?' It was awful to be practical when all she wanted was to drown in his kisses.

'We'll see.'

He pushed down the front of her bodice and his tongue flicked over her nipples. Then he sucked them and she was helpless to fight the desire growing within her like some poisonous blossom. He slowly lifted her skirts and explored her thighs and fork, finding the pleasure nubbin that contained all her desires. She was ashamed that he should feel the wetness that bedewed her cleft, released by his kisses. It was impossible to deny that she was feverish with desire or stop herself from parting her legs in welcome.

'Did you really think you could refuse me or that I would take 'no' for an answer?' he mocked, and thrust his fingers inside her repeatedly till she was mad for more, wanting him to palpate her bud and then push his cock into her.

She was intoxicated with need, writhing in his arms, pushing her pubis against his hand, her needy clit throbbing and on the edge. 'Oh, do it. Go on, I'm almost there!'

He suddenly tumbled her off his lap and she landed in a heap on the carriage floor, crazy with frustrated desire. 'Why did you do that?' she cried shrilly.

'I am your master, or had you forgotten? I say when you'll come or not, according to my whim. You will do everything I command; perform any task, no matter how unpleasant. You can hate me, I really don't care. In fact, I enjoy you more when you hate me. Whatever happens you'll be wise to obey me, especially if you want to continue your journey to Jamaica.'

His eyes glistened in the candle glow and she read an untold depth of experience in them, things that she could only guess at, depravities too deep and dark for her inexperience to comprehend.

'You may keep me prisoner, but you can't stop me hating you,' she retorted.

'Stubborn minx. Will you never learn?'

He pulled her up and forced her across his knees on the velvet seat. She struggled but he was too strong for her, holding her steady with one iron hand while he lifted her skirts high, exposing her bare bottom. She knew what was going to happen. Yearned for it. Her cunt was on fire and her bud aching. She wriggled against his muscular thighs, trying to rub herself to completion. She could feel his erection thrusting against her side, bare and seeping pre-come, and marvelled at his self-control.

Her face was buried in the musty cushions and the air was cool on her naked flesh. The anticipation was dreadful, stretching out like a protracted scream. She heard his voice, above her and close to her ear. 'If you are a well behaved and grateful slave, I may give you what you want.'

She felt him sit up and heard the swish as his hand came down flat on her naked hinds. She yelped but did not dare budge, her bottom on fire. Again and again she felt the impact as his hand, hardened by fighting, slapped down across her reddening skin. The pain was excruciating, but not so bad as the frustrated need to have him frig her to climax and then drive his phallus into her up to the hilt.

She wondered if he would take her to bliss before the coach arrived at its destination. She suffered six more smacks and then he said, 'Will you obey me in everything?'

'Yes, oh yes, finish me off, you devil!' she cried.

The coach jolted and rattled, totally lacking in any form of springs, but Romilly was blind and deaf to anything as he turned her over, kissing her breasts, biting her nipples, and rubbing her bud relentlessly till she plunged into a climax so intense that she blacked out for a second.

When she recovered it was to find him on his knees between her legs, thrusting his cock in and out and coming in a quick rush. The coach stopped, and recovering she saw lights beyond the window and realised they had entered between gates that led to a large, well lit, white-painted house.

'I know you hate and despise me, but how do you feel, seeing Tertius going off with that haughty bitch?' Lafette asked, eyeing Cat shrewdly.

They were still sitting in the taproom and Starling had brought a plate of cold meat and bread, washed down with a quantity of ale. It was getting late but the night was warm, the cicadas chanting their eternal song and the moon high. She was in a maudlin mood; too much booze and too little loving. Although she had fucked Phil, he fumbled about like the inexperienced schoolboy he was, and she had been forced to bring herself off, impatient with his clumsy groping.

127

'How d'you think I feel?' she answered, her head swimming. She didn't usually drink like that but seeing Armand with Romilly had given her a nasty shock.

They were alike as two peas in a pod. Oh, not physically perhaps, that huge man and the petite girl, but inwardly, spiritually maybe. Cat couldn't explain this weird feeling. She might have been depressed about it, but was made of sterner stuff. If she wanted anything as badly as she wanted Armand then she would fight for it, and fight dirty if need be. It had never before occurred to her that he might lose his heart to a woman, though she had realised that eventually he would want to return to his own kind. She knew a little of his story and loved him all the more for it, but secretly feared that one day she might lose him entirely.

A foreboding inside her whispered that the time had come, and that if she wanted to prevent it she must do something about it, even being nice to Lafette, if need be. Perish the thought! She knew that many women adored him, but she had never been able to see his charm. However, it was wise to keep on the right side of such an influential brigand, so she decided to give him a chance to prove his skill as a lover.

It was lonely at nights when all the customers had staggered home, wherever that might be; hut, ship or street corner. She could talk with Starling or Phil but Cat was easily bored, restless, needing a challenging adventure. Lafette, for all his faults and they were many, was never boring. Better to wake with his raffishly handsome face on the pillow than alone. She untied the bandana that covered his head and his stygian locks fell forward, shrouding them both as he kissed her.

'I've always wanted to do this,' he murmured, his breath overlaid with rum.

'And now you have. What next?' She tugged at his gold hoop earring.

'It's your call. I'd not force myself on a lady.' Sometimes he adopted a kind of mock gallantry as if, indeed, he might have come from wealthy stock. She rather suspected that his father

128

had been born into the elite but that his mother was probably a housemaid.

His hands were on her breasts, cupping the warm globes, and though she wished it were Armand she allowed herself to slide into that tipsy state when it didn't much matter. 'In the dark all cats are grey,' she muttered, and led him by the hand to her bedroom above the *Kicking Donkey*. He wasn't Armand, yet he might prove useful. There was a plan working like yeast in her brain.

A tall Negro in green and white livery, who unfolded the step and then stood back so that Romilly might alight, opened the carriage door.

'Well met, Jake,' Armand said, clapping him on the shoulder. 'Is all in order here?'

'Yes sir, running like clockwork.'

'Excellent. Where's Mr Stanley? Ah, there you are.' Armand addressed a dapper little man who was very spruce from the top of his grey peruke to the tips of his highly polished buckled shoes. 'We have guests, as you see. I want them to receive the best of attention during their stay.'

'Yes, sir, of course, sir.'

'He is my steward, and looks after the place during my absence,' Armand informed her.

'You own this house as well as the island?' Romilly was impressed despite her misgivings.

He nodded and gave brisk orders. Soon the baggage had been taken indoors by underlings, and Armand led his enforced guests up a flight of wide, shallow stone steps to a veranda that ran round the lower storey, supported on white pillars. Shutters enclosed many of the narrow windows and lush green creepers twined between them. The perfume from their purple flowers filled the warm air.

'You are wondering how I acquired such a place?' he commented with a cynical smile. 'I won it at the turn of the dice. Dame Fortune favoured me.'

'You're a gambler?' Romilly asked. This wasn't the first time she had heard of men losing fortunes, property, everything they owned at the gaming tables. She sometimes worried about Jamie. What would happen to her if, after they were married, he threw his prospects and her dowry away?

'Occasionally. More so when I was young.'

'What a lovely house!' Alvina was rapidly revising her opinion of him. A person of such obvious taste could not be all bad.

Inside was even better. Candles blazed everywhere, and the hall was tiled in black and white, like a chessboard. A staircase made of delicate ironwork curved aloft. Kitty, Jessica, and the valets were led up to the bedrooms to prepare for their employers. The others were conducted to a magnificent, airy, white-painted reception room where a couple of uniformed mulattos with impassive faces served drinks and sweetmeats.

'This is all very well,' Jamie said suddenly, putting down his crystal goblet of wine and addressing Armand. 'But we came here with one purpose, surely. That of arranging our release.'

'I am well aware of that, *monsieur*.' Armand was dignity itself, leaning elegantly against the marble mantelpiece, looking like a grandee in his silks and white ruffles, his jet-black hair caught back in a queue. He gave a little laugh and spread his hands wide. 'Would you prefer that I cast you into a dungeon or maybe the basement? I see no reason why we should not get along while you are here, providing you don't try to escape. For believe me, I'm no fool and can be quite merciless.'

Romilly shivered. She could well believe it. His behaviour in the coach proved it, and her buttocks stung every time she sat down, a reminder of his strength and passion. She wondered where she would sleep that night – in a guestroom or the master chamber?

Servants arrived to light the guests upstairs.

Romilly had hoped she might share with Alvina, a false

hope as it turned out. She found Jessica waiting for her in a bedroom that excelled itself in grandeur.

'Yes, my lady, it is his,' Jessica said when they were alone.

'He expects me to sleep in *that*?' Romilly pointed at a four-poster so large it resembled the entrance to a mausoleum. 'With *him*?'

'I don't know, your ladyship, and that's for sure, but isn't this a surprise? I was afeared that we'd be staying in that tavern or somewhere equally squalid. He's a man of many parts, and that's no fairytale.'

'He's a pirate. We must never forget that.' Romilly was voicing her own doubts aloud. It would be all too easy to be lulled into a state of false security. 'Where are you sleeping?'

'A little way down the hall, within call should you need me. My dear lady, I have been conversing with Peter Quidley, and he holds Captain Tertius in high esteem.'

'That's as may be,' Romilly answered tersely, seated at the dressing table while Jessica brushed her hair. 'But he's a filibuster, a rogue, a vagabond of the sea, nonetheless. If I show you my spanked backside will you still think kindly of him?'

'Your father used to spank you,' Jessica reminded, smiling at her in the cheval mirror.

'That is an entirely different matter. Armand Tertius is perverse. He enjoys inflicting punishment. It arouses his base desires.'

'Come, come, cheer up, milady. Look what I found in the trunk of clothing he provided,' and she held up a cream silk negligee, lavishly trimmed with lace and almost transparent. 'Do you think he ordered it to be provided for you?'

'I don't know and I don't care.' Romilly clung to the thought of Armand as a vile seducer, determined to lock her bedroom door that night. Jessica had ordered water be delivered and soon a trail of servants came in, filling the wooden tub that stood in a little antechamber. Pails of hot and cold were tipped in and Jessica tested the temperature and, when it suited her

131

fussy requirements, she dismissed them and encouraged Romilly to undress and immerse herself.

'It's nothing like as grand as the pool on the island,' she said, holding up a towel to shield her mistress as she stripped and dipped a toe into the bathtub. 'But at least we're private here, without that saucy jade Sabrina, looking on and blatantly taking her pleasure with Marcus and the like.' She suddenly saw the imprints of Armand's palm and exclaimed, 'Oh, my dear mistress! I see what you mean by his brutality! What ails the man that he needs to master you thus? I'll rub in soothing balm when you've washed.'

'No need for you to bother,' said Armand, as a panel in the wall slid back and he appeared in the opening. 'I'll do what is necessary. Now get out.'

'I need her services,' Romilly protested, holding a sponge in front of her breasts for she was only half submerged.

'Tomorrow,' he said with that sardonic smile. 'I'll look after you tonight.'

'Milady?' Jessica looked at her, hovering uncertainly.

'That's all right. Goodnight, Wade,' Romilly said, terrified that Armand might have her duenna sent to the slave auction.

With a backward glance Jessica scurried away, and when the door closed behind her Armand came closer, staring down at Romilly. 'You are beautiful enough to inspire any artist,' he said, a musing smile playing round his lips. 'I have a friend who would paint you, if I so desired. What do you say? Will you pose for him?'

'You'll give me no option, beating me if I refuse,' she said haughtily. As if he was of little consequence she soaped her shoulders and arms, then lifted her legs from the water one at a time and applied the sponge to them, paying careful attention to her toes.

Armand feasted his eyes on her. 'I'm going to wash your back,' he said, took off his jacket and rolled up the full sleeves of his shirt.

'If you insist.' She handed him the sponge in an offhand

manner. Water dribbled from it onto his breeches.

He took it, his face darkening. 'What an ungrateful bitch you are. One spanking isn't enough, or so it seems. Do you want another?'

'What I want or don't want has nothing to do with it. As you have so rightly said, you're the master.'

'You do well to remember. Stand up.'

She did so, water running down her body in rivulets. There was little use trying to conceal herself. She had nowhere to hide and maidenly modesty did not become her any more. Armand had put paid to that. She out-stared him, her eyes reflecting the chill in his. 'Is this what you want, *master*?'

He ignored her sarcasm, squeezed the sponge and applied it to her pubis. 'Open your legs.' She parted her thighs a little. 'More,' he demanded, and when she slid her feet further on the tub's base he thrust the sponge between, the slippery soap-filled object caressed her crack, and she started at the rush of pleasure it produced.

He moved firmly and her needy clit responded, seeming to have a mind of its own. The rapidly cooling water sloshed round her calves but the rest of her was burning. She put her hand flat against his chest and pushed him away. Then she stepped out, water puddling the carpet beneath her feet. She reached for the towel but he was there first, wrapping her in it and then propelling her towards the bed. She was pushed down on the embroidered quilt and, looking up, saw the astonishing spectacle of her and him reflected in mirrors set in the tester. Her hair was in wild disarray and, as he ripped away the towel, her body was exposed, pink-skinned with heat and shame. Shapely limbs and flat belly, dimpled navel, full breasts with the brownish red nipples standing like the hopeful noses of household pets. Longing for what? His kisses and caresses?

Armand stripped to the waist, a tawny savage, all muscle and sinew and duel-scarred flesh with darkly furred arms and chest. His face was savage too, filled with lust and the

133

arrogance of a conqueror. He forced her to look up, using her hair like a rein.

'See, Lady Romilly. See your naked body so ready for mine. And look,' he turned her over. 'Look at the marks I left on your rump. They've not faded and will soon be joined by others. Doesn't this excite you? Of course it does, but you're too damned stubborn to admit it. I know better. I've had you in my arms, begging me to bring you off. You can't deny it. You may have the soul of a saint but you've the body of a harlot.'

The mirror image seemed to mock her as he did. A beautiful wanton with her legs sprawling and her arms outstretched on the pillow. Her lips were moist and wet, her tongue circling them lasciviously, and breasts that inspired Romilly to touch them. She did so, seeing the woman in the mirror doing the same, pinching the nipples into hard, needy peaks. The man reflected there was handsome, his black hair falling across his face and halfway down his back, and his eyes held all the passion in the world in their depths. His hands hovered over the mirror woman like the talons of an eagle and the figure on the bed lifted her body to meet them.

Romilly closed her eyes, wanting no sensation but that of feeling. To watch herself being made love to by her captor was nothing short of diabolical, but if she could pretend it wasn't really taking place and that she was dreaming, using Nathan as her fictional lover, then it was the acme of pleasure.

Armand slapped her awake. 'Look at me. This is real, Romilly, not some fantasy in your head. I won't share you with anyone. Do you hear? Not even in your secret thoughts. You belong to me.'

He left her momentarily and then returned with manacles. He held her wrists and clapped the cuffs round them, fastening each by chains to the bed-head. She fought him but he was too strong for her, kneeling across her body. Next he put irons on her ankles, spread her legs wide and tethered them to the foot-posts. She was utterly helpless, spread out for him to do with as he willed. He had retained his breeches and top boots, which fitted equally closely. A leather belt spanned his slim waist and he unbuckled it and opened the flap fastening, revealing his eager cock. Romilly moaned and tugged at her bonds, wanting to touch it.

He saw her need and lowered himself so that the tip entered her mouth. She could smell his musky scent, the softness of fabric against her face, and her tongue roved round the ring in his helm. The gold was warm and smooth. So was his phallus. Wetted by her salvia and his jism it felt like silk, like satin, like the richest velvet, and she could not stop licking it. He pushed in harder and she could barely take it all, the end butting her throat till she choked.

'You'll learn how to do this, slave,' he grunted, withdrawing. 'I want to enjoy every part of you and feel you swallow my spunk.'

She followed him with her eyes, imprinting every facet of his face and body on her mind. The room was shadowy and the candles silhouetted him. It made him mysterious, an incubus, a revenant, a demon who stalked women in the dead of night. She waited breathlessly for his next move.

He took up a riding crop and trailed its tip slowly over her face and down the length of her body. Its touch was soft and gentle, a whisper, no more. Her nipples crimped as it circled them and flicked backwards and forwards over the aching peaks. She met and held his eyes, unable to hide her enjoyment of this pliable instrument designed to galvanise a horse into action.

Even the fact that she couldn't move added to her arousal. There was simply nothing she could do but revel in her bondage. He had robbed her of her will. She was no longer answerable for her actions. Someone else was responsible, leaving her free as a bird, able to excuse herself by blaming him for her enslavement. The ferule moved sinuously, tickling her ribs and dipping into her navel. She could hardly breathe, anticipating its tender touch on her slit. Armand did not hurry, making every second tell, using the crop like an extension of his fingers.

'You are learning, *ma belle*,' he whispered. 'Watch yourself, and watch us. It is like looking at another couple fornicating.'

She stared at the mirror overhead, seeing the crop's progress as it moved towards her mound, inch by slow inch. Armand lay by her side, propped up on one elbow as he too witnessed the leather approaching her cleft and tangling with the fair fluff, now darkened by her juices. Then, as delicate as a butterfly's wing, it landed on her rosy, swollen love-bud, which strained from between her labia. Romilly gasped.

'It's that good, eh?' Armand said huskily. He leaned closer, his breath whispering over her sensitive clit. He replaced the crop momentarily with his tongue, teasing the little organ, nibbling it gently till Romilly was almost beside herself with need.

The mirror woman returned her stare, and she too seemed possessed. 'Can that really be me?' Romilly whispered.

Armand straightened, his lips glistening with her dew, and turned the crop, pushing the silver-mounted handle into her fork. She bore down on it, hips angled so it would contact her nubbin. The silver warmed, became a pleasure object, and Armand manipulated it just as he controlled her, lowering it and driving it into her vagina. She was soaking wet and this invasion by an inanimate thing felt strange but not unpleasant. Armand partly withdrew it, and then inserted it again. In and out, like an alien penis. She was ready, clenching her internal muscles round this leather-covered lover, but she needed contact with her clit to make her erupt.

Armand stopped, pulling the handle from her abruptly. 'You're being unfaithful, slut! How dare you climax with anything or anybody except me, your lord and master?'

The air moved as the crop passed through it and landed across the tops of her thighs. She yelled and it fell again, catching her belly this time. Blow after blow landed on her exposed flesh and she saw her mirror image writhing on the bed, tugging at the chains, begging for mercy. The master stood there, dark and menacing, gripping the crop, a cruel snake that dispensed pain as a priest dispenses pardons.

Then his fingers replaced the whip and she was writhing on his fingers... coming... coming in one glorious rush. He loosened her wrists and unfastened her ankles, then turned her over, holding her from behind as he thrust his prick into her cunt and then her arse. He fucked her hard, ending up in her nether hole. A few strokes and he had finished, leaving her as bruised and battered as if she'd been caught in a tornado. It was as if he sucked out her very life, leaving her an empty shell.

He wiped his cock and left the bed, she hoped forever, turning on her side and attempting to pull the covers over her tired body. He returned out of the darkness, dragged the quilt back and proceeded to anoint her bruises with a white, scented balm. It took the sting away and she relaxed against the pillows. His sudden concern touched her, and she enjoyed the feel of his hands, now gentle as a woman's, on her damaged skin.

When he had finished he replaced the lid on the phial and began to dress. Romilly was dozing but his movements roused her. Somehow she had expected him to climb into bed with her and sleep there till morning. She had been looking forward to this closeness and it was a blow to see him fully dressed and buckling on his sword.

'You're leaving?' she said, half sitting up, though every movement cost her dear.

'Business,' he said brusquely.

'At this time of night?' She didn't believe it.

He tapped the side of his nose mysteriously, smiling as he replied, 'A pirate's work is never done.'

'You're going to another woman,' she accused, tears stinging her eyes.

'Am I?' He was maddeningly cool. He paused at the door, looking back with a partly amused, partly annoyed expression.

'And if I am, it has nothing to do with you. Goodnight, Lady Romilly.'

'Oh, you! You!' She hurled a pillow across the room but he had already gone and she was alone and raging in the master chamber, no nearer knowing his heart and mind than when they met at Awan's altar. 'Bastard!' she cursed. 'Bastard! Bastard! If I never clap eyes on you again it will be too soon! And I can't wait to go to Port Royal and escape your odious presence!'

Chapter Nine

Every time a ship put into Cayona merchandise was brought ashore to be sold. The quickest, most profitable and all round satisfying way to do this was to employ the services of an auctioneer who knew his job. Thus the loot of many nations was distributed throughout the Indies.

Romilly walked up two shallow steps and entered the long, low-ceilinged warehouse where almost anything could be acquired. She hadn't wanted to come, but Armand was insistent that she and her friends did so.

'It will open your eyes to how some of us live,' he stated over the breakfast table that morning. 'Have you any idea how to run a business? No? I thought not. You may as well continue your education while you're here,' he added in that sardonic way of his. 'I have already dispatched a letter and there is another ship sailing for Port Royal next week, and Captain Willard will be aboard. Lord and Lady Fenby are expecting you, I understand, and must have been mightily worried as the *May Belle* is overdue. Meanwhile, enjoy Tortuga.'

Enjoy it? Romilly hadn't seen much of him since the night of their arrival. He was capable of taking her, showing her passion that she had never known existed, and then withdrawing completely. Under armed escort she and Alvina had visited the market, been measured for gowns in the workroom of an exiled Parisian tailor, and entertained like royalty at Armand's house, known as Bella Vista.

Now it was the morning of the auction, and a carriage had borne them there. The sale room was already full, with tiered seats for women on one side and men on the other. Alvina was scathing as she looked across at the female buyers.

'I've never seen such a motley collection,' she announced, when they had been taken to a separate area reserved for friends of important clients. 'Heavens, will you look at them! Brothel keepers, I shouldn't wonder.'

Jamie fidgeted. It riled him to have his life arranged by Armand. He sat with George, a supercilious expression on his face and Romilly thought how much more attractive they were without wigs, their own hair growing again. Tom and Gaston danced attendance. They did their best to supply their masters with clean linen under difficult circumstances, as meticulous as they had been in London. Alvina seemed to have accepted her lot better than anyone, waited on by a round-eyed, overexcited Kitty. The maid had been in her element since being captured, surrounded on all sides by admiring men.

'It could be a hundred times worse,' Alvina always said, whenever Romilly started to complain.

Now she flicked open her fan, waving it to cool the air but well versed in that language known to most fashionable ladies, using it as a means of communication and flirtation. She eyed the crowd over the top of it, causing a stir among the ranks. A white woman of her quality was rare indeed, in this hotbed of trade frequented by retired buccaneers turned planters, shady ladies who employed girls to whore for them, pimps who did the same, landlords of taverns and owners of gambling dens.

Armand, who was behind the scenes organising the sale of his wares, had ordered lemonade. It was brought by a pretty mulattress in a print cotton frock and matching turban. Romilly sipped it gratefully, disappointed to find it tepid.

'I'd like a coloured maidservant,' Alvina pronounced languidly. 'Perhaps I'll take one back to England with me.'

'If we ever get there,' Romilly responded gloomily.

There was a platform at one end of the room and a short, stout man with spiky ginger hair and rimless spectacles stood behind a rostrum. 'He's acting as if he's king of the dung heap. Must be the auctioneer,' Alvina remarked, attracting his attention with her fan. He stared across at her bosom and smiled, displaying crooked teeth. She nodded to him, smiling faintly and flustering him even more.

His assistants carried in the items to be sold, holding them aloft for all to see. There were bales of silk, silverware, canes, clothing, books and maps, anything and everything that could be turned into hard cash. Romilly spotted Armand lounging close to the auctioneer. His aristocratic bearing singled him out, though he was casually dressed in linen breeches and a plain shirt with the sleeves rolled back.

The lots were dealt with speedily, customers bidding against one another. Money changed hands and the buyers collected their goods. Romilly was fascinated, and aware of a change in the atmosphere when it came to the traffic in human beings. The women ceased chattering and leaned forward as a strapping Negro wearing nothing but a loincloth was led to the platform. His hands were manacled. Some of the men were interested too, for he was strong and healthy and would have made a useful field hand. Bidding was brisk but the one who outdid everyone else was Cat. She had swept in late, dressed to kill with an enormous feather-trimmed hat set at a jaunty angle on her flaxen locks.

She handed over her money and one of her minions led the new slave away. Then all eyes returned to the platform when a young black woman took his place. 'Strip her! We don't intend to buy a pig in a poke! Let's have a look at her!' demanded members of the audience, both male and female.

This was almost too much for Romilly who was already on edge due to Cat's arrival. Armand was deep in conversation with her and she was smiling and vivacious, leaning into him and holding his arm. Hatred was like a burning brand in Romilly's breast, yet she told herself that she didn't care. They were well suited, a pair of unscrupulous, shameless villains. Hanging was too good for them! She would like to see them suffer a lingering death, perhaps marooned on some deserted island, separately, of course.

'Will you look at her?' she couldn't help remarking to Alvina. 'Not satisfied with purchasing a new slave to take to her bed, she is angling to get her hands on Armand, too.'

'He was rather stunning, wasn't he? The slave, I mean. A magnificent specimen of manhood, and did you note the size of his package? I'm enjoying this. It's better than a play at Drury Lane Theatre.' Alvina was teasing her, hazel eyes sparkling.

'You never take anything seriously,' Romilly returned crossly. 'That woman is a coarse strumpet and Armand seems to dote on her!'

'And you are jealous, dear heart.'

'I'm nothing of the sort. Be quiet, they're putting the girl up for sale.'

The Negress hesitated, hanging back, but a sharp slap on the rump propelled her up the step. Her handler followed her, stripping off the single white garment she wore. A murmur rose from the spectators, especially the men. Her skin was nut-brown, her hair the colour of ebony and she held herself like a queen, even though her rounded belly and heavy breasts betrayed her pregnancy.

'Here you are, ladies and gentlemen,' said the auctioneer in a hectoring voice, sneering at the girl. 'Two slaves for the price of one for she's near her time, and will provide you with a wet nurse, too, feeding her own brat and any baby you may have. And what about you, gentlemen? Haven't you ever wanted to suckle at a warm teat and be treated like an infant? She'll provide you with all manner of delights. What am I bid?'

The men sniggered and the bidding came thick and fast. The pregnant girl stood impassive and Romilly admired her dignity. 'Oh for some money,' she hissed at Alvina. 'I'd buy her myself and look after her and her child. This is monstrously cruel!'

The women were bidding as well as the men, especially those who were flashily dressed and looking for fresh blood for their bordellos. Then she noticed that Cat was in the lead, matching every sum with a higher one. Was there a streak of compassion in her after all? Romilly wondered, disliking the way in which Armand was nodding encouragingly. What were they up to? But a fat man in an elaborate periwig and brocaded jacket was hell-bent on having her, spurred by the auctioneer's artful words, and eventually Cat shook her head and bowed out. The hammer fell and the girl was hauled off to satisfy the desires of her new owner, no matter how perverted.

Romilly had seen enough, but there was no respite until all Armand's goods, including half a dozen prisoners, had been sold. She had a job to stay awake, head drooping as lot followed lot, but at last Armand came to sweep her up and install her in the coach.

'Aren't you glad you're not for sale?' he murmured in her ear.

'I am indeed. Have you any idea how much I despise you for being associated with the slave market?' she retorted, standing outside the building in the hot sun of late afternoon. She directed her comment to include Cat, who was still hanging around him.

'Best be civil, my lady,' Cat returned crisply. 'Or you might find yourself on the block.'

'You wouldn't sell me, would you?' Romilly addressed Armand, but wasn't surprised when he answered.

'I would, if you proved too much of a nuisance.'

She gave them both a withering stare and climbed into the carriage, her annoyance increased when he disappeared from view, arm in arm with Cat.

'Shall we walk in the garden, my lady?' Joshua said to Romilly after supper.

'Thank you, Captain Willard, I'd like that.'

Armand had not returned and her anger was like a burning brand inside her. He was with Cat, she was certain of it, and could imagine them laughing at her, and then copulating. He

143

was a traitor and she would do almost anything to rile him, even though she risked his wrath.

It was dark, a full moon rising in an indigo sky, accompanied by a host of stars. Never had they appeared so bright, even when she was in residence at Harding Hall in the heart of the English countryside. A warm breeze touched her cheek and lifted a strand of her hair. Sabrina had given her citrus oil to stem off the attacks of mosquitoes and, so far, she had remained untroubled by the ubiquitous little pests.

Joshua extended his arm courteously, and she slipped her hand into the bend of his elbow. They strolled on the terrace and then went down the steps to the gravelled path that surrounded the flower-filled parterre. Candlelit lanterns hung from the trees, but as they walked further away from the house, moonlight was the only illumination.

They stopped, hidden from view by a tree. 'I hate to see you upset,' Joshua burst out, driving his fist against the bark.

'How kind, but you mustn't worry about me,' Romilly ventured, alarmed by the change in him. He was no longer the controlled master mariner. Now it seemed as if there was something eating away at his very soul. 'This should be Jamie's problem.'

'Tsh! He's more concerned about the cut of his waistcoat! Of course I worry. I'm not made of stone,' he vowed and, somehow, she found herself in his arms. It was like going home, so safe and comfortable, yet dangerous too. If Armand was to find them it might mean death.

'Captain Willard... Joshua,' she said, struggling to free herself, though not very hard.

'I'm sorry, my lady, but this situation is enough to drive me mad. The way that rogue treats you.' In his anguish he was holding her ever more tightly, straining her slim body against his. She could feel the thudding of his heart and was aware of his penis, a bulge beneath his breeches. An imp of perversity made her press her pubis against it, wriggling up and down. Joshua groaned, a man in torment, and cupped her buttocks

144

in his hands, pressing her ever closer, then he covered her mouth with kisses. She leaned against the tree and surrendered to his insistent lovemaking. Such enthusiasm was flattering and he was like a spring suddenly released, his feelings bottled up too long. He kissed her throat and the naked rise of her breasts, then pushed her bodice down, freed her nipples and tongued them ardently. His fervour carried her away and she wanted to touch his cock, tugging at his breeches, releasing it in all its erect glory.

'My lady... Romilly!' he panted, and hoisted her skirts high, finding the way to her fork. She moaned and spread her legs, welcoming his touch. In the depth of her glowed a spark of revenge; if Armand knew about this he would be furious! Not only that, she was enjoying Joshua, her experience with men limited. How would it feel to have someone other than Armand penetrate her love-channel?

Joshua slipped a hand down between their bodies and found her wet cleft, then rubbed her clitoris. Romilly started that compulsive, blissful journey towards climax, almost forgetting where she was or with whom. Joshua smelt different, felt different, not in the least like Armand, apart from having a knowledge of how to pleasure her. But something was missing. Her master had trained her to expect pain as well as satisfaction. Joshua was too tender, almost worshipping her, whereas Armand demanded that it was he who received adulation.

The bark scratched her back and she welcomed the discomfort. The moon latticed the boughs overhead. Night creatures scurried about in their everlasting search for sustenance, but she wasn't afraid, safe in Joshua's arms. 'Oh, my lady... you wonderful woman,' he panted. 'Am I doing this as you like it? I want to give you pleasure, to feel you spasm in delight.'

'Oh yes, Joshua, that's right. Do it, please do it!' she moaned, totally possessed.

He dipped his finger into her juice, slicked it over her nubbin, increased the speed of his rubbing till she felt herself carried high among those twinkling tropical stars, reaching an ecstatic climax. He was aware of her convulsing round his finger and exclaimed, 'That's it, my dearest! Take your pleasure and then I'll take mine.'

While she was still shaking with the force of orgasm he lifted her from her feet and she clasped her legs round his waist, and her arms round his torso under his jacket. She felt the hardness of his helm pressing into her slippery vagina, and then the full force of his prick as he thrust into her till it seemed to penetrate her womb. Her inner muscles clenched round it involuntarily, grabbing at his manhood. She threw back her head, eyes tight shut, reduced to nothing but sensation. Joshua's control had gone and he worked himself in and out of her, bending at the knees and supporting her at each stroke. She could feel the sweat soaking through the back of his shirt, and the smell of it coupled with their mutual fluids was all part of that primitive mating.

He increased his movements, faster and faster, then barked aloud as he filled Romilly with his libation. He relaxed against her and her legs slid from his waist. She buried her face in his chest, recovering her breath and, with it, her senses.

'What we've just done is dangerous,' she whispered. 'Armand might kill you if he found out.'

'And I should think it well worthwhile. Dear God, Romilly, I think I love you,' he answered, still panting from his exertions. 'I know I have no right to say this to you. I'm a commoner and you are highborn, but the heart makes no distinctions when it comes to love.'

'Don't speak like that,' she begged, putting her clothing straight and trying to pat her hair into place, all the time aware of his semen trickling down her inner thighs. 'It's nothing to do with class or station. I take little heed of that, but I fear Armand and what he may do to you.'

'This shall be our secret for a while.' Recovering his equilibrium, Joshua was making plans. 'First of all I must carry out the task of seeing your aunt and uncle. Then I'll return with the ransom and a ship to take you to Port Royal. Once there we can decide on our course of action. Dare I hope that you care for me, just a little?'

'Of course I do.' She didn't exactly lie. She was fond of him, admired him, but was aware that the spark that had existed between her and Nathan and, later, had burst into flame with Armand, was lacking, not entirely perhaps, but a glimmer compared to a furnace.

'You can't be falling in love, surely? I don't believe it. Not you! Not Armand Tertius, scourge of the seas going soft over a doxy!' Cat was lying beside him in her netting draped four-poster, the sounds of the awakening inn rising from below, augmenting those coming from the port. Morning sunlight streamed in at the dormer windows.

He didn't answer immediately, arms linked beneath his head, relaxed as men are after being milked of their spunk. 'In love with Lady Romilly? I don't think romantic love is quite my style, do you? I can't see myself writing a poem to my mistress's bosom or mooning around, waiting for her smallest sign of encouragement. But I'll admit that she would suit me as a wife, perhaps, given that I was seeking one. She has the right blood in her veins, the right breeding and would give me authentic heirs.'

'Providing they *were* yours, and not the spawn of some underling she'd fucked,' Cat commented, tone sharpening whenever Romilly came into the conversation. 'Ladies like a bit of rough, so I understand; a groom, a gardener, a gypsy… even a pirate, like you,' she added, mocking him because it hurt not to.

He tugged her hair, making her look at him. 'And what do you know about ladies?'

'Damn all. I was born in the gutter, had my child in prison, what chance did I have to better myself? But I don't regret a moment of it, for it led me to you,' she vowed. 'We are good together, you and me. We work well as a team. Can't we keep it that way without some toffee-nosed bitch who was born on the right side of the blanket coming between us?'

'She'll be going soon, off to her rich folk in Jamaica, and she's betrothed to that mincing popinjay Lord James. Do you really think I'd waste my time on her?'

Cat knew him better than he knew himself. For several years they had been occasional lovers but, womanlike, she nurtured a fondness for him that she feared was a lost cause. But hope springs eternal, and she was always tetchy if any other female appeared on the scene. Though it wounded her when he bedded them, she accepted that this was the way of men, just as long as he didn't lose his heart and marry one of them. Sabrina posed no threat, for Armand would want his wife to be white. In any case, the Creole was after what she could get and incapable of sincere feelings.

Cat had been delighted when he chose to spend time with her instead of his beautiful prisoner. She told Lafette to stay away for a while, but they had a plan half formulated and it was necessary for her to keep him sweet, without Armand knowing anything about it. Scheming was life's blood to her and she had found her counterpart in the wily Lafette.

'What is it you find so attractive about this lady?' Cat couldn't help asking, running light fingers through the whorls of hair on his chest.

'She's a spitfire, proud as the very devil, refusing to yield herself to me entirely, and she has a perfect, peach-like derrière ripe for spanking. It glows poppy-red after a few strokes and she tries so hard to resist, screaming that she doesn't like me spanking her but she comes off like a rocket every time I do.' Armand's eyes lit up and his penis started to swell before Cat's eyes and, though she might envy Romilly for having this effect on him, she knew that she would reap the benefit.

He sprawled on his back, his cock standing up straight as a flagpole, and she bent over him, taking it between her luscious breasts. Her skin was slippery and his member slid in and out

148

of that mock vagina in a smooth, silky motion. Cat clamped her legs round his thigh and rubbed her clit against the tanned skin. But there were other ways she wanted to try before either of them climaxed, so she sat up, leaving his cock fully erect, the thick shaft knotted with veins. The foreskin was rolled back and the gold ring glistened with the dew seeping from the slit in his mushroom-like helm.

Slowly, sensuously, Cat leaned over and breathed on it. It bobbed with need and she held it and directed the head into her mouth. Armand made no sound, but she could hear his heart beating rapidly and his cock said it all – swelling, jerking, and pleading for the ultimate sensation. She smiled to herself and started to suck it, cradling his balls in one hand, gently playing with them as they hardened in their hairy sac. She worked eagerly, cheeks drawn in as she increased the suction, and her clitoris echoed the sensations she was giving Armand. She wanted to attend to it, but was absorbed in fellatio.

She often acted the dominatrix, as with Phil, and Lafette wasn't averse to having his backside paddled, but she enjoyed submitting to Armand, her skin stinging with the trauma inflicted on it only last night. This served to excite her all the more, and she rubbed her clit with her free hand whilst slurping at Armand as if his cock was sugar cane. He arched his spine, lifting his penis to her mouth while she fed on it like a babe at the nipple. Cat did not slow her pace, using her tongue on his stem and running the tip round his glens. His cock grew bigger, firmer, and he suddenly spent himself over her face. The milky juice ran down her chin and throat and spattered her breasts. She laughed and massaged it into her skin.

'That's the best beauty lotion you can get,' she pronounced. 'I'm sure it's the elixir of youth. It should be bottled and sold to women who think their looks are fading. There's a fortune to be made.'

'Oh, Cat,' he reached out and ruffled her hair, 'you're

incorrigible.'

But not the one you really, truly want, she thought sadly, but didn't voice it, merely went to the nightstand and poured them two snifters of brandy.

'Where were you last night?' Armand asked, pacing the floor, hands locked behind his back.

On his return to Bella Vista he had ordered that Romilly be brought to him. It was early and she had been in the midst of her toilette and was not yet dressed. She trembled inside, wondering guiltily who had been talking. Was it that weasel, Mr Stanley? He was always watching her with his shifty eyes, a kitchen tyrant who bullied the servants. Could he have spied on her and Joshua? She was no closer to being an independent woman than when she had lived under her father's domination.

'I was here. I had supper, went out onto the terrace for a while and then sought my bed,' she answered, but was sure that he knew she was lying.

He came closer, looming over her. 'Alone?'

'Of course, apart from Wade who helped me prepare for the night.'

'Are you sure? A lady of your principles would not be bending the truth, would she?'

She turned defence into attack. 'Why should you care? Were you not engaged about your own pleasures?'

'That has nothing to do with the case. You belong to me, until such time as I am paid to release you. Was it Captain Willard who fucked you in the garden? I hear that you were seen with him.'

'I don't know what you mean. Your spies were mistaken. I'm astonished that you listen to tattling servants.' It was hard to remain standing there for he was so very large and powerful, and his anger sent waves of excitement flooding her nerves and settling in her loins.

They were in his study, where he entertained cronies and

150

worked on accounts with Henry Moorcross. It was a very masculine place without the smallest concession to softer, more feminine furnishings, and she was alone with him. Though noises came from without, the lively bustle of the household, and the chatter of parakeets and the calls of songbirds drifting in through the open window, she might as well have been on the moon. No help would be forthcoming.

'I form my own judgements,' he said coldly, though reaching out and running a hand down her cheek. 'I believe you capable of any kind of trickery. You play the innocent very well, but are far from it in reality.' His touch turned to steel, seizing her jaw so that she was forced to meet his eyes. 'Now, I want the truth, lady. Did you fornicate with Willard last night?'

At that fraught moment Romilly was glad she was the Earl's daughter. How dare this dog treat her so? 'Let me go!' she shouted, wanting to spit in his face. 'I don't have to answer your questions.'

'Your manner says it all. You are guilty as hell.' He let her go with such force that she stumbled.

'Guilty of what? You're not my husband.'

'And I thank God for it. But while you are here I'll not have you humping other men. You are mine and mine alone. Lay across the desk.'

'What?'

'You heard. Bend over it with your arse bare and raised towards me.'

She hesitated, opened her mouth to protest, but he propelled her to where a large walnut desk stood before one of the windows. He swept papers and ledgers away and forced her down across the shiny, brassbound surface. He pulled off one of the curtain cords and bound her wrists, stretching her arms on the far side and tethering them tightly. Romilly fumed but was helpless to do other than submit. The desk ground into her breasts, but as she struggled to ease her hands the wood rubbed against her nipples and her pubis contacted the metal edge. Armand lifted her negligee and nightgown, hitching them both above her waist. She visualised the lewd sight of herself with a bare bottom and the plump lips of her sex exposed. From where she lay, her face turned to one side, she could glimpse the garden beyond the window. It was glorious under the sunlight, with its brilliant blossoms kept green and fresh by the constant attentions of the slaves who worked there.

Only a few hours ago she and Joshua had transformed it into Eden, and she didn't regret what she'd done. Revenge was sweet and she had succeeded in breaking through the hard shell with which Armand surrounded himself. She sensed more than heard him behind her, bracing herself for what she knew was to come. He didn't hurry, making her wait.

She could feel herself drifting off, getting accustomed to the cord on her wrists and the discomfort of the desk. When he struck it was with the shock of a thunderclap. His hand caught her in that tender place where her buttocks met her upper thighs. The slap and her yelp resounded through the room. She jerked in her bonds, instinct making her attempt to get away, but the second slap flattened her to the wood, pain washing over her. He changed position, slapping her left cheek with a stinging technique that sent tears coursing down her cheeks. He rained blows as light as summer showers, followed by brutally severe ones that almost robbed her of her senses.

'How now, darling?' he murmured, bending over her, his breath tickling her ear. 'Do you regret your rash coupling?'

'I regret nothing,' she declared stubbornly, though her rear was on fire.

He moved away and she wondered if he was finished with her. Then a bolt of lightning shot through her as he lashed her with a leather-covered paddle. She was bereft of the will to scream; it was as much as she could do to draw breath, and there was a deep singing within her, a litany to Armand's mastery. She was achieving the exaltation that martyrs feel at the stake, but then reality hit her and she was aware of nothing except agony.

'This is what you wanted and this is what you get,' Armand muttered, poking the paddle into her crack, then reversing it so that the handle penetrated. 'Say you want it. Repeat after me, "master, I'm a wilful trollop and want you to chastise me".'

'I won't; this is ridiculous,' she managed to say with a show of firmness, while inside she longed to recant, confess, have him punish her as he saw fit.

'How beautiful you are, stretched out to receive your punishment,' he murmured, and his hands drifted over her bruised hinds, cool on the burning skin. 'I could almost lose my heart to you, Lady Romilly,' and he traced her labial groove, his curved forefinger sliding into the tight cleft, the way eased by the moistness of her inner folds.

Her buttocks clenched and she sighed, pain mingling with pleasure. He stroked her little nodule, and Romilly couldn't restrain her gasps and wriggles that indicated he had found his mark. Having thoroughly roused but not satisfied her, Armand turned his caresses into sharp slaps, his palm landing on her thighs, her bottom and her fissure. She didn't know if she was on her head or her heels, one moment in agony, the next rising towards a fulfilment that was never attained.

Armand was controlled, every move worked out, but as he came into sight she noted the erection distorting his breeches and knew that before long he would be forced to empty his cods of their seed. Such activity as that in which he was now engaged excited him to fever pitch. She prayed to deny him, leaving him frustrated, but was in a state of madness where all she wanted was to feel him taking her as harshly and cruelly as he knew how.

The paddle whacked her on her calves, the backs of her knees, everywhere that was exposed to view. When it flicked the parted centre of her crotch she wailed, her mind empty of everything except pain. She was losing her senses, the desktop, the room, the window, the drapes spinning. She felt him behind her, pushing between her legs. She was overwhelmed because he was feeding his cock into her, and his hand was cradling her pubis from the front, his thumb palpating her clitoris. Everywhere hurt. Everything was arousing. She was tossed among sensations.

Armand directed his cock to its goal, pushing it inside, using her love-channel not her arse this time. He could not touch her anywhere without pain augmenting the pleasure. She knew what it was like to be a slave, the need to be mastered, and the idea terrified yet elated her. Sensation overrode sensation; she could taste fear on her lips, smell danger in his sweat and drown in the force of their mutual desire.

She cried out when she came, shuddering with the strength of it, and Armand cupped her pubis and allowed her to enjoy it to the full. His cock pulsed within her, riding towards its end. He dug his hands into her hair, clamping her scalp with the intensity of his gathering passion. He rocked against her, pinched her flesh, bit her neck and she felt his seed flood her. He rested quietly, laying across her, cock still entombed in her cunt.

'You'll not have Willard again,' he grunted. 'He's off to Jamaica and we are going back to Devil's Paradise. I'm being merciful, but if you betray me a second time you'll wish you'd never been born.'

Chapter Ten

Gone were the trips into town. Romilly was virtually a prisoner and Joshua forbidden her presence. He was not even permitted to bid her farewell before embarking for Jamaica.

'It's back to the island for us, then,' Alvina commented, already bored with Cayona, although equipped with made-to-measure gowns and accessories.

'Who cares?' Romilly was wallowing in self-pity. 'Armand neither wants me nor grants me freedom. I'm in limbo and don't know what to expect.'

Alvina looked up from supervising the packing. 'He needles you, doesn't he? These matters wouldn't vex you so much if you were indifferent to him.'

'Poppycock!' Romilly exclaimed, and vented her anger on Jessica who was practically useless these days, wandering around like a lovelorn loon.

'There are wedding bells in the air,' whispered Alvina.

'Peter Quidley?'

'Who else? Do you think he has bedded her yet?'

'Stop it, your mind is like a cess-pit. You think of nothing but coupling.' Romilly sparked up, furious because she, too, was obsessed by visions of sexual encounters.

Armand was impatient to leave. He spent much time with the officers that had accompanied him and it appeared as if there was something important brewing.

'We board this evening and sail at sunrise. Peter says that with a brisk wind behind us we should reach San Juliano at daybreak,' Jessica pronounced sagely.

'Then you'd better shift and stop mooning about,' Romilly snapped. At one time Jessica would have jumped to attention, but these days she walked in a rose-pink daze, immune to all save love.

'It's an affliction,' Romilly raged at Alvina, sotto voce. 'Even the most sensible of women loses control, obsessed by some man's cock.'

'It's part of Dame Nature's plan. We mate and the future of the human race is secured. Not that I want children yet, but one day, perhaps. You're so serious. Be light-hearted like me. There's nothing worth fretting your bowels to fiddle-strings about,' Alvina advised cheerfully.

Armand leapt from the leading longboat when it ground on the sand, splashed through the shallows and headed for the fortress like a man possessed, full of the forthcoming venture. First he called a meeting of every man jack there, dragging them from their comfortable billets with the women who'd thrown in their lot with them.

Sabrina was called to account. 'What's been happening during my absence?' he demanded, pacing the stone flags of the Great Hall.

'Not a lot,' she replied casually. 'Sancho and Browne have kept control and the men have been happy to take it easy, but they're straining at the leash now. What's afoot?'

'There's a Spanish galleon sailing from Mexico with a cargo of gold from the mines. I intend to take her and return loaded with bullion. Are the ships ready to sail?'

'As far as I know.' She lifted her smooth brown shoulders and spread her hands wide, palms up.

'You should make it your business to know. Didn't I leave you in charge?'

'Oh, stop behaving like a bear with a sore arse,' she returned. 'Everything is ship-shape and Bristol fashion. They've finished careening the hulls, the cannons are all in place and the crew eager for action. What more do you want?'

'Right, you've done well,' he said grudgingly. 'Now I charge you to take care of the prisoners, especially Lady Romilly who proves a wilful jade. I'll leave the *Scorpion* and the *Golden Queen* here, and take the *Sirocco*. She's a fast frigate and one is all we need. The galleon will be slow and bulky. It shouldn't present a problem.'

Romilly saw nothing of him. The fort buzzed and there was frantic activity as the pirates prepared. They forgot women, gambling and booze; only the acquisition of wealth was important. Swords and cutlasses were honed to razor-sharp perfection, pistols, matchlocks and muskets primed, gunpowder kegs stacked in readiness, cannonballs loaded by davits, and the cannons themselves lashed into place. The carpenter and his mate were ready to amputate if necessary and Jessica upset because Peter had to go in his capacity as a doctor.

'Stop snivelling!' Romilly snapped, exasperated, as they stood on the beach and watched the ship disappear till it was a dot on the horizon. 'He'll turn up like a bad penny, never fear.'

'It's all very well for you, milady. You're young and beautiful but I'm in my thirties and he's my last chance.'

'Stuff and nonsense! Just think how nice it will be without having to hang around after him.'

'Aren't you concerned about Captain Tertius?'

'I hope some Spaniard runs him through!' Romilly spat viciously, turned on her heel and made for her room. She would lie low for a bit, and when Sabrina least expected it intended to explore the island by herself, or maybe with Jessica in tow.

She missed Joshua, was becoming more and more disenchanted with Jamie, and yearned to escape from Armand. All right, so she was supposed to wait patiently till Joshua returned from Port Royal, but she chaffed at the bit like a high-strung filly longing to take flight. An atmosphere of ennui prevailed. Even Alvina couldn't be bothered to flirt and Jamie and George spent the time lolling in hammocks in the shade, supping rum and playing cards.

The skeleton force left behind to guard the fortress carried out any work on the remaining ships in the morning, then enjoyed a siesta during the afternoons. There was no telling when the *Sirocco* would return, but Romilly knew she mustn't delay if she was to enjoy a measure of freedom. She had given up any idea of running away. It seemed pointless if Lady Fenby would be sending her ransom soon, but she needed to rebel against Armand's dictatorial edicts.

'You are bored, my dear,' Sabrina said, strolling into Romilly's bedroom one noon. Aponi walked several paces behind her, slender as a reed in a colourful sarong.

'Yes, you're right, I'm unaccustomed to idling. Back home there were a myriad things to do... shopping in the Royal Exchange... watching the gentlemen beating each other at indoor tennis... attending the playhouse with a good chance of glimpsing the King and one or other of his mistresses. And when we travelled to Harding Hall, that's the family seat, you understand, we hunted nearly every day during the season and held house parties and played bowls on the lawn and had all manner of fun.'

Sabrina smiled and came closer, breathing out an exotic, spicy perfume. 'Poor child,' she murmured. 'This must seem like another world peopled by crude ruffians and loose women.'

Romilly was relaxing on the daybed close to the window, endeavouring to catch the faintest breeze that would modify the heat. She made no objection when Sabrina sat beside her, resting one hand on her silk-clad thigh and caressing her breasts with the other. Romilly didn't protest, though startled by her own reaction. She was missing human contact, longing for someone to pay attention to her needs, no matter how roughly. Armand had released feelings and emotions that she didn't know she had. It had been days now since a man had touched her and her wanton self yearned for it.

Aponi stood behind them, gently waving a fan over the

couch while Romilly fidgeted under Sabina's artful caresses, but did not withdraw. Emboldened, the Creole trailed her fingers across Romilly's throat, and then up to circle her ear. She examined it, and the pearl-drop that hung from the lobe, then followed this with her tongue, licking and sucking and causing the most pleasant of sensations. It was almost like being aroused by a man, and Romilly was puzzled as she became aware of something hard in Sabrina's crotch.

'Ah,' the Creole said with a wide smile, teeth gleaming in her dusky face. 'You are wondering how I have suddenly grown a prick. No magic, look,' and she stood up and held open her robe all the way. She wore a leather harness strapped round her waist and between her thighs. It fitted her body perfectly and was designed to support a carved wooden replica of an erect cock. She waggled it gleefully. 'You've seen this kind of thing before. It's like the plugs I pushed up your arse.'

She stopped in front of Romilly, the mock-phallus at eye level, and helped her out of her lounging robe. That huge object fascinated Romilly, tingling as she wondered how it would feel inside her. A similar dildo had hurt when thrust into her anus, but that was to be expected as she was a virgin there. She experienced a rush of desire as she tentatively touched the wooden prick rearing from Sabrina's mound. It was remarkable, resembling an erect penis to the very life, but it felt hard and cold, not smooth and warmed by blood like the real thing.

'Would you care to try it, milady?' Sabrina murmured, and she brushed her thumb across Romilly's maidenhair, parted her slit and found the little nodule that rose instantly at her touch.

Romilly was conscious of Aponi watching impassively, but like every white person in the West Indies, had begun to view the slaves as less than human, created to serve and pleasure them. Sabrina's pink tongue licked across Romilly's cheek to her mouth, and very gently parted her lips. Her breath tasted of nutmeg and cinnamon, and Romilly surrendered to its seduction. And all the time the Creole's fingers roused her clit, wooing it into stiffness and setting Romilly's juices flowing.

Aponi set aside the fan and leaned over the daybed, fingers working busily at her own fork. Sabrina glanced at her. 'You'll not be left unsatisfied, wench. I long for another feel of your tight little snatch.'

Her slender fingers continued to play with Romilly's clit, which was overloading with passion, then removed them and said, 'Stretch over the arm of the couch. Bottom towards me.'

'Oh, but… you can't. I was just about to come.' Romilly was frustrated and wanted to cry with disappointment, her bud abandoned at the point of release.

'Stop fretting and enjoy,' said her controller, and pressed the dome of the mock phallus into Romilly's wet and eager vagina. It was satisfyingly huge, stretching her internally and caressing her spasming muscles. It filled her completely, pressing against her cervix, and the sensation was strange for it was so unyielding, not like a man's appendage which, though stiff, still had a certain flexibility. It warmed within her and began to feel more natural as Sabrina moved it carefully in and out, using a clever technique that aped the real thing. Her hands reached under Romilly to cup her breasts and toy with the nipples. Aponi positioned herself so she could carry on licking them, then squirming down and inserting her tongue in Romilly's labial groove, fondling the swollen nubbin.

Romilly throbbed with excitement, intense sensations fanning out from her bud. She arched back against the dildo, riding it fiercely, determined to extract every iota of pleasure. Sabrina gasped as it chaffed her clitoris. Aponi was panting, feeding on Romilly's sex and rubbing her own at the same time.

Romilly started to peak, rising to the glorious heights of orgasm. It roared through her, a searing sensation that seemed to go on forever. She bore down on the dildo and heard Sabrina wail, feeling her shaking as their wooden lover served them both.

Aponi wriggled out from under her and Romilly flung herself on her back. She watched as the slave girl lay on the floor and Sabrina mounted her, driving that inexhaustible prick while Aponi whimpered with joy, wearing a blissful expression that heralded climax.

Heat radiated from Romilly's belly and she wanted another orgasm. She fingered her nipples, hard and pointed, and she wanted to feel Armand's lips on them, her vagina aching for a real cock inside it... Armand's!

Joshua hauled himself from the longboat, climbed the iron ladder and stepped onto the jetty at Port Royal. He was accompanied by Lieutenant Clive Morrison, Henry Moorcross and two hard-featured members of Armand's force. The vessel carried mail and packages between the islands and the coast and was entirely legitimate, though its captain was inclined to turn a blind eye to shady deals if it was worth his while.

The port was a bustling, thriving place that far exceeded Cayona in size and affluence. There were many ships at anchor in its snug harbour and piracy had been outlawed. Only legitimate vessels were welcomed there.

Once ashore Henry conducted Joshua to an inn where a coach could be hired. The accountant held the purse strings. There was no likelihood that Joshua would give him the slip, not that he intended to with Lady Romilly's life in jeopardy.

So resembling a party of respectable merchants, they headed for Seven Oaks, the Fenby plantation in nearby Kingston. Henry was following instructions, having sent a runner ahead to warm Lord and Lady Fenby of their arrival. By now they should have received a letter disclosing the nature of the matter. Kingston was a pleasant, cultivated area not far from the port, and contained plantations belonging to rich settlers who did very well out of the produce raised from the rich soil, living in comfort and served by slaves.

The coach halted at a pair of imposing wrought-iron gates, which were opened by a bare-footed black boy clad in blue livery with a lot of gold trimming. He grinned at them and exchanged banter with the driver. A wide, tree-lined avenue lay ahead, ending at a fine, colonnaded house. A butler greeted them at the ornate front door, looking down his nose superciliously and enquiring their business.

'Lord Fenby should have had a message,' Joshua said firmly. 'We are here with regard to his niece, Lady Romilly Fielding, daughter of the Earl of Stanford.'

The man bowed stiffly and retired, leaving them in the vast hall. Like the exterior of the house it was painted white, a light, airy place, exactly what was required in the tropics. Soft footed male servants wearing uniform and maids in bright cotton dresses went about their tasks. Each was dark-skinned, including the butler. Joshua was distinctly uncomfortable. He hated being associated in any way with the pirates, and it was only his love for Romilly that made him agree to this charade.

As far as he could ascertain the Fenbys lived like kings and could well afford to advance the ransom money. Seven Oaks lay amidst acres of fertile land. They had crossed a river on the way, and seen the cultivated land where field hands garnered cotton and sugar, singing as they toiled. There was no sign of cruelty or neglect. It was apparent that the Fenbys were caring masters, and this encouraged Joshua to continue.

The butler returned, gazing at a point somewhere beyond their heads and announcing, 'Her ladyship will see you now. Please come this way.'

He led them to a reception room and stood back so they might enter. It was furnished in fine style, every item sent from Europe. The French windows opened onto a patio and near them a woman reclined on a gilt-framed couch. She ordered the butler to stay within call, and when he had bowed himself out, looked her visitors up and down and then gestured imperiously to Joshua.

He approached, took her extended hand and placed a kiss on the back of it. The skin was pale, the beringed fingers bony, gripping his a fraction too long, and her bosom, revealed by the décolleté, was full though betraying signs of aging. Her elaborately dressed hair was an unnatural brown that owed much to dye and threaded through with costly pearls, and her mouth was a scarlet-painted cupid's bow.

She's no spring chicken, he thought, alarmed by the hungry look in her eye that spoke of her intention to act like one.

'I'm Lady Fenby. What is your name, sir?' Her voice was stern and she was assessing him shrewdly, paying particular interest to his crotch. He felt like a prize bull or a slave on the block at the auction.

'Captain Joshua Willard, of the *May Belle*, at your service, madame,' he replied, sweating under her regard.

'Ah, yes, my brother wrote weeks ago to say that I was to expect Lady Romilly, her betrothed and friends. Where are they and what happened?'

'Alas, we were hit by a hurricane only a day's journey from here. The ship was wrecked and many crewmembers drowned. Did you not receive a letter concerning this?'

'I did, sir, and took exception to its contents. What's all this nonsense about you being captured by pirates and held captive? And who is this saucy knave who has the temerity to demand money for my niece's safe delivery?'

'His name is Armand Tertius, and he is known throughout the Indies. He owns an island where he rules supreme, and Lady Romilly will come to no harm as long as you accede to his wishes.'

'So I gathered from the letter. He warned me not to take it to the authorities if I wanted to see her again.' She rose to her feet, an intimidating woman dressed as if for a ball at Whitehall Palace. She was an aristocrat to her fingertips, regal in manner. Even Armand's two hellions wilted under her eagle eye. 'And these fellows? Who are they?'

'Lieutenant Morrison, one of my officers, and Henry

163

Moorcroft, an accountant. The other two are bodyguards.'
Clive and Henry bowed, and so did Armand's hellions, though
they had lost their swagger and looked sheepish, doffing
their hats deferentially and moving them around in their big
hands.

'I have discussed the matter with Lord Fenby and he agrees
to speak with you and go into the matter in detail. Meanwhile,
I will accommodate you here. Don't try anything tricky for my
house servants are trained to protect myself and his lordship,
chosen for their strength, agility and loyalty. You have brought
identity papers or other proof of your authenticity?'

Joshua fished in one of his capacious pockets. 'I have, my
lady.'

'Well done. You may stay and show them to me, while the
rest of you follow the butler who will take you to your rooms.
We'll have supper later, by which time my husband and I will
have decided on the best course of action.'

Joshua wanted to leave with the others but concern for
Romilly forced him to comply. Nothing must jeopardise her
safety. 'Your ladyship is too kind,' he murmured insincerely.

'Not at all. Come, sit by me.' She patted the couch then
picked up a cut-glass decanter from the low table and poured
drinks into crystal goblets, adding, 'Join me in a rum punch
and tell me all about England. It's ten years since I visited,
and much has happened since then. One of my sons is being
educated at Oxford University, the other has bought his own
plantation in Virginia and my two daughters have married
into the peerage.'

'Ah, I see,' said Joshua, who didn't understand why she
was recounting her family history. Then he realised that she
was already a little drunk. Did she start at breakfast? he
wondered, having heard that it was the custom among many
ex-patriots, homesick and weary of tropical paradises.

'Do you see? I don't think so. I hunger for London and
yearn for the old house, Harding Hall, where I spent my
girlhood. I even miss my brother, the Earl, though we never

164

got on well. He wanted me to take his daughter for a while. Apparently she is disobedient and high-spirited. Is that so?'

'Indeed yes, my lady, she is strong-minded.'

'And beautiful?'

'Ah yes, very beautiful.'

She picked up on his wistful tone. 'You desire her?' She placed a hand on his knee in an intimate fashion, stroking it through the black woollen breeches. As usual he was soberly and sensibly dressed. Armand had ordered that he be kitted out with suitable attire as befitted a master mariner on an important mission.

He tried to move his leg but she was insistent. Her grip tightened and her cheeks were flushed under the rouge, and her eyes even keener. 'My lady, I wouldn't presume to think of her in that way.'

'Why not?' Her hand was sliding higher, approaching the long finger of cock that lay along the inside of his left thigh.

'I am not of her station. Though I usually wear a sword, it's because I'm a sea captain, not through rank.' Joshua was feeling decidedly uneasy.

She wasn't completely unattractive, and also a very powerful woman, and this had a certain appeal. He'd not had the chance to make love to Romilly again and he was a young man with a young man's needs, his cock aching for relief. But he had to go carefully; one false move and Romilly would remain Armand's hostage and slave forever.

'I never let rank influence me, if I see someone I want,' observed Lady Fenby, and her hand found its goal – his penis. 'My husband spends himself in the cunts of black women from the barracoon. There are several half-breeds with crinkly hair, light skins and the Fenby features running around our plantation. So, since I'm no longer cursed with the monthly flux, I have taken to pleasuring myself with whoever I fancy, of whatever race.'

'What if you're found out?' As she edged closer Joshua started to forget her age. She smelled of rum, scented soap, exotic perfume and woman in a state of arousal.

'My husband dare not accuse me, given his own reputation.'

'But it's different for men.'

'Oh, yes, I'd not have done it earlier, but now I can no longer bear children, no one will know, or if they suspect, nothing will be done about it. The punishment for a young erring wife is severe. If she becomes pregnant and her child is born with dark skin, then it will be smothered and her Negro lover castrated, then burned alive in her sight before she is strangled. It happened to a friend of mine. There's one law for men and one for women, and not only in the Indies.'

He picked up on her bitterness, realising that someone like her, for all her privilege, was unhappy and lonely. She needed to be loved, what with her unfaithful husband and her children scattered far and wide, their offspring denied her by distance.

'That's sad, my lady, but men need to know that the babies their wives produce are really their heirs, not some cuckoo planted in the nest,' he said in mitigation.

She changed the subject. 'Tell me more about Romilly,' she said, refilling their glasses. 'Does she love her betrothed or is it a marriage of convenience, as was mine?'

'He's a gentleman, and the alliance was planned in their infancy.'

'I guessed as much.' She was impatient, leaning her breasts against his shoulder, and stroking his cock. Despite his efforts, he could not stop it becoming thick and hard. 'Is he handsome? Does he fancy women or prefer those of his own sex?'

'I believe he loves her in his own way, and certainly wants the marriage to take place.'

'After her dowry, no doubt. Is she still a virgin?'

Joshua didn't want to answer this question, but said, 'Tertius bedded her, more than once.'

'Did he, the villain? Is he young and handsome? I like my men to be so, can't be doing with old, balding rakes who

166

can't get it up. I fancy being pillaged and raped.' And she laughed loudly, throwing herself into Joshua's arms. He held on to her, for she was tipsy and likely to fall and hurt herself. 'Ah, young man... lovely young man... fuck me,' she crooned.

'But Lady Fenby... I'm a guest in your husband's house.'

'To hell with that. And it's *my* house. Paid for by *my* dot.'

'The servants. They may see and blab.'

'They won't. They know where they stand. I look after them like a mother, feed them, house them, have my own doctor attend them if they're sick and keep families together, not separating them like some owners. But if they misbehave I have them flogged. On occasions I do it myself.' She fumbled under the couch, produced a riding whip and swished it through the air. 'Shall I use it on you? Go on, bare your arse. Let me get at it.'

This was getting steadily worse and the more the scene disintegrated the larger Joshua's cock became. She tugged at his belt, unbuckling it before he could stop her and her fierce need to get at his body acted as an aphrodisiac. He held her hands in his and calmed her, though his heart was thudding madly. 'All right, my lady, be still. Let us take this slowly.'

'Slowly be damned!' She wrenched herself free, sprawled on the couch and lifted her skirts waist-high.

Joshua couldn't help staring at her wide opened legs where the stockings reached the knee, her shapely legs ending in small feet encased in high-heeled shoes. She displayed an expanse of greying pubic hair that covered her mound and edged her swollen labial wings. She reached down and held them apart, showing her pink inner lips and the nubbin that stood out stiffly, large and well developed. He could smell the oceanic odour that belonged exclusively to women, and he was drawn to her, unable to control his instinctive reaction. She had dropped the whip and, without really thinking, he undid his breeches and set his phallus free.

'Oh, what a fine specimen,' she cried, and dragged him on top of her. He was so stiff that she didn't need to guide him into her slippery cleft. He was there before he stopped to consider the consequences.

Romilly was blanked from memory, lost in his compulsive drive towards fulfilment. He was deaf to the voice of reason that tried ineffectively to halt him. He closed his eyes and ears to everything, concentrating on the pleasure, never mind that she was older, better bred, even dangerous should she refuse aid. He was rushing towards orgasm and only death could have stopped him.

'I've got to get out of here,' Romilly said to Jessica early one morning. 'I'll go mad if I don't.'

'I know how you feel, milady.' Jessica fiddled with the breakfast tray. 'I'm so worried about Peter that I can't sleep a wink.'

Distraught though Romilly might be, she had managed a meal of wheat bread and jam, coffee and orange juice. Now she stood at the window, staring out longingly as a caged bird will. The jungle stretched for miles below her, and she had been trying to map out a route, not quite sure what she intended to do if she did give her guards the slip. Sabrina had relaxed her vigilance; confident that there was no way Romilly would brave the wilds.

'Where is she?' She was confident that Jessica would know to whom she referred.

'In bed with Marcus and Aponi.'

'Let's go.' Romilly snatched up a wide-brimmed straw hat, a bag containing a canteen of water, a towel, a shawl and a knife that she had managed to hide.

'Where?' Jessica was at her side, a white coif covering her head and a wrap over her arm.

'To swim,' Romilly said firmly and left the room.

Armand would never have tolerated the slackness that prevailed among the men during his absence. A hush lay over the fortress and its surrounds. There were usually sentries posted, especially at the entrances, but Romilly and Jessica passed through without being challenged. Soon they were following a path that led towards the beach. It wound between escarpments and dipped into routes through the jungle, all unfamiliar and alarming, as were the animal sounds, the rustling, queer cries and the feeling of being watched. Trees towered overhead, hung with trailing orchids and inhabited by monkeys who hurled themselves, arm over arm, under the forest canopy. Jessica, terrified, was on the lookout for snakes, a stick in one hand, ready to swipe at anything that moved.

It was now high noon and they were grateful for the shade that formed a cool haven as they sat on a fallen log and ate the food that Jessica had packed. The cook had been dozing in his rocking chair and the kitchen minions were still abed when she crept down and grabbed a supply of bread, cheese and fruit.

'Can we go back now, my lady?' she asked, worried in case there was news of Peter and she wasn't there to hear it.

'No, I haven't found a pool yet.' Romilly lay back on the short grass and stared up at the trees. The sun formed a golden nimbus among the leaves.

'But we must return before nightfall. It's too dangerous.' Most times Jessica acted as if she was still Romilly's chaperone. In a way this was true, as she had never been dismissed from her post.

'I don't want to.' Romilly's lower lip rolled out in a way that Jessica dreaded. She was as stubborn as her father. She jumped up and brushed twigs from her skirt. 'Let's go just a bit further. It's so lovely here.'

Jessica was forced to concede to her wishes. She couldn't stay there on her own, so she trudged along behind her mistress. The way became rougher. They scrambled over large boulders and pushed cautiously through thickets, always on the alert for snakes or spiders or other poisonous creatures.

The afternoon was drawing to a close. 'We should really be retracing our steps,' Jessica said, then she jumped. 'What was that?'

'A stick snapping somewhere over there,' Romilly answered, on the alert.

It was too late, the shrubs became men and the men proved to be warriors, like the ones who had taken Romilly to Awan weeks ago. And there he was, that great, ugly man with his flat nose and slanting eyes, grinning all over his face at the sight of her.

'Lady... lady...' he managed to get out, and his warriors surrounded her and Jessica, and Awan picked her up and hoisted her over his shoulder.

His feathered cloak tickled her nose. He smelt of sweat and animal fur, and he was like some jolly giant, joking with his stalwarts as they jogged along, heading for their camp. She could hear Jessica protesting loudly as she was similarly treated.

Oh, sweet Jesus, I've been a fool, she thought. I'd forgotten all about Awan. Isn't he afraid of incurring Armand's wrath? Apparently not, if his ebullience is anything to go by. Has he a short memory or is he totally stupid? Will he expect to consummate our interrupted marriage?

Yet, secretly, her wilful little demon was clapping its hands with glee. That would pay Armand back for neglecting her for Cat and his piratical exploits, and his refusal to take her seriously. She wanted to hug the native chief for giving her this opportunity to take her revenge and show that she could be as cold and calculating as Armand.

The village was much as she remembered it, and the same crowd of women and old people streamed out to welcome the warriors home, exclaiming in wonderment when they saw captives. Romilly was put down and instantly recognised by Riku and Mahil.

'I knew you would return,' said the shaman. 'The gods told me so.'

'And what of the wrath of Captain Tertius?' she asked, standing in the grasp of Awan. Now she understood how the elders could speak the English tongue. It was through their

170

association with the pirates and other settlers before them.

'Are you his wife?' Riku made his way round her in rhythmical movements, shaking the gourd and muttering incantations.

'No.'

'But he has taken your virginity?'

'Yes. I'm his prisoner.'

'Why are you wandering here, so close to danger?'

'He thinks he owns me, but I'm no man's slave.'

'We dare not help you. We can shelter you and take you to fortress in the morning.'

'Thank you.'

Awan spat out a torrent of words in their own language, his gestures indicating that he was not amused. The shaman and wise-woman went into a huddle, and Romilly held Jessica's hand and waited, admired on all sides by the tribe. Eventually Riku returned to them and said, 'Awan wants you to share his hut, feast with him and give yourself to him in return.'

'Well, that's not very gentlemanly,' Jessica piped indignantly.

'It's all right, leave it to me,' Romilly soothed. She was curious about the chief, her sex tingling as she imagined him taking her. She recalled his huge erection when she lay bound to the altar. At that time she was still a virgin with no idea of what it meant to be possessed by a man. Now she knew and anticipated the night she would spend with Awan, a little fearful of what to expect, but this added to the excitement.

Jacy ran up to her, a happy smile on her face. 'So glad, lady,' she said. 'Me wash you? Dress you?'

Romilly blushed as she recalled vividly the heated moments she had spent with the lovely native girl. 'Yes, thank you,' she said, and entered the chief's hut to be prepared for him, accompanied by a reluctant Jessica to whom this was all very strange. 'They won't hurt us,' Romilly assured her. 'I've told you how they found us when we were cast ashore, but the chief and I have some unfinished business.'

171

'I don't understand,' said Jessica, totally bewildered.

'He wanted to make me his wife, or rather one of his wives for he has several, but Armand broke into the camp and took me away. He intrigues me, and I'd like to know what it is like to be made love to by a native.'

'Lady Romilly! For heaven's sake! Goodness knows what the Earl would make of all this.'

'He'd disinherit me, I expect,' and, so saying, she gave herself up to being washed, pampered and generally prepared for the belated nuptials of herself and Awan.

The hut was large and divided into a main room and the one she now occupied at the back. The walls were hung with woven blankets and animal skins, the floors bare wood, swept clean and very tidy. There was a mirror resting on a cupboard, and she wondered how these articles had been acquired, maybe through trading or perhaps washed up on the shore after a vessel had been shipwrecked. Maybe they even came from the *May Belle*. The thought of Joshua arrested her and she wished he was there, almost wanted to cry off from her forthcoming encounter with Awan.

Jacy had a bowl of warm water brought in, offering palm-oil soap so that Romilly might clean away the sweat of the day. She kept her distance for Jessica was there, insisting on helping her mistress, looking down on the native girl. Romilly's clothing was simple, consisting of a calf-length, loose cotton shift and thonged sandals. Gone were stays and lacy petticoats and fine dresses. Unadorned garments were so much more practical on the island. The French tailor had made her gowns in his atelier, and she had worn them in Cayona, but since Armand was no longer there she pleased herself, attired like a naiad and enjoying the freedom.

'Don't wash my hair,' she said. 'It doesn't need it and I still intend to swim either in the sea or a pool before I leave here.'

Jessica used a comb and Romilly's locks fell about her shoulders in a curling mass. She stared in the mirror and was satisfied. Jacy brought across bead necklaces and a wreath of flowers, and Romilly tried them, liking the effect and keeping them on. She could hear sounds from the larger room, her nose responding to the delicious smells as the meal was brought in. Riku appeared in the doorway, wearing a horned headdress and an animal-teeth necklace. He was holding a calabash, nodding to indicate that she should drink its contents.

It tasted sweet, but was decidedly alcoholic, made of fermented fruit juice. It went to her head and distanced her from what was really happening. Drums throbbed, flutes wailed and Romilly stepped across the threshold to meet her bridegroom.

'No,' said Riku, when Jessica went to follow her. 'Come to other hut. Never fear, we care for you.'

Romilly was alone, apart from Awan who reclined on a heap of skins by an upended log that served as a table. A smoky flare was attached to a beam and the light softened his harsh features. His smile, too, made her warm to him. He seemed genuinely pleased to see her. He patted the space next to him and she sank down, tucking her legs under her. He offered her food that consisted of cooked grain covered in a mixture of meat and vegetables. She realised that she was hungry and ate it with her fingers, as he did, sucking them clean. He was eager to please her, peeling fruit and putting it to her lips, nodding and making remarks that she couldn't understand. Soon he stopped talking or feeding her, reaching out and touching her breasts.

He stood up and removed the leather thong that was all he wore. Romilly, still seated, looked at the huge phallus that reared above her. It was fully erect, a being in its own right, rising to his navel and beyond. It twitched, the shaft knotted with veins, the helm twin-lobed and shining with juice. He stroked it, made it even larger, and then fondled the weighty balls that hung below it. He stepped close, a colossus of a man, and pushed his cock into her face.

She breathed in his odour, that sour-sweet smell of male

virility, and opened her mouth, taking the bulging glans inside. He was huge, moving slowly, going deeper into her throat, making her gag. She pulled away, shaking her head and saying, 'No, it's too much.'

He frowned, his dark eyes flashing, then turned her away from him, pushed her into a bending position and introduced that mighty weapon to her anus. She struggled but he held her still and poked into her orifice with a stubby finger. It was dry and she yelped. He pulled back and swung her round, looking into her face in a disconcerted way with his brows drawn into a frown. She wished she could tell him to go slowly and insure that she was wet, the language barrier spoiling her enjoyment. He seemed angry and puzzled and took up a switch that lay beside the makeshift couch.

'Oh, no,' she said, realising what was coming.

He sat on the log and pulled her, facedown, across his mighty thighs, her clothing flung over her shoulders. His cock pierced her side, an upright spear that dribbled wetness over her. When he had her settled he examined her crack, running a finger up it, and penetrating both orifices, withdrawing his finger and lifting it to his nostrils, then nodding, satisfied. His prick jerked but retained its tribute.

The switch landed with a rush and Romilly shrieked. This fired Awan and he repeated his blows, getting more and more excited. At last, unable to wait, he raised her, spread her buttocks and thrust his rampant beast within her vagina. At first she felt nothing but pain, the switch turning her hinds to fire, the largeness of his weapon seeming to penetrate her to the heart. She was soaked with dew, the beating rousing her to a frenzy, and Awan was intent only on his own pleasure. She reached down and stimulated her clitoris in time to his thrusts.

Pain was now lost in pleasure. His was the largest prick she had encountered, almost too big for comfort, but the stretching and plunging now added to her enjoyment. She circled her bud, rubbed it, spread her juices over it from where he was entering her, and was beginning to climb the mountain towards that sunlit peak of orgasm.

Awan grunted and she responded to his savage jolts. She was close to her apogee, brought about by her own fingers and that monstrosity inside her. His excitement intensified. He neighed like a stallion, driving into her with all his strength, skewering her on his phallus. It was as if he was riding her, then the role reversed and she was riding *him*, taking her joy of his prick, whipping him into a fever, working up their spiralling passion until her climax galloped through her.

He bellowed as his cock spewed, flooding her with his tribute. At that moment of release he sank his teeth into her neck, and she knew the satisfaction of bringing this mighty man to his knees, putty in her hands. Like all the rest of them his cock ruled him, and she fell with him onto the ground, his phallus still a prisoner within her.

Chapter Eleven

Where am I? was Romilly's first thought on waking. Then memory returned and with it shame and regret. She lay on the primitive couch with Awan, his feather cloak spread over them. The lamp had gone out and daylight crept through the curtainless windows. A rooster crowed somewhere and a dog barked irritatingly. Awan was curled up at her back. She could feel his semi-hard tool pressing into her bottom crease, seemingly untiring. Now that she had tried him and found that he wasn't what she was looking for, she wanted to leave the village as soon as possible but doubted he would let her go. Once again her impetuosity had led her into trouble.

She sat up, doing her best not to disturb him, but at once he was alert, big brown arms dragging her back into the sweaty heat of his body. The smell of him made her feel sick. She pummelled him. 'Get off me, you great lump! I need to pass water.'

He couldn't understand, but gave an amiable, sleepy grin and released her. She dragged her dress over her head and pushed aside the woven grass matting that hung at the door. Riku was squatting outside. It looked as if he had been there all night. A circle had been drawn in the dust in front of him and small bones were scattered within it.

He looked up at her and shook his head mournfully. 'You will be leaving. Not Awan's wife.'

'No,' she said, stepping past him. 'Where is my maid, Jessica?'

'I'm here, my lady.' The duenna appeared from a nearby hut, yawning and stretching. 'What a night! I didn't sleep a wink. Are we going? I can't get away from these savages

176

quickly enough.'

'We'll go, just as soon as I've answered the call of nature.' Romilly ran behind some bushes, then squatted, sighing with relief.

By the time she returned Awan was standing arguing with Riku. He looked angry enough to kill the shaman but didn't dare, terrified of evoking the vengeance of the gods. A crowd had begun to gather, and Mahil was stirring them up, foretelling disaster.

Awan kept glaring at Romilly, but eventually calmed down, listening to the elders. 'What's he saying?' Romilly asked Riku.

He brushed a bunch of twigs over her from head to foot. 'This to drive away evil. He unhappy to lose you, but I say not to anger Captain Tertius or it be bad for tribe. You go... now... before he change his mind.'

'I came here determined to swim in the sea,' she said, grateful to the old man for soothing Awan's wounded pride.

'I tell warriors to take you there, then lead you to fortress.'

'Thank you,' Romilly said and, leaning forward, kissed him impulsively on the purple patterned cheek. Then she stretched on tiptoe and saluted Awan too, astonished to see tears in his dark eyes.

This odd episode was over and she knew she must get back, hoping that she'd not been missed already. It was early, a haze over the forest and she walked with Jessica, guarded on each side by the chattering, brightly hued men, their bodies painted with weird designs. They were naked and armed with spears, and she got used to seeing their cocks bobbing as they trotted along. Jessica kept her eyes fixed firmly ahead.

They soon reached a secluded bay and the men tactfully withdrew, leaving Romilly free to undress behind some large boulders. 'Are you coming in, Wade?' The gentle swell of the azure sea was tempting Romilly to hurry.

'No, my lady, I'll stand on the edge and hold your towel.'

'You're so stuffy. Have you no sense of adventure? It's a

177

glorious morning and this is a marvellous place. Look at the cliffs and the white sand, and the trees and shrubs and wild flowers.'

'I'm not unaware of its charm. As for adventure, well, I'm not impressed with what you were up to last night with yon savage. A pirate was bad enough, but at least he is from France,' Jessica returned smartly. Disapproval was written in every line of her face.

'I don't care what you say. I'm for a dip in the sea.' Romilly was naked now, but she wrapped the towel around her and ran down the beach, aware of an exhilarating sense of freedom.

Jessica followed her to the edge and Romilly waded in, giving little shrieks as the wavelets tickled her ankles and, as she ventured further, reached her thighs and sent impudent fingers inching into her fork. She struck out and was soon swimming strongly, shouting back to Jessica. 'It's so nice. The water is warm, you really should join me, Wade.'

'Don't go too far, my lady!'

Romilly floated on her back, hair spread out around her head, her nipples crimped and pointing to the sky, her wet triangle of pubic floss darkened. She wanted to stay there forever, rocked by the sea. Her eyelids closed and she was filled with a sense of well-being. Then Jessica's scream jerked her out of her reverie. They were no longer alone. A crowd of men came streaming across the sand and she recognised their leader.

He cupped his hands round his mouth and bellowed, 'Come in, Lady Romilly. It is I, Lafette.'

It was the swaggering bully who had duelled with Armand in the *Kicking Donkey*. She bottomed it, but kept the water level above her breasts, facing him, pushing back her streaming hair. 'Why are you here?' she shouted, calmer now she could see that Jessica was unharmed.

'I've come to rescue you from Tertius.' Lafette approached, the waves washing over his black leather sea-boots. 'Never fear, my lady, you are safe with me. Can I tempt you to leave

178

the ocean, rising like Venus from the deep?'

Despite his pretty turn of phrase, Romilly suspected him of dark motives, but she had no alternative but to leave the screening water and walk naked towards the group of lecherously leering men.

'I want my towel,' she demanded, every inch the goddess he had mentioned.

He seized it from Jessica and waded in till the water reached the tops of his thighs. As he came closer Romilly was not blind to his flashing dark eyes and white teeth, his bold, gypsy looks and olive skin. He was a handsome, devil-may-care rapscallion, and she could feel her cheeks reddening at the blatant symbol of desire rising in his breeches that were rendered even tighter by being saturated. Dear God, she had just got rid of one ardent swain only to be confronted by another!

'Give me the towel.' She snatched it rudely, but he only laughed and picked her up like a stranded mermaid and splashed towards the shore.

She struggled to keep a part of the towel over her vital bits, but it kept slipping and sliding. The dozen men who had accompanied him hooted and guffawed, slapping him on the shoulder as he reached them. Romilly's feet sank into sand, but with Jessica's help was able to adjust her covering. The duenna had elbowed the men aside, giving them a tongue-lashing as she went to her mistress's aid. They teased the straight-faced woman, rolling their eyes and grimacing, but she ignored them, severe as a teacher in a dame school.

There was stirring in the bushes and the leader of Awan's warriors poked his head above them. He shouted at the pirates and waved his spear threateningly. His troop did the same, leaping up and down, shouting and brandishing their weapons, but a few random shots soon had them running, and it was doubtful if they would be back.

'Don't hurt them,' Romilly pleaded. 'They are kindly and have treated me with respect.'

'Savages. They'd better not try anything with me.' Lafette's intentions were crystal clear. He couldn't stop touching Romilly, even though she slapped his roving hands away. 'I can't wait to get you to my ship,' he said. 'I'll treat you like a queen... my pirate queen.'

'How dare you think of such a thing?' she rounded on him briskly. 'Are you not afraid of what Armand will do? Your life won't be worth a groat if he gets his hands on you.'

Lafette pretended to stagger, overcome with fright. 'Oh, that's awesome! Can't you see me shaking like an aspen?' Then he sobered suddenly and grabbed her in his arms, his breath tainted with alcohol. 'Shall I fuck you here on the sand, in front of my men and your maid? Or shall I make you wait till we reach my ship?'

'Armand will find you. He'll be sending a search party out to look for me.'

'He is away chasing a Spanish treasure ship.'

'Where did you hear this? It was not general information.'

'Cat told me all about his plans. He's been rogering her, or didn't you know?' he rejoined, his hands on her breasts, the towel thrust down.

His words stabbed through her like a butcher's knife. Cat and Armand? It was as she had suspected. 'You think I give a tinker's cuss about that?' she snapped, trying unsuccessfully to wriggle free of him.

'She does, even if you don't. She's madly in love with him and financed my ship to come here during his absence and take you away so he would never find you, leaving the field clear for her.'

'And you agreed? You bastard!' Had he been more sensitive her tone would have turned him into a pillar of ice.

'Not for her sake, but for my own. I've wanted you since the first moment I saw you. Now you are mine. I can keep you, sell you into slavery, give you to my crew... your fate will be in my hands.' He hauled her into his arms, shouting to his men, 'Back to the longboat, the *Stella Mare* and the open

180

seas. We'll celebrate the nuptials of Lady Romilly and myself. I'll have Father John marry us. Will you do that, John?' He addressed the largest, fattest, most heavily armed individual in the group.

'Aye, aye, cap'n,' he said. 'If I can remember the service from my days as a vicar.'

'It's like learning to swim; you never forget,' Lafette joked, happy swinging Romilly aloft and starting off along the beach to where a clump of rocks led into the next bay.

There lay a longboat in the charge of armed men and, not far out, rode a ship at anchor, a fine, sleek, warlike vessel with the carved figurehead of a striking women in blue – Stella, the star of the sea.

Lafette swung Romilly up and waded into the water, then dumped her into the bows while Father John did the same with a protesting Jessica. The men leapt in after them, laughing and shouting, pushing off, taking up the oars and rowing swiftly to where the vessel waited. Romilly sat shivering. Spray spewed up, wetting her thoroughly and stinging her eyes. The ship grew even larger, the steep sides looming over them. Father John helped Jessica climb the swaying ladder and Romilly's numb hands clung to the wet harshness of the rope as she hauled herself painfully up, glad of Lafette's arms about her and his lean body pressed to hers for support.

She was helped over the side, eager hands seizing her. Her nearly naked state inspired a cheer from the throats of Lafette's hellions. He gave orders to set sail and then took her to his quarters in the stern. The ship wasn't half as fine as the *Scorpion*, but then its commander wasn't Armand, simply an opportunist who would do almost anything for gain.

Jessica pleaded to be allowed to go with them, but she was hustled into a small cabin close to the main one that was Lafette's. Once inside he closed the door firmly, kicked off his soggy boots and breeches and pulled Romilly down to his narrow bed, whipping the towel away. His shirt covered his cock, but it lifted the fabric as he feasted his eyes on her,

181

examining her all over as if she was a rare piece of porcelain that had fallen into his greedy hands.

'This is the first time I've had a real lady,' he murmured. 'Is your cunt different to that of ordinary women? Do you come, as they do?'

'Please,' Romilly was soaked and exhausted, 'let me dry myself.'

'I'll do it for you.' He produced a quality white towel and started to rub her hair. Such a gallant action surprised her, but the pirates were full of surprises, not entirely the debased beasts they were reputed to be.

He ran his hands over her mane of tangled locks. 'Don't look so angry with me. What I have done has been through love of you.'

'Indeed!' A handful of months ago Romilly might have believed him, green as grass and falling for flattery. Now she doubted every man who crossed her path. 'Love? Lust more like.'

'And don't you lust, too? Or is a lady bereft of such base feelings?'

She faced him full on. 'You have no idea what a "lady", as you call me, wants.'

'Then show me,' he said, and his sensual lips glistened where his tongue had passed over them. She imagined them slurping at her clitoris and her slit was moist with more than just salt water. She could hear the sounds of feet and noises as the sailors got the ship under sail. Timbers creaked and winches squealed as the anchor was weighed. Lafette was taking her away from San Juliano and she had no idea of her destination. Would Armand rescue her? It would be best to keep Lafette sweet if she wanted to see her homeland again.

'Where are we heading?' she asked, making no protest as he lowered his head and nibbled her breasts, his erection pressing against her.

'Tortuga, but on the far side where Tertius will never find us.'

He was well built but slighter than Armand, a man who would have turned heads among her friends in London, quite possibly passing himself off as a gentleman. She wondered what twist of fate had brought him to his present position as a freebooter.

So, he was taking her to Tortuga but not Cayona. Armand and Cat. Horrible visions of them together haunted Romilly. And she had been fool enough to consider harbouring gentle feelings towards him. She was bitterly humiliated and her list of grievances against Armand grew ever longer. It made Lafette an attractive proposition. Word was bound to spread that she was now his mistress. With any luck Armand would hear of it and be needled, at the very least.

She laid back and Lafette bent over her, showing his teeth in a wolfish grin. 'You want me to force you? Is that it? So you can blame me and say I raped you?'

It was violence she needed to rouse her fully – the kind of treatment she had come to expect from Armand. She lashed out at him, putting up a fight, and Lafette entered into the game, swearing when she raked his face with her nails, then tethering her wrists together above her head. She jabbed him with her knee, narrowly missing his balls, and he smacked her hard across the thighs. He was rapidly losing his temper, scowling into her face, trying to kiss her while she snapped at him.

'Goddamn, woman, you can't win so give up trying!' He lifted his shirt and showed his cock. It was thin but long and stiff. He kneed her legs apart and thrust into her slit.

Romilly wasn't ready, nowhere near climax. He hadn't touch her love-bud and she doubted that he even knew about it. In desperation, she avoided his attempt at penetration and started to rub herself. Their struggle had excited her and she wanted relief. Lafette was all male, sinewy, strong, a pirate leader, appealing to her wild side, but what use was he if ignorant of woman's seat of sensation?

'No, let me,' he said, proving her wrong, and he positioned

183

himself between her legs, facing her cleft. He subjected her to an amazing tongue-fuck, his hands reaching up and stimulating her nipples. Romilly strained towards his cunning lips and tongue, crying out as she reached her peak. He let her come, then withdrew and introduced his swarthy-skinned prick to her vulva... and thrust. She was beyond caring who was driving the engine, desperate to clasp a hard object inside her, convulsing round it in the final throes of an orgasm that left her breathless.

Lafette seemed stunned by her passionate reaction, lying beside her and smoothing her hair. 'So, what do you think of ladies and fornication now?' she asked, glad that she'd had him, and not only for revenge. If they had met at a different time and place she might well have fallen in love with him.

He laughed, very pleased with himself. 'I shall not be satisfied with anything less in future. Father John will marry us. I want you with me forever.'

'Forever is a long time,' she murmured. 'I'm learning that Fate is a fickle jade, and one can't rely on her.'

'Then we must enjoy every moment,' he said, his penis stirring again.

She felt soft and sentimental, almost loving the man in her arms, and had noticed that this seemed to follow every sexual encounter. She had felt it strongly for Joshua and even Awan. With Armand it was more uncontrolled; she wanted to serve him, to be enslaved by him, and thought that it may have been because he was the first to take her virginity.

Lafette played with her breasts. 'I've never seen such milk-white skin. It's so fine and delicate.'

'Not when Armand has been spanking me,' she rejoined, sighing under his caresses.

'He spanks you? And you like it?' He was amused and excited.

'I didn't at first, but it stirs strange feelings in me, makes me want him more.'

'I shall try it,' he declared and sat up, legs over the side of

184

the bed, pulling her across his lap.

She gave herself up to pleasure, never mind that the ship was noisy, the cabin crowded and none too clean and the man himself in need of a bath and shave, his stubble chaffing her. She lay across his knees and waited in a state of fear and anticipation.

His first slap was hesitant, but her reaction made him increase the force of the next. Then he beat a brisk tattoo on her bare bottom. 'It's turning pink!' he exclaimed excitedly, and spanked her harder.

Romilly lay yelping each time his palm landed flat on her rump. Pain and heat shot through her, and so did desire. But soon she'd had enough, wanting him to take her in the anus. Lafette wanted to continue, fascinated by the change of colour that now saturated her rump from pale pink to red, to scarlet, to crimson and the deep, ripe colour of a plum, and he would not let her go till he was ready.

Then he flung her over onto her face so he might keep on admiring his imprints and, while doing this, was inspired to enter her most private place, wetting it from their mutual juices. He slipped a hand under her, cupped her mound and applied a finger to her clitoris. Just for an instant she thought she had died and gone straight to heaven.

Armand's rage almost shook the island to its foundations. He strode into the fortress, fully expecting Romilly to be there, and was greeted by Sabrina who threw herself down, clasped him round the legs and begged to be forgiven.

'She has run away! I don't know where. When I woke she was gone and we've searched all over but can't find her. Her duenna is missing, too!'

'Stupid bitch!' Armand knocked her to the floor where she lay, grovelling. 'I told you to keep her safe. Where were you instead of performing your task? Rogering, I suppose. Sleeping with one of your slaves, or maybe two. You're useless! Take her to the dungeons,' he ordered Johnson. 'Chain her up.

Keep her on bread and water.'

'What will you do?' questioned Peter, concerned about Jessica.

'Search for her, of course. The *Sirocco* is to be unloaded and repaired, so I'll take the *Scorpion* and fresh lads and search every bay and inlet, going into the interior if need be, leaving no stone unturned until I find her.'

'You need to rest, sir,' Peter advised. 'It's been a strenuous trip and you didn't get off unscathed.' He indicated the bandage on Armand's left arm.

'It's a scratch, nothing more,' Armand dismissed it. 'We did what we intended, took the galleon's cargo and anything else we fancied and then set her loose. The captain was so grateful to be alive that he would have kissed my boots. No doubt he'll get a wigging from his superiors for losing such valuable treasure.'

'May I come with you? Mrs Wade is with Lady Romilly, by all accounts.'

'You have the wounded to attend.'

'I've done my best for them and my assistant can carry on from here. There weren't too many casualties and no deaths, thank God.'

'Do what the hell you want,' Armand said abstractedly, and rushed of as if the devils of hell were after him.

The *Stella Mare* was racing across the ocean, a stiff breeze behind her and her sails full-bellied. Romilly stood with Lafette on deck while he took the helm, his hands confident on the wheel. Jessica had been permitted to join them. She was crumpled but unharmed.

'You're not really going to wed him, are you, milady?' she asked, horror-struck at the idea.

'What do you think?' Romilly replied, eyes sparkling with mischief. 'I doubt very much whether Father John is still qualified to perform a ceremony. He's probably been defrocked or whatever they do to naughty priests. What d'you think of

186

my garb?'

Jessica stared at the costume Romilly was wearing. She looked like a keen-hipped lad in velvet breeches, leather boots, a wide, striped sash spanning her slender waist, an open-necked shirt showing her cleavage, and a scarf tied round her head, pirate fashion.

'Where did you get those clothes?' Jessica asked, tight-lipped.

'Lafette gave them to me, and these hoop earrings.' She shook her head so that the gold glittered. 'He says he'll find me a sword and teach me how to fence.'

'Hardly a fitting occupation for a genteel young lady.'

'Do I merit that name now? I don't think so.' Romilly stared ahead, watching the wide expanse of blue above and below, the racing white horses, the gulls screaming overhead. 'I could settle for this life,' she remarked.

But with Lafette? She wasn't too sure. At the moment he was like a child with a new toy and couldn't do too much for her, but would it last? And what would happen when he tired of her? He didn't know it, but she had no intention of staying long enough to find out. A way of escape would present itself, she was sure.

It came sooner than she anticipated.

The sun was high in the heavens when the lookout shouted, 'A vessel astern of us, bearing down at full speed!'

Lafette reached for a telescope, squinting in the direction indicated. 'God's blood!' he muttered.

'What is it?' Romilly wanted to snatch it from him but he wouldn't let go.

'We're being followed.' His tanned face had paled, his confidence shaken.

'By whom?' She dared to hope, yet feared the truth.

'The *Scorpion*.'

'Armand's ship?'

'The very same.' He turned from her, bellowing orders through a leather speaking trumpet, addressing his boatswain

187

and gunners, but the pursuing vessel was gaining on them.

There was a patch of white smoke from the stranger, and a loud boom followed by a shower of spray flung up by a roundshot that hurtled across the prow of the *Stella Mare*. Pandemonium reigned on the decks. Lafette was shouting commands, ordering the crew to reef the sails and bring the ship up to the wind so that her guns might be fired.

The attacker was lowering and raising her topsail. 'What's that for?' Romilly rounded on Lafette.

'It's a signal to heave to.'

'Will you do so?'

'Not on your sweet life,' he replied grimly. 'Get below, out of the way.'

She took no notice of him. Armand was coming for her! And while her heart sang, so she was terrified. He would be in a terrible rage. These might be her last few hours on earth. It was too late for her to seek shelter. Cannon boomed and the *Stella Mare* shuddered under the heavy impact as she was hit. Romilly was flung against a bulwark as the ship yawned uncontrollably. Another direct hit took away the shrouds.

'The rudder is smashed!' the boatswain shouted. 'The steering tackle is out of action!'

'Hell and damnation!' Lafette swore, his face grim. 'With the helm out of control she'll yaw as the wind takes her.'

Romilly watched as the attacker bore down on them at a fierce rate of knots. She was already shortening sail in readiness for boarding. The *Stella Mare* gave returning fire but the aim was faulty, the damaged ship yielding to the breeze, firing into the void. A great black flag with a golden falcon was run up in savage challenge. It streamed from the masthead – Armand's symbol by which his fleet was recognised throughout the lawless regions of the islands. The *Scorpion* had further shortened sail and was creeping towards her victim, the sunlight gradually eclipsed by her black hull.

Her bulwarks were lined with men as she glided up astern,

casting her shadow over the doomed vessel. There was a shattering impact, the rending of timbers, the clank of grappling hooks and the staccato rattle of musket fire. Then the assailants were aboard, swinging across on ropes, and Armand was in the lead, sword in hand. There were shouts and screams mingled with the clash of steel and the din of gunfire as his men took over, killing those who resisted, showing mercy to the ones who surrendered.

Armand saw Romilly and their eyes met over the smoke and chaos. His stare went straight to her heart and she wanted him to take her then and there, on the blood-slippery deck, amidst the noise of battle. Awan, Joshua and Lafette were as nothing compared to him, puppets who became invisible as soon as he appeared.

'Where's Lafette, you troublesome bitch?' he shouted, indicting that he hated and despised her. A bubble of misery lodged in her chest. She shook her head and didn't reply.

At that moment Lafette jumped from the carved rail of the poop deck, swinging his sword at Armand who parried the blow. Lafette snarled viciously, mad with rage at the loss of his ship and Romilly. This gave him a disadvantage, making him careless so that he laid himself open, but Armand took his time, wanting to make him sweat. Lafette retreated, trying to keep out of the way of that blade that pursued him mercilessly. The dazzling point seemed to be everywhere at once, and realising he was mastered, a look of terror passed across his face.

Romilly stood motionless, with a hand pressed to her throat and skirmishes taking place all around, her mind concentrating on the conflict between two men who had each known the bounty of her flesh. Her hopes, prayers and fears were for Armand. Lafette might never have existed. They feinted and parried, their feet beating out a tattoo on the deck, their men fighting all around them. Then with a quick twist of his wrist Armand spun Lafette's rapier from his grasp and lunged.

He let his blade slide in softly, entering Lafette's chest,

pushing until his sword appeared through his back and the hilt rested on his ribs. He was skewered like a butterfly on a pin. When Armand withdrew his blade Lafette slumped to the deck, coughing up blood. Romilly ran to his side, dropping to her knees and taking his hand in hers. Armand watched them, his sword lowered.

'It was not her fault,' Lafette gasped. 'Blame Cat. She put me up to this.'

'Cat? Why?'

'She is jealous of you, my friend. Take good care of this lady,' and with that he choked on more blood, coughed violently and breathed his last.

Armand's eyes met hers, and amidst the tumult and confusion she read in their depths an icy contempt that froze her. She held out her hands to him. 'Armand, it's true. Cat is to blame.'

'You ran away. It was nothing to do with her. Chance led you to Lafette. Why did you run from me? Why break your promise to wait for Captain Willard and the money?'

'I can explain...'

'Later,' and he turned on his heel.

Demoralised by their leader's death, his men threw down their arms and surrendered. They were given permission to sew his body in a canvas shroud weighted with lead-shot, and Father John said a few prayers before it was committed to the deep.

Afterwards Armand addressed them. 'I have no quarrel with you and my score with Lafette has been settled. I suggest you limp back to Cayona and sort the ship out. We'll leave you to it.'

'You've been hurt,' Romilly said, seeing the stained bandage and alarmed for him.

'During our trip. It's nothing. Peter has seen to it.'

'Is he here, sir? Oh, can I see him?' begged Jessica, clinging to Romilly.

'He's on the *Scorpion,* ready to patch up wounds. You can

help him. Make yourself useful.'

'What about me?' Romilly asked.

'A man has just died because of you,' he replied brusquely. 'And all you can think about is yourself. I shall guard you more closely now, *mademoiselle*. No more tricks. And you'll be in chains until I decide what punishment to give you.'

He signalled to Johnson, who dug a pair of manacles from the depths of his pocket and passed them to him. Armand clapped them round her wrists and then she was taken to the *Scorpion* and thrust into the hold.

Chapter Twelve

Romilly crouched in a corner of the dungeon, brooding on what had happened. There was no escaping Armand's wrath. He was furious and she dreaded to think what he planned for her. As he said, a man had died because of her, and it wasn't a pleasant feeling. She kept remembering how she had enjoyed Lafette's lovemaking and her conscience smote her. She should never have left the fortress and explored the island. Nothing had come of it but ill luck.

The ship's hold had been uncomfortable enough, a damp, smelly home for rats, and she was kept without food or water. But when they arrived at Devil's Paradise she was hauled forth and marched into the fortress. Sabrina had been there, scoffing and hitting out at her, blaming her for the beating she'd received. In a condemnatory silence she was frogmarched into the dungeon and the heavy bars and bolts rammed into place. She was left in almost total darkness, mitigated by the flicker of a small lamp. All that was there was a bucket for bodily functions.

She was hungry, thirsty and miserable, chained and unable go far from the pool of light, but the place was familiar. Armand had taken her there the first time he chastised her. It was the night when she lost her virginity and, she now confessed to herself, became his slave. Willing or unwilling, it didn't matter: the end result was the same. Why was she fighting it?

As the hours dragged by she became desperate, shouting and begging to be released. No one answered, and she collapsed on the heap of dirty straw that formed a bed, leaned her head on her upraised knees, and cried. It was then that the grille in the door slid back and someone peered through.

'Johnson here, Lady Romilly,' he said, his harsh voice music to her ears. 'You're to come out now.' She jumped up, tiredness gone, as the fastenings slid back. She had never been more pleased to see anything than his bearded, weather-beaten face.

'Where am I going?' she asked.

'I've orders to take you to him.' Johnson inserted a key into the manacles attached to a ring in the wall and she flexed her released arms.

'Is there any news from Captain Willard?' she said as he gripped her elbow in his knobbly fist and they started up the winding stone steps to where blessed daylight streamed through an arched window.

'Not that I've heard,' he replied, and her heart sank.

The stillness was broken by sounds issuing from the Great Hall, men's voices, the clank of swords dangling in scabbards and the scuffing of feet. These ceased as Romilly appeared under the massive arch of the doorway and every eye turned to her. They were intimidating, but the most fearsome person of all was Armand. She caught a quick glimpse of Jamie and George, and an anxious looking Alvina, but couldn't stop staring at her captor.

'How pale you are, Lady Romilly. Is it confinement underground or fear, I wonder?' Armand said in a sneering tone. 'But so slender, just like the boy you pretend to be. Those clothes become you, showing your arse to perfection. Such a shame to remove them, but this must be done.'

Sabrina came forward, and although Romilly fought her like a she-cat, she succeeded in subduing and stripping her with the help of Marcus and Aponi. Despite their wariness of their leader, the watching men wolf-whistled when she was rendered stark naked. She was too proud to cringe under this crude regard, so stiffened her spine, held her head high and lifted her ribcage to thrust her breasts forward. Let them look and lust, the damned bastards. None of them were worthy of her, and that included Armand!

193

'Is this what you what?' she shouted at him. 'Is this how a gentleman behaves?'

His face hardened and he snapped his fingers. At once curtains were pulled open at the back of the hall revealing a gaunt, menacing crosspiece. Excitement ripped through the crowd and Armand watched them cynically. He had given them free rein. Men grabbed at the subservient girls and some fingered the boys. Cocks were bared, ready to plunge into whichever orifice presented itself. Sabrina led the orgy, while Johnson, Armand and Peter kept an eye on the situation lest it became too violent. Fights were always breaking out among the quarrelsome men, each of whom considered himself to be the strongest and most virile.

Alvina and Jamie stood close, supporting one another. George was becoming aroused as he saw the young male slaves bending over with no option but to offer their arses to hirsute pirates who sought gratification with someone of their own gender. Peter was protecting Jessica; hand on his sword hilt, daring anyone to even think of touching her.

And Romilly was to provide the entertainment.

'Why did you do it?' Alvina cried as Romilly was dragged towards the crosspiece by a couple of hefty servants.

'I had to try,' she answered, but could say no more, the breath knocked out of her as she was fastened to the post, her arms stretched high and her legs spread and tied tightly. A roar came from the throat of every man there, even those reaching their zenith like rutting beasts.

Armand strolled over to her, lifting her breasts familiarly, then bending to take one in his mouth, licking the nipple and causing a furore in her loins. She groaned, easing her back against the wooden struts, straining on her toes to relieve the drag on her manacled arms. He stood to his full height and looked at her with those cold grey eyes that yet held a fiery glow in their depths.

'You are too beautiful, *ma belle*. A man could lose his soul in your embrace,' he murmured, and she ached with longing

194

for him.

'Release me. Take me to your bed and I will show you how much I love you,' she pleaded, losing the last remnants of self-respect. Love him? Could she really mean that? She was very much afraid that she did.

'You hope to soften me, perhaps?' he replied sardonically. 'Not even you can escape punishment. You caused me a great deal of trouble and must learn that I will not be defied. As for love? That is only for poets and fools.'

'Not so,' she insisted, remembering Nathan and the timbre of his voice when he stood on stage and spoke Shakespeare's words. *Romeo and Juliet* had been magical and she refused to believe that true love didn't exist.

He turned away, gesturing to Johnson who handed him a tawse. Romilly caught a fleeting glimpse of the leather instrument that was cut into strips at the end. She clenched her fists, closed her eyes and waited. The crowd were silent. Time seemed to have stopped. Then the tawse sent a rush of agony through her. She yelled and bucked against the wooden cross, but there was no escape. Armand raised his arm again and subjected her to another blow, higher this time, streaking across her belly and leaving a trail of red marks.

'No more!' she pleaded. 'Have mercy… master!'

He changed the tawse to his injured left arm, then slid a hand under her crotch and flicked her clitoris with his middle finger. 'You're wet,' he muttered. 'Your body betrays your arousal.'

'Don't add to my humiliation,' she sobbed.

'You did that by copulating with Awan, though I suppose he could be called a noble savage, but then you debased yourself with that scum Lafette. You merit little consideration.'

The spectators roared their agreement, but Alvina was loud in her condemnation. 'Let her go, you rogue!' she cried. 'By God, sir, you're expecting a large sum of money for her… for all of us. What more d'you want?'

He gave her a cold, level stare, then deliberately raised the

195

tawse and brought it down across Romilly's legs with extra force. She hung there, head bowed to her chest, arms nearly wrenched from their sockets, every inch of her seeming to have its own particular sting. There was no use in pleading. All she could do was suffer and hope he'd grow tired of this cruel sport.

Then he suddenly stepped back and allowed his followers to touch her, but added a stern warning. 'No one is to stick his cock in her cunt or arse or mouth. That's my prerogative and she is my property.'

She felt fingers on her breasts and cleft, old men and young, faces almost idiot with lust, exclaiming as they handled her. Strangers' hands, dirty hands, some gentle, some harsh, all wanting to poke her, open her labia wide, play with the slick-wet folds, rub her nubbin and tickle her anus. Not only men. There were women, too, debased sluts who, through choice or coercion, gave themselves to anyone. Romilly was too far gone to care. Why add to Armand's satisfaction by complaining? She remained motionless, showing no reaction, and they soon moved away.

His tall shadow fell across her and she was released. She could barely stand but shook off his hand and dragged the cloak he offered about her abused and battered body. 'I suppose you'll expect to fuck me now,' she grated.

'You are more than ready for it,' he replied coolly, and she realised she was.

He gathered her close, then swept her up in her arms, supporting her effortlessly. She choked back a cry of pain as he walked towards a couch and ordered its occupants to leave. He laid her on a heap of cushions and whipped away the cloak. A growl rose from the audience and some of them pressed closer.

'You can't... not here, in front of all these people,' Romilly gasped, horrified.

'No? Just watch me,' Armand said, lowering his breeches and kneeling over her. He kissed her and parted her thighs,

196

and his hair fell over her like a black curtain and she felt the hardness of the ring that penetrated his flange.

It no longer mattered that every movement hurt, that friends and enemies alike were watching her; nothing was of significance save that Armand was caressing her bud. His cock was poised for action, but he controlled it, bringing her to full bloom so that her orgasm burst, showering her with pleasure. He tore off his shirt and plunged into her, the cock-ring sliding over her cervix. He moved faster, supporting his weight on his hands placed flat on the mattress beneath them. She lifted her legs and clasped them round his waist, raising her pelvis to take more and more of him. She wound her arms round his neck and his pace increased, his dominance exciting her so that she could feel herself rising towards ecstasy again.

She clawed his back, wanting to hurt him as he had hurt her, leaving bloody scratches while he rode her wildly, spurred on by the cheering crowd. Romilly wanted to come again most desperately, driving her clitoris against his penis root, but she couldn't quite achieve the right motion. She felt the tension mounting in him and lowered a hand, giving her bud the friction it needed to bring her off. No longer concerned about him she cried out as she came again, and he too gave a sharp bark, pumping her full of his semen.

He slumped on her and there was a second's silence before the hall resounded with a burst of applause.

Joshua relaxed in a brocaded armchair in the main bedchamber of Seven Oaks House. He had a slender glass of punch in one hand and a cheroot in the other. Life had never been so easy, and he liked it.

Always conscientious and hard working, he had discovered a completely different side to him – the good-looking, virile stud of a middle-aged woman. There was nothing required of him save that he was on hand to attend to her sexual requirements and act as her escort if she travelled to town. He could be as lazy and idle and non-productive as he pleased;

in fact Lady Fenby preferred him that way.

He had been introduced to Lord Fenby, a stout, red-faced individual who was almost permanently drunk. On the rare occasions when he was sober his loud, hectoring voice could be heard upbraiding the servants and, a genial host, he treated his guests to lengthy, complicated and mostly fictitious tales of his exploits. As his wife had told Joshua, he didn't sleep in her bed but chose to be with his coloured mistresses who took advantage of him, queening it over the slave quarters. There was little love lost between the couple.

'You wouldn't neglect me like that, would you, Joshua?' Lady Fenby said, gliding over to wind her arms around his neck. She was wearing a lacy-trimmed, diaphanous robe that flattered her thickening waist and heavy thighs.

'I shan't be here much longer,' he reminded, his face muffled in her flounces as she cocooned him between her large breasts. 'Have you talked to your bankers? Will they provide the money for the release of the hostages?'

'Oh, yes, don't fret. It's all arranged,' she said, sitting on his knee and worming her fingers into his shirt. 'Are you so eager to leave me?' Her painted lips pouted.

'Of course not,' he answered, and this was partly true. He knew that he stood little chance of making Romilly his wife. The social gulf was too wide. His future as a seaman would be an insecure one. Oh, he'd be master of merchant ships, but the pay wasn't much and the work hard and dangerous. He might well end up in Davey Jones's locker, food for the fish.

She held his face between her hands and looked deep into his eyes, and his arms tightened about the still attractive woman. 'I've a proposition to put to you,' she began, her voice warm and sincere. 'Why don't you stay here? No, don't stop me. Hear me out. I've been happier with you over the past precious days than I have been for a long, long time. We get along well, don't we?'

'We do,' he replied, resting a hand on her breast, and it was true; she was like an indulgent mother that he could fuck.

'Well then, go to Cayona with the money, return with Romilly and her friends and, when they sail for England, remain here with me. You can have your own ship and be her captain. We do much trading between the islands and the coast and I need a reliable man like you. My husband is killing himself with drink and when he finally dies I shall be an exceedingly wealthy widow. After a decent time of mourning we could be married. When I finally leave this world you would inherit everything. What d'you say?'

Joshua was dumbstruck. His first reaction was to refuse. She was too old. He'd be a laughing-stock, but as he thought about it the advantages outweighed the disadvantages. He was fond of her and she knew many sexual tricks that intrigued and excited him. Like now, for example. She was sitting across his lap with her thighs stretched on either side and her pubis rubbing against the burgeoning erection in his breeches. They could play together at any time. There was no likelihood of her becoming pregnant. He might want children later, but when she died he'd be able to marry a young, fertile wife.

If he went back to London with Romilly and her party, all that was in store was to see her wedded to Lord James and gradually lose all contact with her. This way he'd be his own man with money in his pocket and a ship. In return he would keep his part of the bargain, looking after her and being faithful. Lady Fenby would have no cause to complain.

She was nobody's fool and knew exactly what was going through his head. She reached into his breeches and bared his cock. Running her hand over it expertly, she lingered on the helm and anointed it with the dew already seeping from its tip. 'Think about it,' she whispered, then ran her tongue over his foreskin.

'I will,' he promised, utterly controlled by the urge for release.

'It's siesta time,' she purred. 'Let's to bed, my darling boy.'

Armand treated Romilly like a pariah. The harsh punishment she had received at his hands had not dissipated his anger.

Alvina had a theory about this.

'He's acting like a man who is wildly jealous. You upset his apple cart when you fucked Awan and Lafette. He's probably as annoyed with himself as with you, furious because you've hurt him.'

'I wounded his male pride?' Romilly sat up in bed, for it was early and they were breakfasting there before the heat of the day.

'More than that, sweeting. Maybe he loves you.'

'I would that it were so,' Romilly sighed, but did she really want to have this fiery individual harbouring undying passion for her? She'd never be free of him.

'Dearest, men can be such a nuisance,' Alvina sighed, setting the tray aside and wriggling under the quilt beside her. 'Take your fiancé for instance. Is he really interested in you or just after your dowry? As for George… I've caught him with Clive more than once, playing the hump-backed beast, yet he likes to fuck me. I've had more pleasure with Marcus. He doesn't pretend to love me, simply fucking me, and that's far more honest.'

'I wish it was a year ago when I hadn't embarked on this merry-go-round. I was innocent then, and far, far happier, my head filled with girlish fancies.'

'Until you dallied with Nathan.'

'That's true, and look where it led me… here, in a pirate stronghold.' Romilly was close to tears and happy to feel Alvina's arms around her.

She was a reminder of home and security, those carefree hours they had spent together, shopping, giggling, flirting behind their fans. To be cuddled by her was comforting, and the heat she felt in her loins an added bonus. She had experienced the pleasure women could give each other and welcomed Alvina's hands moving gently over her, reaching her thighs.

'My God!' she exclaimed, and pulled back the covering, staring at Romilly's bruises. 'His brand hasn't yet faded!'

'I know,' Romilly sighed. 'He beat me sore.'

'I was there, remember? And you don't hate him for it. We women are strange cattle, to be sure. We often despise the men who are nice to us, and desire the one who will treat us badly, both physically and mentally. It must be something to do with choosing a strong mate to father our offspring and protect us.'

She caressed the bruised skin tenderly and her fingers wandered across to Romilly's fork, parting the feathery lips and stroking her most private place. They said nothing more, giving themselves up to pleasure, fondling and soothing, using lips and fingers to arouse, each knowing what the other needed to bring her to orgasm. Romilly, though once hesitant about touching a woman's genitals, now took delight in doing so. She licked Alvina's cleft, tasting her salty juices and inhaling her piscine odour. To suck at her beautiful breasts was to revert to infancy when she enjoyed the bounty of a wet-nurse's milk. To hear her gasp and feel her shudder as she reached fulfilment made her proud to be the one who had made this possible.

When Alvina paid her the same compliment in return, she received it gratefully. Such an uncomplicated experience, similar to masturbation, and she didn't miss a man's penetration or even that of a dildo. Later they lay in each other's arms and slept peacefully.

The time had come for them to return to Cayona. Joshua was expected any day. Armand trusted few and, disappointed in Sabrina, put Johnson in command of Devil's Paradise. He had deliberately stayed away from Romilly, not simply to take her down a peg and damage her pride, but because he distrusted his own feelings regarding her. She would be leaving for Jamaica shortly and they would never meet again. He didn't like to dwell on this.

He saw her from a distance, gave her orders through Sabrina, though was on speaking terms with Jamie and George and even Alvina, though he suspected that she would relay his every word to Romilly. He had closed down his emotions, was short-tempered and sarcastic and not any better when the *Golden Queen* anchored in Cayona bay.

Once assured that his hostages were in the coach and on their way to Bella Vista, he went in search of Cat. She was behind the bar in the tavern, but stopped serving as soon as Armand came in. 'Take over, Starling,' she said and reached for a bottle of rum. She filled a glass and slid it towards Armand over the polished surface.

'No, thanks,' he said. 'I've a crow to pluck with you.'

She guessed what it was and tried to make light of it, saying, 'You'd better come out the back,' though doubting the wisdom of being on her own with him. He was very controlled, but she knew him well enough to recognise that beneath the calm exterior he was seething with rage.

Once in her parlour she offered him a seat, but he said, 'I prefer to stand. This won't take long.'

'Sounds serious,' she replied, trying to make light of it. 'What's wrong?'

'I thought you were my friend,' he began, looking so handsome that her heart did a summersault in her chest.

'I am,' she protested.

'You plotted with Lafette to rob me of Lady Romilly. He's dead, slain by me. Or didn't you know?'

'I knew,' she whispered. 'Some of his men got back here with his damaged ship. They told me what took place.'

'You had my trust.' He sounded deeply hurt. 'I'm disappointed in you, Cat.'

She stood up, a tall woman but nowhere near as tall as him. It was time to tell the truth. 'I'll admit it. Yes, I did fund him so that he might steal her away. I could see you were growing too attached to her, and I didn't want to lose what we had together.'

He raised an eyebrow and stared down at her. 'And what was that? You're a doxy who owns a tavern. I visited you on occasion and we enjoyed copulating. There was not and never would be anything more to it.'

'Not on your part, perhaps, but what of me? D'you know how much I'd like to better myself, to become someone other than a money-lender and fence, a receiver of stolen goods?'

'I promised you nothing.'

Cat could feel tears burning behind her eyes but wasn't going to demean herself by shedding them. Her heart ached with love for him, and she longed to fling herself into his arms and have him give her a good hiding for plotting with Lafette, and then make savage love to her. For years now she had lived for his rare visits, her other lovers meaning nothing. But on seeing him looking at Lady Romilly she'd known deep inside that her days with him were numbered.

'You want to marry her?' she whispered brokenly.

Anger flashed across his haughty face and he clenched his fists. 'Don't be ridiculous! She'll be leaving soon and returning to her old life.'

Hope surged and she gripped the front of his coat, shaking him in her eagerness. 'Then you'll come to see me?'

He took her hands in an iron grip and prised them away. 'No, Cat.'

There was such finality in his voice that she stood before him stunned, emptiness spreading around her, the years stretching ahead into an uncertain future bereft of his presence.

She was still standing when he turned his back to her, tall, straight and indifferent, and walked out of the door. She choked back the tears and ran her hands through her tousled hair. Starling's ugly face and misshapen form appeared.

'Are you all right, mistress?' he asked, and she was glad to see him, a friend she could rely on, a starveling who had turned up on her doorstep. She had taken him in and given him employment. The inn was the only home he had ever known.

'I shall survive,' she said, sniffing and running her hand

over her eyes.

'Master Paul will be back from the mission on Saturday,' he ventured, striving to cheer her.

'So he will. Thanks for reminding me.' She was beginning to feel better, then said, 'Send Phil to me.'

Starling hobbled out and Cat lay down on the couch, raised her skirts to her waist and consoled herself against the vicissitudes of life by stroking her bud while she waited the arrival of her young lover.

'What now, I wonder?' Alvina asked, as she sat with the other hostages in the grand reception room of Bella Vista. 'How does Armand know that Joshua will soon be here?'

'He gave him a date by which to return, one that he dared not miss for our sakes,' Jamie replied, stopping his restless pacing and staring discontentedly out of the opened windows. They led on to a paved terrace under a colonnade. The garden beyond blazed with colour and the slaves sang as they worked among the flowers, their voices mingling with the sounds of birds.

'Zounds, but I'm weary of this,' George complained. 'Just think, we could be strolling in Covent Garden at this very moment, meeting our friends in a coffee house or visiting our tailors or going to the club and indulging in a little gambling. How is it that people don't die of boredom in such a backwater?'

'I can't think, my dear fellow,' Jamie answered, handing across his snuffbox after taking a sniff and dabbing delicately at his nostrils.

'There is more to life than the social round,' Romilly said impatiently, finding him more and more annoying, the thought of spending the rest of her life with him hateful. She was in a gloomy frame of mind, not knowing what she wanted.

She had gone through the routine of breakfasting and then having Jessica attire her in one of the gowns made last time she was there. Armand had paid the bill, but she supposed that this would be added to the money he demanded. They were treated well at Bella Vista, and she could almost forget that it belonged to a pirate, bought with his ill-gotten gains.

He no longer had her sharing his bedroom. She had been placed in another further down the corridor, a grand chamber but not half as impressive as his.

She had spent the night alone, tossing and turning, ears strained to catch the sound of his approach.

She listened in vain.

Where was he, with that hussy, Cat? She speculated but without answers and, on rising, found herself paying particular attention to her toilette, adding little feminine touches, despising herself for wanting to catch his eye.

Now it was lunchtime, and they were about to adjourn to the dining room when there was a commotion in the hall and then the door opened and Armand ushered Joshua in. Peter Quidley followed them and Jessica turned pink, her eyes like stars.

'Well met,' Jamie shouted, going across and wringing his hand. Joshua seemed embarrassed but returned the greeting and that of George, too.

'Captain Willard,' exclaimed Alvina, extending her hand to him without rising from her seat. 'Was your mission successful?'

'Very much so, my lady,' he answered with a bow.

'You met Lady Fenby? She has agreed to help free us?' Romilly asked, glad to see this fresh-faced, clean-shaven man whose upright bearing typified a naval officer.

'She has indeed,' he replied, kissing the back of her hand, and she noticed something different about him. He had changed in a subtle way that she couldn't define. Then he added, 'I shan't be returning to England. Lady Fenby has offered me employment and I have accepted.'

This was a shock and Romilly realised how much she would miss him. 'Are you sure this is a wise decision?' she asked, surprised because she was upset. Had he forgotten how close they had been for a while? Had his vows of love meant nothing?'

He smiled at her and she caught a tinge of regret in his voice as he answered, 'I'm sure, my lady. I shall be master of my own boat, a person in my own right.'

'Never mind about all that; when are we free to leave?' Jamie cried impatiently.

'So anxious to go?' Armand remarked mockingly. 'I take it that you've not enjoyed your visit and won't be returning.'

'I think not, sir,' Jamie said with exaggerated politeness. 'I shall be happy if I never clap eyes on the place again.'

'When can we leave?' Alvina was almost dancing round the room. 'Oh, Captain Willard, what is Port Royal like? Are there shops and parties and jollifications?'

'It is lively, my lady, and so is Kingston. The Fenbys live in fine style and are so looking forward to seeing you all. Lady Fenby has arranged a welcome soirée.'

'Not so fast,' Armand cut in. 'I've yet to count the money.'

'It's all there, sir, I've checked it myself,' Henry Moorcross assured him. 'I've not taken my eyes from the chest wherein it lies.'

'Once I'm satisfied that the ransom has been paid in full, I'll make arrangements for you to board ship. How did you get here, Captain Willard? Was it by packet-boat?'

'No, sir, the Fenbys own several sloops and ordered a Captain Fox to bring us back here, and wait till everyone is ready to depart.'

'So we could leave now!' Romilly jumped up, unwilling to spend another hour in Armand's odious company.

'Tomorrow, *mademoiselle*,' he said. 'One has to wait for the tide.'

'Can't we go onboard tonight?' Jamie was eager to be off.

Armand nodded coolly. 'That can be arranged. See to it that you're packed and ready.'

'My jewel case and its contents; you've not returned it.' Alvina never lost sight of her possessions if she could

206

possibly help it.

'I shall arrange that this is done. Now, if you'll excuse me I must check the moneybags. Come, Henry.' He turned to leave the room without even looking at Romilly, but was delayed by Peter.

'Jessica Wade will be staying, sir,' he said. 'She has done me the great honour of consenting to be my wife.' Jessica crept over and he took her hand. 'Do you give your permission?'

'Does she realise that you are an outlaw, and she'll live with you among the pirates on San Juliano?'

'Yes, sir, I know that,' she murmured. 'I'm happy with this, all too happy to be with him. I love him, you see.'

Armand hesitated, and his stern expression softened. 'Very well, I have no objection. You will be able to help him nurse our wounded when we come back from taking ships.' He looked over her head to where Romilly was watching, then stalked from the room.

Jessica flew to Romilly's side. 'Oh, my lady, I don't want to leave you, but you understand, don't you?'

'Yes, yes, you're lucky to have found love,' Romilly said, devastated by Armand's coldness.

'I'll help you pack,' Jessica offered, but on her own terms. She was no longer a servant, but soon to be married to a doctor, one who came from a good family. Only the sons of the rich could afford to be educated and follow a medical career.

'Come along, don't stand there looking as if you've lost a guinea and found sixpence.' Alvina hustled Romilly upstairs. 'Port Royal awaits us! We shall be the talk of the town, and when we get to London tales of our adventures will enliven many a supper party. Why, if King Charles hears about it we may be invited to the palace to regale him. There's so much to look forward to!'

Romilly trailed after her. Never had she felt so miserable, envying Jessica who had found her heart's desire, and wishing that she could feel as gay and excited as Alvina. Of course she wanted to see her father again, and it would be pleasant to meet her aunt.

As for her marriage to Jamie? Perhaps she could persuade him that they were not suited and help him to find another heiress. Maybe in Kingston he might meet the daughters of colonials far wealthier even than the Earl, although he had expressed his desire to be in London. Alvina would help, she was sure, unless she, too, became enraptured with Jamaica and found a husband there.

And Joshua? Something had taken place while he was away, and although she was relieved in many ways, she missed his adoration He had behaved differently when they met briefly. In all, there was little for her to look forward to, but she refused to accept that it was her feelings for Armand that were causing this knot of unhappiness lodged in the region of her heart.

All went according to plan. Within a short time one coach carried their luggage, along with Kitty and the valets, and Romilly, Alvina, Jamie and George occupied another. Joshua and Clive rode horses supplied by Bella Vista's stables.

Jessica bade them a tearful farewell, hanging on Peter's arm, but there was no sign of Armand. The drivers cracked the whips and the vehicles rolled into motion. That's it then, Romilly thought, leaning back against the padded seat. I shall never see him again.

'Thank God we're free!' Jamie chortled, gripping her hand in his sweaty palm. 'We'll forget this episode and start again, shall we, sweetheart?'

She didn't reply, watching the trees and bushes pass the window, while the coach jolted and rattled over the uneven road. Cayona was fast approaching and she wished time would stop. At the quayside Joshua guided them to the right ship and soon their goods were stowed aboard. Alvina lifted her skirts, showing a shapely ankle as she was helped up the gangplank.

'Come along, Romilly, you sluggard,' she called back.

'Give me a moment.' Romilly couldn't move. It was as if her feet were glued to the wharf. Everyone else passed on to the sloop's deck, and still she hesitated.

Then as if in answer to her prayer she saw Armand's carriage drive in, the finest of the lot with a crest emblazoned on the door. Without hesitation Romilly ran towards it, ignoring the hulking coachman who wanted to know her business, dragged open the door and hauled herself up and in.

It was dark but her hands reached out and found him. 'Armand... oh, Armand...' she whispered, the tears running unchecked down her face.

She flung her arms round him, leaning into him as he sat there motionless. Then he gripped her by the hair, dragging her closer to the window so that he might read her expression. 'What do you want?' he grated.

'To stay with you,' she gasped.

'Is that true, Lady Romilly?' He was so close, his eyes, his hair, everything about him sending bolts of desire shooting through her. 'You want to stay with me, a pirate, a scoundrel, as you've so often dubbed me? Is this a game you're playing?'

He was hurting her, his fingers digging into the tender flesh of her arms. She would carry his bruises for days. 'No game,' she said breathlessly, feeling the heat and hardness of his body and never wanting to know anything else.

He shrugged, but pulled her closer. 'It means nothing to me. You know me for what I am. My plans don't include love.'

'It doesn't matter. Let the others sail to Jamaica. I want to go back to the island with you.'

'To be my slave?' His lips were on her face, her throat, her breasts and she was in heaven.

'Whatever you wish,' and she relaxed across his lap, her face buried in his chest, enjoying the moment.

He suddenly reached up and rapped on the roof of the coach with a cane. 'I shall use this on *you* when we get to Bella Vista,' he warned with a throaty laugh, as the vehicle swayed into motion.

'Oh, don't hurt me, master,' she said, but they both knew she didn't mean it.

'Hot-arsed wench!' he muttered, and pulled up her skirts, displaying her naked belly and fair bush. 'Why should I be bothered with you, eh? I thought I'd got shot of you for good.'

'Is that what you really want?'

'I never do anything I don't want.'

Soon they were driving between the gates that led to the house and he helped her descend, and then hurried her to his bedchamber. Within seconds she was pushed across the bed, her vulnerable backside bared to receive his slaps. Not at once – he made her wait, the tension building till she wanted to scream at him to begin.

She felt his hands on her, running over every inch as if committing it to memory. He was behind her, standing between her legs. She wanted to turn and look at him, imprinting his image on her brain, but he held her down, subjecting her to the scrutiny of his fingers.

He was so clever, keeping her on the rack, unsure of his next move. Was he about to give her bliss or agony?

He swept her hair up from her neck and placed his lips there. Then she felt cold steel as he took his dagger to the lacing of her bodice and stays, cool air inching across as the material fell open.

His hands coasted up and down her spine, making her writhe with the tingling pleasure of it.

'Tell me how much you want to experience that rare pottage of pain and joy,' he murmured in that low, richly accented voice.

'I can't... I don't...' she wasn't sure, utterly confused.

The air rustled as his palm descended upon her buttocks. She moaned at that all too familiar sensation, like fire striking through her to her loins.

He spanked her again, harder this time, and she revelled in

the power emanating from him. He was her master, in truth, deny it though she might. Feelings rushed through her like the ocean that lapped the island's shore. They were every bit as primitive and overwhelming as anything Nature could design.

His hand fused with her tender flesh, as if they were part of one being. Then he stopped chastising her and plunged his cock into her warm, wet vagina, at the same time slipping a hand beneath her and palpating her love-bud.

Riding her he chased his end, and she climaxed with a violence that shocked through both of them. She heard the sounds of his coming on his breath, and felt his seed pouring into her. This time he didn't leave her when the spasms were done, but took off his clothes and lay with her, arms folding her close as she drifted into sleep.

Sometime later Armand woke Romilly and said, 'You must write a letter to your aunt, explaining why you are not with the rest. I'll send a messenger with it before the ship sails at dawn.'

'What shall I say?' She was still bemused with sleep and quite delirious with happiness, waking in his arms and in his bed. 'And will you return my ransom money?'

'Tell her the truth,' he said, and provided paper, a quill, sander and an inkwell. 'As for the money? Ask her if you may keep it as a loan. I'm sure your father wouldn't want you to go short.'

'He won't care, and will be angry if I've disobeyed him and refused to marry Jamie.'

After much quill sucking and deliberation, she wrote,

Dear Lady Fenby, Honoured Aunt,
Thank You for providing money for Me. I beg to inform You that I have had a change of Heart and shall be Remaining here. So will my Chaperone, Jessica Wade, as she is betrothed to a doctor. It is my Sincere hope to visit You in Kingston ere

211

long.
  I am Well, as I Trust You are.
  I remain, Your Affectionate Niece,
  Lady Romilly Fielding.

212

Epilogue

The theatre was packed. King Charles was attending the opening night of a new play by his friend, Lord Rochester. Rumour had it that the audience could expect to be titillated by another of that rakish nobleman's bawdy works.

There was a stirring in the ranks of the foplings and painted ladies in the pit as a couple arrived and took their place in a stage box. 'D'you see who has just come in?' twittered one, all lovelocks and laces, a beauty patch covering a pockmark near his chin.

'Who is it? Do tell,' begged another, tweaking the exposed nipples of the whore at his side.

'My dear, don't you *know*?' The eyebrows of the first speaker shot up to his curly fringe. 'That's the Comte de Tertius and his Comtess. Most frightfully rich, so 'tis said, and what's more he made his money through piracy. What d'you make of that?'

'Ha! There are enough pirates in business or politics or the law courts as it is. One more won't make all that difference. But, tell me, wasn't she Lady Romilly Fielding, daughter of the Earl of Stanford?'

'You're right, and she was once betrothed to Viscount Milward, but something happened when they went to the Indies.'

'She's as brown as a gypsy. Most unfashionable. Ladies like to have white skin or it looks as if they have to work on farms for a living,' said one of the women spitefully.

'La, how unfortunate! That will never happen to me, unless my debt collector catches up with me, and even then father will bail me out. He'll be pushing me into finding a wife soon.

In fact, he has one in his sights. She's old, all of twenty-five, my dear, and plain as a pike-staff, but has a large dowry so that's all right.'

Romilly looked down with a smile, knowing that she was the subject of much gossip and speculation. She and Armand had only just arrived in town, having spent several months in Paris or on his estate in the Loire Valley. He had achieved the object for which he'd striven so hard, that of buying a pardon from the French government. The fact that her father was an Earl had helped the situation and she could see that this was one of the reasons why he had married her. After the ceremony they left Devil's Paradise, heading for Europe, his days as a pirate over. As comte and comtess they had been received by King Louis XIV at the Palace of Versailles.

Armand's chateau was enchanting and the peasants glad to see him, for they had suffered under his mercenary relatives. Though Romilly might miss the freedom of San Juliano, it came naturally to her to be lady of the manor, besides which, Armand was a restless person and would want to go travelling again. She anticipated seeing Italy and Spain and Austria, when he took her on the Grand Tour.

The Earl had forgiven her, accepting and even liking his son-in-law. Alvina and Jamie had both made good matches in Jamaica, and George had returned to his stamping ground in London. Jessica was now Mrs Quidley and had given birth to a son. Peter, too, had been pardoned through Lady Fenby's intervention, and they now resided in Port Royal where he had a flourishing practice.

It was only after Romilly had been with Armand for some time, that she realised how much he wanted to go home. With the money he had accrued, he could afford to employ lawyers to fight his case and restore the family chateau and lands that were rightfully his. San Juliano was empty of pirates now, reverting to the jungle and Awan's tribe. Johnson and the others had been absorbed into the Indies, following their unlawful trade, with the exception of Henry Moorcross who now worked for Lady Fenby as her accountant, Joshua was in charge of her little flotilla, and Sabrina, Armand's one-time concubine, had joined forces with Cat and opened a brothel.

Romilly found it unbelievable to be sitting with Armand waiting for the performance to begin. Nathan was taking the leading male role and she was eager to see him and test her reaction, the whole episode taking on a dreamlike quality. The King had not yet arrived, and nothing could start until he did, but being their sovereign he took his time. Romilly and Armand had been invited to partake of refreshments with him after the show. News of their adventures had reached his ears via Alvina, who had dragged her colonial husband back to England.

Romilly glanced sideways at Armand, sure that every woman present would be lusting after him. He was dressed in the height of fashion, as indeed was she. He wore a suit of claret velvet, with a cassock coat that reached his knees, slit on either side and trimmed with sparkling buttons. Under it was a waistcoat, lavishly braided and breeches that fitted his muscled thighs. She couldn't resist resting her hand on the one nearest to her, feeling his instant reaction even though he was controlled. She worked her gloved fingers higher, feeling a throb that emanated from his groin. He turned and smiled faintly, his cravat and ruffles startlingly white against his tanned skin.

They were alone, and her buttocks ached with the remembrance of his latest spanking. It happened as they were preparing for the evening, alone in their bedroom at her father's townhouse, maid and valet dismissed. Now, almost within sight of the noisy audience awaiting their king, he inserted a hand under her voluminous skirts and landed unerringly on her mound. Romilly didn't betray her arousal, accustomed to this by now. He chose the most inappropriate places, and they had even fucked in the conservatory at a ball given by King Louis. As Armand's slave she was bound to obey, no matter the time or place. She found such spontaneity exciting. It kept her on her toes and didn't allow for complacency.

His aristocratic fingers combed through her bush, and she recalled how they had held the sword that killed Lafette. Also memories of those selfsame hands wielding a whip, a tawse, a paddle, were enough to raise the fine hair on her limbs and wet her cleft with honeydew. Even when the King took his place in the royal box with that informality he enjoyed so much, Romilly was hardly aware, more concerned about having an orgasm before Armand decided to tease her by stopping. She had assured he wouldn't do this by resting her hand on his cock and rotating the ring through his tight breeches, causing his member to swell larger. He'd need to put that somewhere, and soon.

She was on the point of coming when the curtains parted and Nathan stood there, speaking the prologue. Romilly placed her hand on top of Armand's, stopping him rubbing her for a moment, and stared at the man who had introduced her to her own deeply passionate self. He was as handsome as ever, but no one could ever eclipse Armand in her sight, or treat her to that inflammatory mixture of sensuality and bondage.

'Go on,' she whispered, breathing in the scent of Armand's hair and feeling his cock twitch under her hand. At once his slippery middle digit continued its slow, delicious frottage.

She didn't hear the rest of Nathan's speech, hardly aware that he had left the stage and that it was now filled with other actors going through their paces. She came, silently, giving nothing away as he had taught her, and as she did so thanked the fates who had cast her away on the shores of Devil's Paradise.

More exciting titles available from Chimera

All **Chimera** titles are available from your local bookshop or newsagent, or direct from our mail order department. Please send your order with your credit card details, a cheque or postal order (made payable to *Chimera Publishing Ltd*) to: **Chimera Publishing Ltd., Readers' Services, PO Box 152, Waterlooville, Hants, PO8 9FS.** Or call our **24 hour telephone/fax credit card hotline: +44 (0)23 92 646062** (Visa, Mastercard, Switch, JCB and Solo only).

UK & BFPO - Aimed delivery within three working days.
- A delivery charge of £3.00.
- An item charge of £0.20 per item, up to a maximum of five items.

For example, a customer ordering two items for delivery within the UK will be charged £3.00 delivery + £0.40 items charge, totalling a delivery charge of £3.40. The maximum delivery cost for a UK customer is £4.00. Therefore if you order more than five items for delivery within the UK you will not be charged more than a total of £4.00 for delivery.

Western Europe - Aimed delivery within five to ten working days.
- A delivery charge of £3.00.
- An item charge of £1.25 per item.

For example, a customer ordering two items for delivery to W. Europe, will be charged £3.00 delivery + £2.50 items charge, totalling a delivery charge of £5.50.

USA - Aimed delivery within twelve to fifteen working days.
- A delivery charge of £3.00.
- An item charge of £2.00 per item.

For example, a customer ordering two items for delivery to the USA, will be charged £3.00 delivery + £4.00 item charge, totalling a delivery charge of £7.00.

Rest of the World - Aimed delivery within fifteen to twenty-two working days.
- A delivery charge of £3.00.
- An item charge of £2.75 per item.

For example, a customer ordering two items for delivery to the ROW, will be charged £3.00 delivery + £5.50 item charge, totalling a delivery charge of £8.50.

Chimera Publishing Ltd

PO Box 152
Waterlooville
Hants
PO8 9FS

www.chimerabooks.co.uk
info@chimerabooks.co.uk
www.chimera-connections.com

***

Sales and Distribution in the USA and Canada

Client Distribution Services, Inc
193 Edwards Drive
Jackson
TN 38301
USA

***

Sales and Distribution in Australia

Dennis Jones & Associates Pty Ltd
19a Michellan Ct
Bayswater
Victoria
Australia 3153